NO CHOICE

A CHRISTIAN FANTASY

TERESA HOLMAN

Light Walker Publishing

LIGHT WALKER PUBLISHING

CONTENTS

I CAN'T SEE

"**M**y vision is blurry, honey, but don't worry. I'm going to take the next exit." Jeff rubbed his eyes again, glancing at the rearview mirror.

"My eyes are super bloodshot, that's really the worst symptom besides the headache." He didn't want to say too much. Jazlyn was a worrier.

The wives of Navy SEALs had plenty to keep them awake at night; he didn't want her living that life. It's why he still hadn't proposed, at least that's what he told himself.

Jazlyn sighed into the phone. "You've been awake far too long! You need to sleep! Jeff! Please, get off the freeway!"

Attempting to control her panic, she twisted her long hair in one hand, twirling it around her index finger.

"Jaz, you know I'm used to no sleep. And...I'm never sick. I'll kick this whatever it is; you worry too much. Let's focus on our future. I'm out, I'm never going back."

Jazlyn's gut knotted. This strong man who never complained was complaining. Her chest tightened; of course, all she wanted to do was finally think about their future, but with her stomach tied in knots; it was hard to ignore her instincts, or intuition or whatever it was. She almost whispered, pleading with him.

"I-45 and blurred vision should not be in the same sentence. Jeff, I'm begging you to pull over."

Jeff was nodding at the truth of the comment, even though Jazlyn couldn't see him.

"I know. I am, honey. I promise. I'm headed to your house. In thirty, I can finally wrap my arms around you, give or take five minutes,

and depending on crazy traffic."

Jeff dropped his cell into the cup holder of the big SUV. Squeezing his eyes, still begging them to clear, everything went black for a moment. He blinked again, heart racing into his throat. He watched the line of cars in front of him. "You'd think that after ten p.m. there wouldn't be so much traffic!" He switched off the radio, hoping the silence would help him concentrate. His vision darkened again, moving in a tight circle, leaving only a pinprick. There wasn't more than a second before the pinprick went completely black. He heard the engine as it barreled off the bridge. He never saw his Range Rover hurtling into nothing, but he felt his own weightlessness when his vehicle went airborne, plummeting eighty feet before it splashed into the bay.

Jazlyn paced from the living area to the kitchen. "Thirty" had come and gone, and Jeff was no longer answering his phone. She plopped back onto the sofa and automatically called his cell again. It went straight to voicemail; twelve times, it had gone straight to voicemail. "Jeff! Don't do this to me! Answer, please, please pick up!" She left another pointless message. This time, she couldn't keep her voice from quivering. Twisting her long hair, and pacing, she was past leaving the "please call me" messages. "Jeff, honey, please. I'm really worried. You should be here! Where are you? I don't know if I should call the police or keep waiting." Jazyln shook her head, closing her eyes. Her dark hair fell over her face and into her lap, her tiny frame shook with each sob.

She thought of how long she had waited for Jeff. His years in the service, always deployed, always somewhere far away...and dangerous. His constant reassurance that he would leave the navy, then they could be together, figure out their future... But Uncle Sam always had a more important need for men like Jeff. He was a SEAL, and he was definitely one of the "few good men" she had ever known. She had known more men than she cared to admit, but none of them she would categorize as good.

It was true, she was sort of a "wild girl" most of her teenage years, then the freedom of college unleashed someone she herself was surprised by. When those days ended, she was totally burned out of dating. Men wanted one thing, and she was no longer in the business of providing it. She hadn't dated in four years when her best friends, Britton and Asha, set her up with Jeff. He was nothing like any of the men she had dated in the past. His big brown eyes shined with honesty. She felt in her heart, no, in her soul. He was different. He was "the one." When she questioned his motives once, he said, "Jeff H. Cooper, that H stands for honorable." If it had been any other man, she would've thought it was a joke. But...Jeff didn't joke about his character. She never doubted him again.

Whispering into the silence of the night, she laid her head back. "Be safe, Jeff. I can't live without you!" Picking up her cell phone again, she begged it to ring, praying to hear his voice. Jeff always calmed her. He was her anchor; he was her constant. The cell phone's black face betrayed all her hopes, refusing to ring no matter how much she pleaded. Her tears could not be stopped, neither could the worry. Both pummeled her mind into dark places...making her feel sick and exhausted. Leaning against the pillow, her eyelids pulled down with the weight of the news she needed to share. It had already been a long month waiting for him. Knowing Jeff was coming home had given her the energy she needed to get through. Her eyelids closed, and her body forced her mind to stop thinking long enough for a short reprieve.

"Beeping, what is beeping?" Jazlyn scrambled to pick up the phone, but it was already in her hand. Glancing down, all she thought was, not Jeff, an unknown caller. Her heart sank. "Hello?" Her voice croaked, betraying the sleep she hadn't risen from completely.

"Mrs. Cooper?" The caller didn't say more, and Jazlyn wasn't waking up fast enough to keep up with her racing pulse.

"Yes, well no! This is Ms. Berman! But...I hope... How is he?"

The caller hesitated, attempting to gather the words. "This is the emergency department at John Sealy Hospital in Galveston, Texas. You are listed as the emergency contact for Jeff Cooper." The sharp intake of air slowed the caller's rehearsed message. "Ms. Berman, are you there?"

Jazlyn stopped the tears that were pouring across her lips, wiping them away. "Yes, yes, I'm here. Is he okay?"

The caller hesitated. Listening to the woman's voice shake made the rehearsed message feel trite. "He is in ICU." Her voice softened. Gently she added, "His car went over the bridge and into the bay. He's lucky that onlookers saw the accident and dialed 911. I don't have any other information." The woman paused, the tension stuck in her throat. She swallowed hard, waiting for the questions that usually came, but she only heard sobbing. "Mrs. Cooper, I mean, Ms. Berman, do you know where the hospital is located?"

Jazlyn stopped her spiral into the unknowns, replying, "Yes, yes, I've seen it. But he's alive? You're telling me he is alive?"

The rehearsed reply came out harsher than intended. "Yes, Ms. Berman. H*e is in the ICU.*"

Jazlyn hung up and allowed the hope that he was still alive to calm her teeth chattering.

"He's alive! He's alive." She stood on shaky legs and held onto the wall. She would need a few things. Jeff was alive, and that's all that mattered.

CHAPTER ONE

A VIRUS

"**B**ritton, come and look at this!" Asha stood in front of the television, her hands on her hips, eyes wide. The broadcast interrupted the Christmas program she was watching with the kids. "They're talking about some kind of virus! Seems it's causing blindness and even deafness."

Britton called from the other room, "I'll be right there, almost finished!"

Asha continued spilling the information she already heard. "Most of the victims have traveled overseas...but still, it's so bizarre!"

Britton came out of the workroom, he looked like he had been somewhere far away. Asha smirked at how lost he often was in his work.

"I was making lesson plans for the other therapists." He ran one hand through his curlyhair, then clarified. "For while we are gone, I want them to be easy to follow."

Asha smiled at his glazed eyes and disheveled clothes. The man was always over prepared. But his over used mantra rang in her ears.

"When you work with those affected by autism, you are never "over prepared."

It wasn't only a job to Britton, the Therapy Center was his passion. He'd been open five years now, and his reputation for that passion created a waiting list he was always trying to make room for.

Britton and Asha stood wide eyed, watching the reporter outside of John Sealy Hospital, reporting live.

"That's not far from here, is it?" Asha turned to stare and saw the concern in Britton's squinted eyes. He wrapped both arms around her; he didn't want her stressed out. There was so much to do to prepare a whole family for two weeks in another country. He hugged her tighter.

"Nowhere is far enough when you're talking about an airborne virus." Britton turned worried eyes that locked on Asha's.

"Did they say how it spreads?"

They both listened when the wind blown reporter answered his question.

"Authorities from the CDC have quarantined this area. So far there are not many answers to where this virus has come from or how it is spread. CDC

officials announced only moments ago that they have not been able to identify the virus yet. Top virologists working around the clock have yet to give

it a name or classification."

The reporter stood in front of the CDC, the audience watched as he was handed papers by someone in a headset. He looked, with serious eyes, directly at the camera. "This is the most current update, folks. There appears to be six hundred confirmed cases inside the United States. More than

four hundred of them have traveled to the Middle East in the last six weeks." Asha squeezed Britton's arms around her, and she felt him

swallow. "Travelers are urged to carefully wager their need to visit specific locations. So far, travel bans have not been issued, but are expected in the

next few hours. Israel, Iran, and Iraq will be top of the list. It is a difficult decision for President Holden."

The reporter stared with troubled eyes, looking out at his unseen audience. He anxiously interlaced his fingers, then slid them apart

and continued. "With many Americans traveling to Jerusalem during the holiday season... Officials have added a 'visit at your own risk' advisory.

There is also no guarantee of being allowed back into the country once departed. How quickly this virus may spread is still unknown.
"

Asha drew a sharp intake, spinning around to see the fear spark in Britton's eyes.

The Christmas program abruptly came back on, and in the middle of a happy chant of "Rudolph the

Red Nosed Reindeer.

Their five year old, Maddie, jumped up and cheered. The ten year old, Britton Jr., looked over his glasses with barely an expression at all. Asha turned

slowly allowing Britton to take her in his arms.

"Oh no! Britton! How will we travel? How will we know if we are at risk? The kids, how will we take the kids?"

CHAPTER TWO

TOUGH CHOICES

B ritton set his backpack on the security conveyor belt. It was a long flight to Jerusalem. Almost 15 hours, with a stop in Washington. He nodded at the TSA agent who pushed his bag on through while he stood spread eagle in the scanner. The machine whirled around him, there was no privacy in this world anymore.

He mumbled, "I'm glad my underwear is clean. Who knows what all this machine exposes." He stepped out and tossed the pack over his shoulder. It was heavy, but his conscience was heavier. Was he doing the right thing? Was this fair to his wife, to his children? He sighed, swallowed, and kept moving forward.

For the next hour and a half he could watch the news scare everyone into staying home. Taking risks was not so difficult for him, the life he lived before this one...life as a "defective" made normal life feel tame. Looking at his phone, at least Asha hadn't called again. She was not happy about his plan, he was not feeling so great about it either. It separated him from his family, definitely not ideal. But during Christmas?

He had no more than found a seat and pulled out his phone, when he saw her face on the screen. He hit the "FaceTime" tab and heard the children giggling. "Hello, Daddy!" Any worry melted when he looked at those beautiful faces.

"Hey there, pumpkin heads! Did you already forget about your lonely daddy?" Britton Jr. rolled his very serious ten year old eyes, but little Maddie's big emerald eyes grew serious.

"We could never forget you, Daddy! Besides, you were already here today. We don't forget so fast!" That child was so literal, he chuckled.

"So true, and I'll be back before you know it!"

Maddie jumped up and down, circling a big red box that was wrapped with a shiny green bow. Asha leaned her head into the picture, her big green eyes looked darker with the purple moons underneath them. That look in her eyes always caused him to squirm. "This gift was delivered a few minutes ago, it says to the best kids a daddy ever had! Merry Christmas." She raised her eyebrows. "Is this something I should allow them to open now, or wait till Christmas day?" She knew the answer, but she wanted the kids to know their daddy was the good guy.

He heard the children chime in together, "Now, now, Daddy, now!"

Asha paused and then whispered, "I'm pretty sure I've heard a tiny bit of meowing." Britton smiled at her...it melted her, and he knew it. Even when she disagreed with him, that smile always bought him grace.

"I wanted to get them something really special, and since, well since you have always loved cats." He inhaled, pushing against the relentless guilt. The kids would love this kitten, but Asha would care for her. Feeding her, and being the incredible pet owner she'd always been. "Yes, please let me watch them open it."

Asha looked at him, pursing her lips, she tried not to say what she wanted to. But the words pushed hard against her heart, so she whispered, "Why does this feel like a guilt offering for leaving us at home for Christmas?" If green eyes were lit on fire, Britton saw exactly what they would look like. Before he could defend himself, Maddie jumped up and down, doing a circle around the box. Britton Jr. sat down cross legged, his ever reserved, yet patient nature, allowing his sister's antics with only a few sighs.

Asha watched them both, lips rolled between her teeth, she was trembling. She couldn't decide if she was more angry or more afraid. "Maddie, why don't you sit down beside your brother? You untie the bow and let Britton Jr. lift the lid." Maddie promptly plopped down almost on her brother's lap, red curls flying, tearing the bow before Asha could yell, "GO!" Maddie effectively caused Britton Jr. to straighten his clothes and inhale, like the miniature adult he often was. When Maddie allowed him to lift the lid, a tiny grey and white ball of fur curiously set both paws on the edge of the box.

The big blue eyes were the color of the Caribbean sea, the size of large coins. They gave an almost comic look to the kitten's face, reminding Asha of a recent children's movie where the cat made a big eyed kitten face that was impossible to resist.

The kitten tilted her tiny head to one side, causing the red collar of jingle bells to softly ring with each movement. Maddie jumped to grab the tiny prize and pulled her into a hug. Britton Jr. cautioned his small sister with the persistence of an old soul. "Be careful, Maddie, she isn't a toy. Maddie, she is real." The warning did little to discourage Maddie's jumping and hopping with the kitten in tow.

She held the big eyed kitten tightly and sang, "Jingle bells, jingle bells! Thank you, Daddy, we love her. We love Jingle Bells!" Britton Jr. attempted to intercede. He had not even held their gift yet, and already Maddie had given her a name.

"Maddie, her name isn't jingle bells, she just has bells on her collar. We need to give her a proper name."

But Maddie spun away when he tried to take the kitten. Flipping her hair, and singing, her own private dance. "Her name is Jingle Bells, can't you hear it?" She spun away from him again and again, effectively keeping the kitten out of his reach. Britton Jr. knew there was not much chance of reasoning with his strong willed sister, so he threw up his hands.

"Can I at least scratch her behind the ears? Cats really like to be scratched. He reached around Maddie and gently ran his fingers through her soft fur while Maddie did her best to be still. The tiny kitten lifted her head to enjoy the scratching and began to purr.

Britton watched the wonderful Christmas moment and sighed heavily. "Well, I guess you will see to it that Britton Jr. gets to hold their Christmas gift later." Britton chuckled at the sing song chant of Jingle Bells in the background.

"Yes, of course, Maddie will likely get tired of her new 'gift' in an hour or so. She is certainly a determined child!" Asha sighed with the grief of the situation, they both felt the heaviness of it. "No need to worry, I will coax her at the right moment. She also has a short attention span." Asha quickly added, "I can't imagine where she gets that." She spun the phone around so he could watch Maddie wrap the kitten in a dishcloth for a blanket and Britton Jr. cautioning and guiding his overzealous sister.

Asha tried to carefully form her words in case one of them was listening. "So any news about the 'issues' we discussed earlier? Any precautions from the TSA?" Britton turned away from his phone, turned back, and noticed the lines already forming around her eyes. She really did worry a lot for someone who used to be so easy going.

"Hey, Ash, breathe for a minute." He watched her close her eyes, he still marveled at her long, beautiful eyelashes. The green of her eyes was vibrant, not like a grey green. Her eyes were more like the color of a new leaf. He took a breath, praying he could instill some faith, some confidence in the plan they had agreed was the best course of action.

"Where has my red headed wild child gone? That carefree, throw caution to the wind, tiger I married." He looked at the emerald eyes, and he saw all that loving him had cost her. His mind brought memories of her forward, memories of when he was still nonverbal, living inside his mind. He thought she wore an air of aloof mystery, almost like a cloud of perfume that hung heavy around her. She seemed exotic and unreachable back then. He never wanted to forget the gift she was, how hard he prayed that she could see past his disabilities. From where he was at the time, that was the same as praying for a miracle. But oh, how he longed to reach her...and that never had changed.

He felt that same strong desire now. Last night he held her trembling body as she sobbed over the thought that they would be apart at Christmas. He would be more than an ocean away, and she would feel like a single parent...it was a horrible situation. He tried to vanquish her fears with more confidence than he really felt. He was good at that, at least he thought he was until today.

His best weapon against life's anxieties was usually comic relief. His Kool-Aid smile drew her to look at him. He teased her, "I hate to admit it, but I think I have truly domesticated that tiger." The sad eyes stared deeply into his soul, then she brushed away the tears that threatened to roll down her cheeks. She chuckled at his comparison, he always made her laugh, even in the worst situation.

"Are you trying to say my green eyes and red hair were better suited to the wild?" She smiled, lifting that one eyebrow. The butterflies danced in his gut everytime he realized she was really his wife, his soulmate...the woman Adonai chose for him.

"You need to take a look at the carnage going on since you escaped." Asha slowly moved the phone across the living area. Gift box opened and lid off, Christmas tree crowded into one corner, the kitchen island a mess with icing in reds, whites, greens...cookies still cooling. Asha came back on the screen. "I'm pretty sure this is much closer to a zoo!" She smirked again, and Britton laughed, the heaviness of the mood began to lift.

He needed to be sure, completely sure, they were in agreement with this decision. "Asha! I promise to keep you informed of the smallest detail. So far there has been nothing. I'd say, from the house to the airport...strictly routine."

The words were hardly out of his mouth when the voice blasted over the airport intercom. "Travelers for flight 2015 will kindly line up to sign CDC consent forms before boarding the flight to Jerusalem. There will be no exceptions. CDC officials are available to answer questions." Britton watched the lines growing longer while Asha's anxiety washed back over her face.

"Are you sure about this, Britton? Can't you just wait? We can figure out a way for you to go after the new year!" She felt a shaky sense of dread, suddenly she couldn't remember why she had agreed this was a good plan. The question hung between them...a bomb that might explode with the slightest move. Neither of them said more.

Britton stood in the line holding his breath, all it would take was the slightest nudge for him to change his mind....his phone dangled from his ear, he struggled to hold his backpack. The tension grew, and finally he heard Asha exhale her acceptance, he cautiously took a breath.

"Asha we've been through all the possibilities. It's important I see the new program they are running. The conference at the Jerusalem Center is THE conference, and it is only once a year!" He tossed his hair out of his eyes, so sure he needed to be there. Not only for himself, but for his clients. "I could come back home, go another time. But...I am the keynote speaker. We both know it wouldn't be the same, if I left them to find someone else. Would they ever invite me back? Not to mention, our clients need all the newest information we can get for them, now. I know you agree, at least you did last night. We've been through this over and over."

Britton nodded to the lady at the counter, he leaned over to look at the documents. "Asha, I know you wanted to visit your uncle, see some old friends, this is definitely not what either of us planned. But we could really use the money from my presentations, and can our clients really wait another year?" He nodded at the woman behind the counter, picked up the documents, and tried to make some sense of them. The phone hung on his ear, and Asha couldn't see anything but his chin.

"With the government reopening the Autism Projects again, Asha, I have to do something. We both know what that could mean for all of our clients. We have lived that nightmare…" He took the phone back in his hand and looked at the despair on her face. His heart jerked, his first responsibility was to his own family, but… "Their only real hope is to be able to prove they have value. I have to try and make that happen. This is the only way I know to give them a chance. I, I promised…" He let the truth of that sit between them.

Asha smirked, but she wiped away a tear. "No pressure." He chuckled but his heart wasn't in it. Never ever did he expect he would need to choose between his family and his clients. She loved their clients as much as he did. It was a passion they shared. They were both totally committed. Sure, he had been defective. That was a game changer for him. But with the possibility of the government taking complete control of everyone with autism again, someone had to do something.

Standing at the counter he tried to focus on the paperwork. "Asha, are you still there?" Asha let the tears slide down her face.

"Yes, we've been through your reasons. I just feel, I feel this is more about YOU. I'm not trying to sway you by being cruel, but really, Britton. But isn't this more about what you need than anything else?"

The anger flared in her eyes, not so much at him, just at the awful situation. But she was lashing out, she whispered the unspoken truth. "It's always about proving that you are enough. Proving that all those the world labels "Defective" are enough. That's how it always feels to me." She choked on her tears. "I wish you understood, I wish my love, your family's love, made you feel like you were enough, and if not that, then Adonai's love." Britton felt the words, a gut punch of raw honesty and emotion. There was way too much truth in her words to ignore, but he resisted with everything he had.

There was no pretending she wasn't right on some level. He stared at her distraught face, the phone began to tremble in his hand. Her eyes poured tears... Rethinking his whole practical plan, he began to back pedal. "Look, let's just forget this whole crazy scheme. I'll use the ticket another time. I'm sure the travel agent can give me a credit." He stepped out of line, leaving the waiver lying on the counter. He walked over to the wall and pressed his back against it for support. "I thought we had decided this, Asha. Did I make this decision on my own? I thought we agreed."

He listened to her sniffing, closed his eyes, second guessing himself again. Asha swallowed the giant knot that choked her, but finally she answered, "How do we spend Christmas without you? I feel so selfish even asking you, but the kids, Britton. How can you leave the kids? We haven't been apart once since, well since the night we said, 'I do.' The rational, practical wife inside me knows it's the best decision. But my heart, Britton. My heart tells me that this is so much bigger than either of us knows. Before you ask, I don't have any better ideas. Just a horrible feeling in my gut."

Britton was nodding, everything she said made sense. It dug the knife of guilt in deep. He knew it wasn't her intention, she was being honest. If she couldn't tell him how she really felt, who could she tell? But he needed to be sure that no matter how hard this was, they both agreed this was the best decision, for them, for all the "Defective" that depended on them.

"I don't want this anymore than you do, Ash." Did he? Was speaking in front of hundreds of therapists the real driving force? His never ending need to put to rest the constant assumption by so many that he was just another "high functioning Defective." Could he really be so shallow after all he had lived through? He bit his bottom lip, the questions built inside like a thunderstorm. Was he doing this for all the wrong reasons? Missing Christmas with his family, flying into a restricted zone! An unknown virus causing deafness and blindness, it was a big risk.

Using his empty hand to rub the worry lines forming on his forehead... He prayed out loud, "Adonai, please help us know clearly Your will!" He waited only a moment, then tried to make the decision with all those possible motives exposed and looming. "So, am I getting on that plane, Asha?" He watched the line dwindle out of the corner of his eye, it was down to only a few travelers. "I want to know we both feel in our guts that this is the right choice."

She gritted her teeth and nodded. "Okay, okay...if you are sure, then I'm sure."

He watched the line, there were two travelers left. "If I'm going, I will need to go now. I'll call you back the second I'm seated on the plane."

He hung up, but not before the kids chimed in, "We love you, Daddy!"

Asha whispered, "I love you, Britton, more than life." It was the last thing he heard before she hung up. He knew the strain in her voice would stay with him till he returned home safely. Still it was hard to make the choice to get on that plane. He felt the pull on the cord linking them together forever, heard it strain. He prayed it didn't snap.

Britton stared at the document in front of him once more, mumbling the disclaimers, "You must be willing to take full responsibility, with the complete understanding that an unknown virus has been detected in the region that you are traveling to. The CDC recommends that you postpone your trip until

after the virus has been isolated, and a treatment found. "Blah blah blah...where is my sister when I need a lawyer?" The thought made him

laugh. Kate, his "baby" sister, a respected lawyer, was adamant that he never sign anything she

hadn't approved first. He thought about it as he finished writing his name. Not even a lawyer's

advice was going to do him much good today.

He handed the papers to the CDC Representative. She nodded when he showed his boarding pass to the gate attendant.

Everyone on the plane seemed subdued while finding their seats and putting bags into the overhead bins. Not the usual hustle and chit chat. Signing

the waiver made the risk more real, and each person let thoughts of the virus and the possible side effects begin to sink in.

Blindness, a horrific headache that no medication could touch, the first cases also lost hearing, and who knew what else would happen? Was this a

risk he should really take? His gut twisted and turned, he slowed his breathing, and prayed, "Adonai, help."

He found his seat and noticed that his hands had begun to tremble. His stomach was tied into knots bigger than the ones Little Maddie had in her

shoe laces.

He threw his backpack under the seat in front of him, grateful he opted to pay for the window seat. He couldn't be stuck in the middle seat all the way

to Jerusalem, though there were no window seats available for the second leg. He pushed his backpack under the seat with his foot, giving it a shove.

They were both stuck in a space they couldn't fit in. He certainly knew what it was like not to fit in.

All the years he couldn't speak, all the years everyone around him assumed he had the intellect of a three-year-old. He inhaled and laid his head back.

"Adonai, please let me be making the right decision. The clients at the center count on me. You healed me. You gave me my voice back. I want so

much to do the same for as many of the 'Defective' as I can."

Dropping his head back, he closed his eyes. He really wasn't sure if he was putting his clients, his dreams, and everything else in

front of his own family. What kind of dad, a father, had he become? "Adonai, forgive me for any selfishness involved in my decision. I'm asking you to

make something good out of this bad situation. We both know that's Your specialty."

CHAPTER THREE

SEE IN THE DARK

S tartled awake, Britton felt the pressure of the plane descending. For the last eight hours, he barely remembered waking more than once, when the flight attendant offered him a pillow and blanket. He hoped he hadn't snored too loudly. Looking around at the other passengers within earshot, he couldn't believe he had slept so hard on an airplane. It sure wasn't his favorite place to be, but making the plans and all the stress of missing a Christmas with his family... "Adonai, how can this be happening?"

The flight attendant began her spiel about seat belts and landing when she unceremoniously went off script and began to show them each a mask they would be required to wear. "Just a precaution to add extra safety."

Britton blinked. He thought he saw...but surely not. He squinted and leaned out into the aisle. The darkness behind the attendant was definitely there. A foul stench began floating overhead, it was a smell he remembered from his past. He shook his head, blinking his eyes to clear his vision. "Adonai, I need to know that You are with me, that I'm in the right place at the right time."

The prayer had barely risen in a swirl of purples and blues when the dark figure raced at him, grabbing the prayer and extinguishing it as if it were no more than smoke. Britton watched him, and in a reflex, he yelled and grabbed at the creature when it got directly overhead. "No! You have no right to do that!" He snatched at the dark shape before he realized people all around him were staring. He pulled his hand down in a flash and mumbled self consciously, "I was dreaming. I'm so sorry, it was just a dream." He sat back in his seat, trying to calm his racing heart. He wondered...how long had it been since he had pulled a sword from across the veil? It felt like a lifetime ago. Probably the last time one of the dark ones had the chutzpah to show itself. It was years ago, when he lived that other life...when he was autistic himself.

"What is true? What is real?" The silent questions slipped into his mind with little notice. He let them hang in the fogginess of sleep. Wondering what else was in his heart? He shuddered, remembering with vivid detail what it was like being nonverbal.

How difficult life was for those the world believed were so defective they shouldn't be allowed to live. Thinking of his life before wasn't something he dwelt on more than he had to. Adonai healed him. Why, he sure didn't know. But he had spent every moment since training and teaching all those who were willing to believe in the "Defective" population. He was the living proof that they were intelligent human beings, locked inside of damaged bodies.

His mind refocused on the present. Taking the masks from the flight attendant, he passed the other two to his row mates. They each timidly took a mask from him...The "weirdo" who slept nonstop for the whole flight and then grabbed at an invisible attacker. He hoped they thought he wasn't quite awake and was still dreaming.

He kept his head down, grabbed his backpack, and refused to look anyone in the eyes. Even waiting for one piece of luggage, folks were instructed to stand at least six feet away from each other. "In case anyone was infected and didn't realize it." It might be the one time he was grateful for the distance. His face still burned red. He hadn't experienced something so dark, so spiritual in such a long time. He rolled the luggage to the curb and hitched his heavy backpack up on his shoulder. He continued to look down. He didn't want to meet any questioning eyes. His mind was rushing through possibilities like an automatic rifle. He needed to slow his breathing, find some peace. He gazed up at the sky, a soft purple with the coming rain. It turned the mountains on the horizon a rich blue. "What a beautiful city." His breathing slowed, he reached one hand back, massaging his neck, the tension loosened.

When he got to the taxi lane, it was a big surprise to see how many travelers and residents wore the flimsy masks. Britton pulled his mask off. He couldn't imagine how something made of paper would make much of a difference. He was suffocating, not only from the mask, everything was so overwhelming. A virus of the magnitude they described wouldn't be stopped by hand washing and a thin layer of cotton. He rolled the small suitcase to the curb and was about to hail one of the taxis in the long line when he heard someone calling his name.

"Britton. Hey Britton, I'm your ride!" He saw a tall, thin man with red and silver waves stuffed in a white beanie. His heart did a little flip, he stared. Momentarily paralyzed, staring, not replying.

The red hair, the white beanie...he looked a lot like...but no, that couldn't be.

"Hey, Britton, are you coming with me?" It was the jolt he needed. He took the handle of his luggage, hitched the backpack up one more time, and wove his way through the vehicles, all jockeying for position. With an impatient "tsk" to himself, he shoved the possibilities away.

Chapter Four
UNKNOWN

J azlyn watched the monitors counting the number of breaths, listening to the steady beeping. It was at least an assurance that there was hope.

Jeff didn't look like himself at all. His eyes were swollen shut, there were tubes, well they were everywhere. Her overstressed

mind conjured some kind of strange octopus, flapping and struggling not to be tangled in an unseen net.

The virus had taken his vision, and now his hearing. He didn't respond to much of anything. Standing beside the bed, she wondered if she should even

touch him.

Inexplicable grief swamped her, but she was determined to swim above it. She leaned over him, pushing his hair back out of his unseeing eyes,

adjusting his oxygen tubing. Her tears dropped onto his face. He flinched, she held her breath grateful for any type of response. She sat down in the one tiny metal chair, twisting her hair around her fingers, raw from so much washing.

The hospital insisted she wear a paper gown and a thick cotton mask. She wished to tear it all off so she could feel his skin. She drew the line when

they handed her the gloves. That was just a NO! So they reluctantly allowed her to scrub her hands like she was about to perform surgery. She had to

repeat the procedure anytime she entered or exited the room.

She was allowed in fifteen minutes every hour. Even with the smell of cleaning chemicals, if she leaned over him, gently laying her face on his chest,

the faint smell of him was distinctive and calming. Not his aftershave, or shaving cream, or soap. Maybe it was a combination of some of those things.

But mostly it was him, the scent that clung to him. She would miss his scent for a lifetime if she had to live without ever smelling it again. She

laid her head on his chest and sobbed.

****

Asha

Asha took the elevator to the eleventh floor. The elevator bell was loud on a floor where everyone talked in whispers. She donned the paper gown, hat,

and gloves. They issued everyone the protective garb as they exited the elevator.

When asked which patient, she barely whispered, "Jeff Cooper, he's the one with the virus." It was all over the news, now she was unsure if they were even allowing Jeff visitors. The nurse frowned. In a moment of panic, she wished for the hundredth time she'd been able to reach Jazlyn before

coming. She'd come to the conclusion that Jazlyn's phone must be turned off. Jazlyn had no family here. Asha decided to take her chances. Deep

inside the strong possibility that Jazlyn would need her, drove her...she needed to be there.

The steel grey of the nurse's stern eyes stared over the top of her mask. When you can't see someone's smile or a smirk, it is difficult to determine

who they are, or how they really feel towards you. "One visitor at a time. You will need to speak with his wife, or his *girlfriend,* she never

leaves, ever." The nurse spoke in harsh tones and rolled her eyes. "He is in room 362. Give me a minute and I'll point the way."

Asha wondered if the woman had been in the military, her bright blue scrubs a bit cheery for such a forbidding exterior. Asha only nodded, explaining,

"I'm really here to speak with his...with Jazlyn. Of course, I'd love to visit him as well. I will ask her if she's willing to step out with me for a few minutes."

The nurse didn't appear to be listening, but she nodded, waving her away like a pesky mosquito. Asha whispered to herself as she looked down the

long hallway. Under her breath she whispered.

"Definitely not the friendly type."

Asha's mind struggled with the nurse's coarse response. She looked to be late forties, but all the lines that were chiseled onto her face made

her appear much older. Asha mumbled as she scanned the series of room numbers. "What kind of person is cut out for such an intense job?"

Asha shuddered, trying to forget the thick cords on the woman's neck. They flexed and protruded each time she spoke. Her voice was a snarl, her

words a warning. "I'm right down the hall. I'll be watching you."

Asha realized the nurse was still speaking, and she had not been listening to anything she said. Instead...she was staring. Eyes wide at the snake-like

pupils that were there, and then not there. She reached up and wiped the sweat off her forehead. She couldn't grasp what she was seeing. She wasn't

sleeping much without Britton being home. She chalked it up to stress and no sleep...she had to be mistaken. She rubbed the back of her shoulders,

reminding herself to relax them away from her ears. In, a vain attempt to untwist the knots...a constant since Britton got on that plane.

When she looked back, the nurse had moved around the counter and sat back at the computer desk. But she continued watching Asha out of the

corner of her eyes.

Asha whispered a prayer, "Adonai, help! You know Jazlyn needs me. But I'm exhausted. Please, help me say the right things." She paused, still wondering about the snake eyes she thought she'd seen. She squeezed her eyes closed. "And help me sleep tonight." She took a breath. She needed

to finish this prayer before finding Jazlyn. "If I am encountering something, ummm otherworldly, help me understand. And please, Adonai, help me be

brave. I sense a storm coming."

The woman jerked her eyes away from the computer screen, sneering at Asha the moment she said "amen." She curled her top lip up and hissed. Asha

stepped back, blinking, trying hard not to show the fear that was coiling itself around her throat. Shaking, she took a deep breath, sucking in hospital

air, she coughed. It carried the heavy aroma of antiseptic straight into her lungs, and she coughed again. With so much happening in her life, and in

the world...she wanted to run away. Out of this hospital, out of this city, out of this crazy messed up world.

She stopped, held the wall for a moment. The thin knife of anxiety and subsequent shame tried to slide around her ribs...suffocating her.

"Adonai, help me. Jazlyn needs me. I feel so emotionally drained and raw. My sweet friend needs her family. Strengthen me to be that for her."

Asha walked away from the nurse. The snake eyes made holes in her back. She walked through the endless corridors reading off room numbers,

talking to herself, praying, and refusing to care who was watching or listening. She was committed to do what Adonai asked her to do.

"I am all she has. I will not run! I know this game. You have frightened me away before, but not today. Love holds me steady." Asha walked with

renewed determination. The closer she got, the stronger she felt. "Adonai, bless my friends, heal Jeff's body. I shudder to think of him trying to

heal in an environment riddled with the dark ones. Here it is!" Pausing at the door, Asha heard whispers. She spun to see who was there, she looked

back, expecting to be met with the snake-eyed nurse. "No one! Well, no one of flesh that is!" She made fists with her hands. "Vermin of

the Netherworld scurry back to where you came from. I walked through your smoke and mirrors...I will not leave Jazlyn to you! "

Peering through the tiny glass window on the door, she watched Jazlyn hover over Jeff. He was definitely the man of Jazlyn's dreams...knowing that

put a big lump in Asha's throat. She remembered the night Britton and Jeff came in from seeing some macho superhero movie. She and Jazlyn were

working on programming changes for the Therapy Center. Asha giggled, remembering the look on Jeff's face when he first saw Jazlyn. A bittersweet

memory right now.

Tapping on the glass with one finger, she whispered, "Jazlyn?" Jazlyn looked up, almost as if she couldn't imagine someone saying her name.

"Asha? Oh my goodness, I can't believe you're here!" Jazlyn reached for the door, opening it wide, motioning Asha in.

"Should I come in, do you need to come out? There's a...a pretty bossy nurse that says we can't both be in the room at the same time."Jazlyn looked

at Jeff, she only left him when they made her. But...maybe she could take a few minutes.

Jeff's nurse watched over him and Jazlyn, as if they were family. She kept a militant vigil right outside his door. But this nurse's eyes smiled, and she

motioned for Jazlyn to go. "I promise to stay right here, Jazlyn. Please don't worry." Jazlyn nervously made fists with her hands. His situation was very

serious and required constant surveillance. Jazlyn stared at his nurse. Covered in "protective" paper, the startling green eyes with thick lashes,

"smiled" assurance. Jazlyn tiptoed out wondering how many days she had been at the hospital? She thought it was a week, but it might be two or a

year...she would have to ask the nurse. The nurse had become her source of sanity. "What day is it? What time is it? What planet are we on?" She

shook away the madness, and followed Asha out the door.

Chapter Five

QUESTIONS

Asha followed Jazlyn into an unoccupied waiting area that was in front of the main reception. There were multiple stainless steel chairs with bright

turquoise upholstery. They were cold and fitting for a cold, hard situation. But there was also a brown leather sofa covered in white patches, where the

leather was worn off, it might've been in anyone's gameroom. She imagined teenagers drinking soda, and watching a game...It looked out of place, but

a lot warmer than the chairs.

Asha motioned toward the sofa. "Looks like they had a decorator that got started and then in a moment of insanity, bought a sofa from a dorm room."

Jazlyn opened her eyes wide, she'd walked through the waiting area hundreds of times, never even noticing the decor. Truth was,

she hadn't noticed much of anything.

The place wasn't exactly run-down, just weary. It needed a fresh coat of paint, maybe a brighter color. They both chose the homier sofa without

voicing why, dropping down onto the worn spots. Jazlyn felt the tightness in her neck and shoulders, they had been up

by her ears for so long.

"Jazlyn, I would've come sooner, but I just wasn't sure. Your phone must be off." Asha raised her eyebrows, asking, "I've been worried. I couldn't

imagine you ignoring my calls on purpose, but then, I knew you were dealing with so much." Jazlyn looked sort of confused, then remembered.

"Oh, cell phones are not allowed in the room with Jeff, so I just turned it off. I didn't even think. I don't know why I've not turned it

back on. I better call my parents...maybe I better call Jeff's dad too." Her face reddened. "I'm not his wife, but you know, I'm the closest thing he's got

to family here." She leaned forward and whispered, "He listed me as his wife on all his legal documents. I...I was sort of surprised to

learn that." She smiled weakly, and Asha noticed how tired her beautiful brown eyes were.

"Jazlyn, you know he loves you. He's just... The truth is no one knows why there's not a ring on your finger. But there's no question that man's eyes

light up when you walk into a room. There's no doubt you're the only woman he sees." They were both silent for several seconds.

The serious situation made the right words hard to find. Scooting in closer, Asha reached over.

"Let me hug you, oh my goodness, girl, you are cold as ice." Jazlyn relaxed into Asha's embrace. The paper gowns rustled, giving no warmth, Jazlyn

shivered.

"It's just good to be hugging someone who is hugging me back." Her voice broke. The words stung like a thousand bees, a muffled sob escaped her

throat. She stuttered, "How can I even think of such selfish things when Jeff is lying in there, so sick?" The waves

washed over her, the pain was alive, and Asha felt it seep into her own heart. Jazlyn clung to Asha, squeezing her, weeping for all that should've been.

"Jazlyn, we are all praying for you. It's not selfish at all, you love him, you want him to wake up and hug you and tell you it will all be okay. It's what

anyone would want." She patted Jazlyn's back, remembering what it felt like to find the one you love unreachable.

She didn't open that box of memories very often, but this situation forced the lid off.

Jazlyn finally slowed her sobbing and sat up, wiping her eyes on her sleeve. Tears still dripped off her chin. In spite of how hard she tried to contain

them. They fell thicker and faster.

She willed them to stop, mopping at them with her fists. "I can't seem to quit crying since this whole nightmare began. I'm acting like a little girl...I'm

trying to get a grip, I really am."

She curled over and tucked her hands between her thighs, all the way up to her mid forearm. "My parents were going to come and spend Hanukkah

with us this year. Of course they cancelled. I begged them to come, anyway. I straight out told my mom I needed her here with me!" Asha had no kind

reply to that. She wouldn't lie to Jazlyn. The few times she had met Jazlyn's mother, she found her emotionally empty. Asha decided to keep her

ugly thoughts to herself, Jazlyn didn't seem to notice that Asha was quiet. "We both know my parents are not big family people. It's their status, their

social life that's most important." She squeezed her eyes tight, trying to keep the truth from oozing out. She winced at that repugnant truth, she hated

knowing it.

"Yep! Rather than spend the holiday with their only daughter, they will be climbing on their social ladder, making the rounds of all the 'important

people' that matter more to them." Jazlyn rolled her bloodshot eyes. "Mom, did make a point of saying that if I had some 'news' for

her, if "that soldier" would ever propose...she'd be willing to come!" She lifted her left hand, moved her ring finger back and forth, and burst into tears.

"It doesn't seem important anymore. I just want "that soldier" to be okay, to come back to me!"

Asha chewed on the inside of her cheek, bouncing her right foot double time. She desperately wished she knew what Jeff had been waiting for. But

the truth was, no one seemed to know except Jeff. She focused on what she knew was true.

"Jeff is such a strong man, I'm so hopeful he is going to come out of this even stronger! He has survived every other impossible mission he's tackled."

Asha felt heat on her neck. She had asked Britton about a hundred times if he knew what Jeff was waiting for. Britton said that it wasn't his business

to go prying into Jeff's love life. It's how men did things, she guessed. Talked about everything except what was really important. Resentment rose

up, fluttering through her chest like it had wings.

"When I was talking to Britton this morning, he said he spoke with Rabbi Jacob. They will be offering prayers for Jeff in the synagogue." Tears began to

run off Jazlyn's chin and land on her legs, leaving dark blue spots on her jeans.

"My emotions seemed to have morphed into something a little brittle." Jazlyn's cheeks reddened. I'm just...I'm so sorry. I'll get a hold of myself any

minute now." She leaned down and actually picked up her own shirt to wipe her face. "Why are there never any tissues when

you need them?"

Asha pulled her into a hug again, holding her in silence, allowing her a safe place to grieve. She prayed that just being here helped somehow. That

Jazlyn felt safe to grieve such intense loss while holding on to that fragile cord of hope that might unravel any second.

Jeff's nurse walked into the waiting area and motioned Jazlyn back to the room. Jazlyn glanced at Asha, her face blushed, she turned to the nurse.

"Jeff flinched a moment ago. I meant to tell you. My...uh..my tears fell onto his face, and he flinched." She reached up and twisted her hair

around her fingers. She never noticed that she was doing it. It was something she had done since she was a little girl. It easy to tell when she was

nervous. She stood to follow the nurse, her red eyes large with her questions. She forced her eyelids to close for a moment, she was so used to

holding them open. She stared at the nurse, refusing to blink again. "I was hoping, it meant something...anything." She looked down at her hands,

feeling guilty for clinging to such a tiny shred of hope.

Asha stood up beside Jazlyn; they followed the nurse back toward the room. The nurse motioned them both in, so Asha followed quickly behind

Jazlyn. The desk was empty, no sign of the scary nurse with the snake eyes, Asha hurried.

There was only one chair, which Jazlyn quickly sat in. Asha suspected she'd been there every chance she got. Asha tried her best to press herself out

of the way in the tiny room. The nurse chatted calmly, "I'm just going to check his IV and all his vitals. See if I get any response." Jazlyn watched her every move, checking the monitors, making sure each tube came and went from the right place.

When the nurse was satisfied, she turned to speak to Jazlyn, it was a speech she was accustomed to reciting. "The flinching is most likely a reflex. We

all do that even when we are sleeping." It probably wasn't noticeable, but Jazlyn easily detected the rote sound in the nurse's voice. The

hope drained from Jazlyn's eyes. The nurse added gently, "But it's definitely far more positive than not flinching." She patted Jazlyn's back. Heading

out, she held the heavy door, adding, "If you need anything, I'm right outside." They both watched her go, like they had some private

business to discuss that had to wait till there were no other ears.

Jazlyn stood and stretched, arms overhead, her sweatshirt riding up, revealing a tiny waist that showed every rib.

"Jazlyn, when was the last time you ate? Girl, I can count your ribs!" Jazlyn dropped her heavy arms and her head, letting it fall to one side.

"I just...I just don't have an appetite, Asha. I mean, how do I eat without Jeff?" She dropped back into the chair, her sigh loud and heavy.

Asha felt the weight of the grief Jazlyn carried, so heavy it made the air in the room thick. She had been through some scary stuff when she first met

Britton. Even though it felt like a lifetime ago, she would never forget the terror that clawed at her heart. It could squeeze out all her hope, and leave no

room for anything good.

Compassion was all she had to give, and she wanted to offer it. "Hey, why don't you go eat something, anything? I'll sit here with Jeff and pray or read

or just chat...with him. Would that help?" Jazlyn squirmed a little.

"I can't leave him, Asha. I can't, not for longer than the bathroom. If I leave... " Her eyes filled, and she struggled to stop the flow again. The

awkward silence hung in the air, stronger than the smell of antiseptic. Jazlyn fidgeted with her hair, and then dropped her hands to her lap. Finally she

had someone she could ask the looming questions. Someone who wouldn't judge her. "Look, could we talk? I mean, can we really talk? I need to ask

all the questions... My mind is just going so fast. These doubts, these fears...but there aren't really answers are there?"

She had a thousand questions. She wrestled them in the darkest hours of the night.

Since the accident, she hadn't found any answers that gave her peace. "These questions, they are the only things that have been going through my

mind. Endless hours., and only questions!" The words sizzled with confusion and accusations. Jazlyn began wringing her hands, and Asha noticed

they were dry and chapped from the constant motion.

A tingle raced up Asha's spine. This was the conversation Adonai wanted them to have. If she'd had any doubts, the key birthmark, which she rarely

noticed anymore, began to heat.

How long it had been since she felt EL's spirit stir her to action? Now her heart leapt. How could she be honest and not offend? How did she tell Jazlyn

to believe when she stood at the darkest moment of her life. These were the things she wished to talk to Jaz about but...she

prayed Adonai would guard her words. Without thinking, she reached over to place her palm on the birthmark, drawing courage from the energy she

felt there.

Asha met Jazlyn's family the first year they were roommates. They were supposedly Orthodox Jews. But Jazlyn's mom never ceased to turn every

possible holiday into a party that would move her family up the social ladder. It seemed like her beliefs were strong and solid on

one hand. She never missed an opportunity to tell Asha, "Our beliefs do not include Adonai, at least not as Messiah." Asha never brought it up to

Jazlyn, the time, never felt right. But right now, her heart fluttered. The assurance that she needed to be as open and genuine as she could.

Asha prompted, "Which questions should we start with?" Jazlyn's eyes instantly became glassy.

"I'm not sure. I don't want you to think of me as a faithless person."

Asha lifted a finger. "Shall I begin with my list?"

Jazlyn made a face. "You have a list? Is there a list for this sort of gut wrenching, soul

search?" Asha nodded, smiling a sad smile.

"The enemy always comes after our weak spots. The places we feel the most vulnerable. I remember the questions well after my dad disappeared,

and I was just a little girl. They haunted me again when Britton was taken to the Government Autism Project. After all these years, I can still tell you my

list."

Asha shuddered at the memory. She kept that drawer closed tightly, but she would open it now. If she could help Jazlyn, she would slide it open and

let those spiders of doubt come crawling out.

Her heart was scarred. When she thought about all that happened to Britton, to all the "Defectives," it burned like acid through the tenderest parts of

her soul...sizzling and crackling.

"I almost lost Britton at the Government Autism facility, even now the dark memories can steal my sleep." She nervously ran her shaky fingers through

her mess of curls.

"I'll start with the questions that I struggled with the most. You let me know if I need to add anything to the list. Here goes...Where is EL in all this? Has

EL abandoned me? How could He allow this to happen? Am I being punished? Am I being paid back for my sins? Is EL angry with me? "

Jazlyn's bottom lip trembled. "It is great that you understand. But I confess to feeling totally exposed. I used to think of myself as a strong woman, maybe even brave." She dropped her head and grabbed some tissues to mop up the deluge of tears. "I've embraced my Jewish

faith all my life. I'm supposed to know that EL is good." She started shaking her head side to side, and began to tremble. "I have always gone to

synagogue faithfully. I have been taught all the old stories of suffering and EL's great miracles. I'm telling you I know that He loves His

people...and...that He loves me. But this...this has to be some kind of horrific punishment for my sins!"

A shiver made its way up Jazyln's neck, then her shoulders shook. Asha looked around.

"Do you have a blanket, a sweater, something to keep you warm in this icebox?" Asha stood and reached for the blanket folded on the bottom of Jeff's

bed. "Can we use this?" Jazlyn nodded. Asha shook open the thin blanket. "It feels like wool." She rolled her eyes. "Or

sandpaper. Can you make a blanket out of sandpaper?" She halfway smiled and wrapped Jazlyn like she was a small child.

"I know we say things, like take better care of yourself...but you have to Jaz." She leaned over and looked Jazlyn directly in the eyes. "You're freezing,

and apparently starving! How is that going to help Jeff? Those are some pretty serious dark circles under your eyes. Did I mention I could easily count

every rib?"

Asha was lifting her eyebrows, wearing her "mother face" while she lectured. Jazlyn's body began to relax with her friend's love and concern..

Taking care of other people was innate in Asha. Even during their college years, Asha had been Jazlyn's protector, her "big sister." Having two small

children had sharpened the edges of Asha's natural instinct. Jazlyn had made more than one comment about her mom not being the nurturing type.

Living with Asha really emphasized to Jazlyn how little "mothering" she had received. It was more "sit up straight, wear the right clothes, speak

correctly, and make the right impression." It was Asha that made her understand what real nurturing looked like. She valued their friendship, truly

cherished it.

"Thank you, Asha, with you here, I feel like I have family." She closed her eyes, pulling the blanket tighter. It didn't stop the tears that made streaks

down her chin. She opened her eyes to Asha, handing her the last two tissues in the box.

"I better go see if they have anymore." Jazlyn nodded, half smiling in an attempt to lighten the mood.

"Of course, of course. I'm sure I'll need them." Asha locked eyes with her, and Jazlyn rolled hers. How Asha loved this sweet girl, well woman. They

were women now, closer than friends, maybe even closer than sisters.

Asha turned to leave and then she turned back. "Jazlyn, I want to tell you a story." She paused and waited to see if she was sure of this nudge that prodded her. "I want to tell you the story of how Britton and Jeff first met." She held her gaze. "I know it isn't something Britton or

Jeff ever talk about. But it's not like it is a secret." Asha shrugged. "Have you ever heard the story?" Jazlyn sat back, shaking her head no, a little

stunned that she didn't know, had never asked.

"They met in college, didn't they?"

Asha leaned against the wall, clasping her hands in front of her. "There's so much to tell, and even though all is well that ends well, I guess...it doesn't

change the difficulties a person has endured." Jazlyn's eyes grew large, she couldn't believe she'd never heard, never knew this story. She pulled the

blanket tighter and placed her hand across Jeff's arm. She squeezed her fingers around his.

"There are so many 'stories' that Jeff doesn't talk about. He never talks about his parents. Well, his mom, but he lost her so young. And of course, he

was always out on some kind of top secret mission. I guess I learned not to ask."

Asha felt Adonai pushing her ahead, so she relaxed her back against the wall. She needed to carefully listen with her spirit and be accurate with every

detail. "When Britton was first healed..." She stopped and gave Jazlyn a side glance. Her heart was pounding a frightened rhythm, fear knotted itself in her throat. Jazlyn nodded her on.

"Whatever it is, Ash, I want to know."

Asha swallowed, trying to at least make the elephant in the room show himself. She braced and then dove in headfirst. "Lots of people know the big

story, that Britton was one of the 'Defectives.' Not many people really listen when he talks about how it happened, or what his life was like before he

was healed.

As Asha watched Jazlyn nervously twisting her hair, she prayed silently. "Adonai, please guide me to only say what will help." As close as they were,

the strong faith she embraced since Britton's healing was not a line she had been able to cross with Jazlyn. She had always gone to church. Yes, she

believed in EL. But after having seen Britton's healing, whether she believed in God was not a question, it was a given. Maybe now was the moment,

but she still squirmed. It could be a deal breaker for some friendships. The birthmark burned and pulsed, her heart pounded like a bongo drum.

Clasping her hands and then unclasping them, she sputtered, "I don't know how to tell this story and have you believe it. Sometimes when I repeat it,

it sounds more like a fairy tale than the truth. I want you to know that I get that. But you know me, Jaz, I don't make things

up, I don't lie. I don't even embellish."

Jazlyn reached her hand out to hold Asha's. "Look, I'd believe you if you said the sky was purple. I know that about you. That you would only tell me the truth." She squeezed Asha's hand, and that was enough encouragement for Asha to truly begin.

"When Britton was first healed, a lot of people were interested in his story. He had only begun to talk. I mean, because before...well, I'm sure you know

the story, he couldn't talk at all for the first twenty-five years of his life. He truly was completely nonverbal. Just like so many of our clients at the

center, he was just like them. He was severely autistic. He and I were not a 'thing,' how could we be? I was his therapist, his teacher. I knew him when

he was 'defective.' It's no small thing, Jazlyn. He was as autistic as a person can be."

She waited, she needed to let that sink in. The details of that time, she kept close because the world just didn't have the courage to hear the truth of it

all. Maybe it wasn't her story to tell. Someday maybe Britton would fill in the details for Jazlyn, but for now, this would be enough.

"Britton traveled a lot right after he was healed, speaking on radio programs and television. He was speaking to just about anyone who would listen.

He was determined that the world would know, and finally understand, that being a "Defective" did not mean you weren't as human as everyone else.

He was living proof of that."

She watched Jazlyn curl her lips under and bite on them and, as always, twist her hair. How could she tell her about the supernatural when she didn't even believe in Adonai in the first place? But she felt very strongly this was Adonai's idea, so she pushed ahead.

"Britton was speaking in Chicago at the University of Illinois. The lecture had gone okay, but when it came to the question and answers, the students

became hostile and angry. Some of them didn't believe him. They felt he was a fraud. How could someone so well spoken ever have been one of the

'Defective'? Asha began pacing, talking with her hands. "Some of them walked behind him to the parking lot, jeering and pushing him. Jeff was

working security on the campus, that was before his military career. Back then, he called himself a 'rent-a-cop.' She smirked, rolling her eyes at his

derogatory description.

"Anyway, Jeff heard the commotion and rushed over to intervene. Britton had been

shoved to the ground and kicked several times. His nose was broken, and one student had a baseball bat that he was just about to use. Jeff got there

and grabbed the bat." This was it, the moment she was dreading. She swallowed again and locked eyes with Jazlyn.

Jazlyn stared back at her.

"Asha, just tell me!" Asha took in a heavy breath, nodding. This was it, all cards on the table.

"So when Jeff got there and stepped through the crowd to inter vene...there was a streak of light, and a warrior landed in front of Britton and stood over him. The angry students were knocked to the ground. Jeff saw it all. He saw the warrior with his own eyes."

Asha rushed to the finale, she needed to finish before she lost the courage. "So...the Light Warrior, his name is Raphael." She stopped a little

shiver made gooseflesh on her arms. "Britton knows Raphel, from his days as a 'Defective.' He...he often protected him. Apparently, Britton is his..."

She knew that in the Old Testament, Light Warriors were included in the stories. She opened her mouth to say it, and Jazlyn finished for her. "He is

Britton's guardian angel." Asha winced at the reference, but nodded. Jazlyn didn't seem stunned by the story at all. She explained to Asha.

"There are angels all throughout the Talmud. They are a huge part of EL's story. They serve Him, and they protect us."

The giant lump swelled in Asha's throat. "The most amazing thing is that the warrior spoke to Jeff, Jazlyn. He said... Well, I'm pretty sure I have it

memorized:

"Hail Jeff, warrior of God's peace. I charge you to protect this servant of Adonai. You

were chosen for this mission. The day will come when you will dwell in great darkness. Blind to

Adonai's love, He will speak many mysteries. In the darkness, you will find the light!"

Neither of them moved. The tension held, so Asha spun. "I'm going to get those tissues now." When Asha left the room, her thoughts were heavy, but

her spirit danced. One part of her felt like skipping, but the emotions were like toting sand bags. How would this help her dearest friend? She had no

clue how the story even mattered now. "Adonai, I sure hope I understood. That I was hearing Your voice, that it was You guiding me. Please help Jaz

and bring healing to Jeff's body. Help him find You in the darkness!"

Jazlyn dropped her head the second Asha left the room. She had been praying almost nonstop since Jeff was hurt. She didn't feel a religious

obligation, there just was no one else to talk to. She twisted a lock of her hair with both hands. It was getting easier to talk to the

"invisible God." But still, somehow, she felt awkward. "Thank you, El, thank you for this story. I don't understand it at all. I don't understand any of this,

to be honest. But I'm learning to trust You. Thank you for listening. Thank you for sending Asha to be with me in the darkness."

She stared at Jeff's unconscious form. Her deepest worries choked out, "I didn't think...I hoped...I mean, I worried that this was Your way of punishing

him, or me. This story of Jeff as Your warrior, it isn't something I ever considered. It makes so much sense, though. His drive,

his relentless determination to protect others. But he...he has never served you. His whole life has been filled with boobie traps and landmines. You know about his mom dying, and how cruel his father can be."

Jazlyn trembled, she felt a presence, and she somehow knew she had been heard.

Believing that the God of the Universe would listen to her seemed so far fetched, and yet she

felt strongly He was there. The heartfelt confession broke her, and the weight, the crush of her

own betrayals squeezed her heart.

"How quickly I have blamed You. All these years my parents have taken me to the synagogue. You know I have listened hard to Your words. I've never

felt good enough to speak to You. We both know I don't deserve Your forgiveness. But I'm going to ask You anyway. Would You please forgive me? I

want to know You, the way Asha does! The way Britton does." Her throat closed on her emotions, tight, and full...But her heart would not let her

hold back. "And Your son, if he is Your son. Is Adonai Your son?" A love she had never known filled her, overpowered her. She laughed and cried at the

same time. Dropping her head into her hands, elbows on her knees, she whispered, "I want to believe You are Messiah, and I want to believe Asha's

story...help me believe it."

Asha came back into the room with three boxes of tissues. "Hospital tissues, Jaz...they are likely to sand all the skin off your face." She noticed Jazlyn curled over on herself crying again. It was hard to know if she should say anything, or just pat her back. Asha placed the boxes of tissues on the floor,

there really was nowhere else to put anything. She leaned down to open the box on the top when Jazlyn surprised her with a memory.

"Asha, do you remember that first apartment we shared? The one with the cockroaches bigger than a chihuahua?" They both laughed, and tension

eased around the difficult situation.

"Have I ever told you how grateful I am that we met? I don't know if I would've ever had the courage to fly across an ocean for a job interview if it

hadn't been for you." She sniffed, twisting her hair into a thick rope, pulling back on the emotions that engulfed her constantly.

Asha smiled and took hold of Jazlyn's hand.

"Look, the feeling has always been mutual. I mean, I'm so grateful you trusted me enough to come. She took Jazlyn's hand and squeezed it. "The risk

you took coming to work for a fledgling Autism Center." She used her fingers to make air quotes. "With questionable ideas and hopes that so few in

our field have embraced." They both chuckled, Asha was quoting a newspaper editorial done by a big advocate for any therapy but the one they

offered.

Jazyln squeezed Asha's hand back and then nodded. Without warning, an image of Jeff's huge smile blossomed inside her mind. The realization, the truth gripped her gut. "I never would've met Jeff!" She choked on the tears again, the shock of how important that one decision had been to her life,

her future. Her back straightened, and she twisted her hair with both hands. Her life had been guided. Here she was, believing that powerful truth for

the first time. "Maybe what you said about EL ordering our steps could be true. No matter, I will always be grateful I came."

Tilting her head back, gravity betrayed, hot tears ran down both cheeks. "I've wondered

since I got here if God is a lie I told myself, or if I just don't matter much to Him." Asha handed her more tissues and gulped, her sweet friend was

cracking, breaking under the intense pressure. Leaning forward, she hugged her and patted her back.

"I've got to leave pretty soon. I need to go pick up the kids from school." Standing back up she felt an overwhelming need to pray. "I really want to pray

for you, for me, for all of us." Her eyes shifted to the unmoving form in the bed. "I want to pray for Jeff. I know that you don't necessarily pray to

Adonai, but we can both pray for the Spirit of Truth to invade this situation."

She lifted her eyebrows, questioning, hoping that Jazlyn would be okay with the more generic prayer. It was certainly Asha's desire to be respectful of

Jazlyn's beliefs. She would never take advantage of the situation to press her own views of how anyone should pray, or to whom. Dropping her head,

Jazlyn let the tears land on the blanket. "Yes, please, let's pray."

CHAPTER SIX

NIGHTMARES

B ritton lay on the stretcher, his hands bound by heavy straps that allowed about an inch of movement. A woman with dark eyes and silver streaked hair stood over him. Her eyes glowed with a fire that caused him to turn his face toward the wall. "You can't kill me again! I'm not 'Defective,' I'm not 'Defective!'" Britton's screams echoed back at him. There was no one willing to listen.

"We will need blood samples, a muscle biopsy, and a spinal tap." The woman's pupils were not quite right, the shape, he peered into the past, "snake eyes!"

In the half twilight of almost awake, Asha groaned, sweat on both her temples; thrashing, she rolled over. The dream scratched at her, leaving blood and raw skin." There is an answer here. If we have to open up his brain, we will find what we need." The woman pursed her lips and tried not to smile. She chattered her thoughts through gritted teeth. "Getting rid of one of the 'Defective' and calling it research, it's the icing on the cake." Asha watched her smile, a sinister smirk that seemed too big for her thin face. Somehow, Asha knew she cherished the memory of taking Britton's life, and now she planned to savor it again. "You will not get out of my sight, not this time. No more smoke and mirrors, or magic tricks to save you." She snarled, "This time, you stay dead."

Asha moaned, "No, no, NO!" She watched it in slow motion. Her perspective divided almost like she was in two places at once. She was watching it from above, Britton's hair stuck to his head from sweat. He looked so vulnerable. His eyes were closed, and his hands were in fists. The desperation caused her to whisper, "I love you." But the words were lost, hidden behind the moaning, buried by evil.

She loved him as much as any woman ever loved a man. She looked into the aquamarine color of his eyes and knew that he was worth her whole heart. Yes, he was special, but being with him made her special, too. They fit together. He would say he was the yin to her yang. She reached to touch him...but he was too far away.

The woman with the snake's eyes cackled, causing Asha to shiver. The fear moved through her like lightning across the sky...seering and hot. It burned her mind, and everything else disappeared, except the grief. She felt like someone scooped her heart out with a shovel. A warm hand squeezed her shoulder. Asha turned tear glazed eyes to gaze into the face of Adonai. His gentle words helped her breathe. "Do you trust me, Asha?" Tears fell, she reached for Him, His face faded and was gone.

A sliver of panic exploded in Asha's chest. She grabbed at her heart with closed fists. Her eyes flipped open, and she couldn't catch her breath. Gasping, she blinked, attempting to believe it was not real. "It's only a dream, it's not true! It's only a dream!" But the dream was so vivid, she watched her hands shake. It had been years since the dark ones tormented her sleep, but these dreams, and all the horrible thoughts, were covered in their fingerprints.

That's when she noticed a tiny form under the covers. "Maddie? Oh sweet girl, you're so cold. When did you crawl into bed with Mommy?" She swept the red curls off Maddie's slick forehead and noticed she was sweating. Asha placed her cheek next to her tiny child's face. She was cool, so perhaps Maddie had been dreaming, too. Dropping her head back onto the pillow, she stared, watching the ceiling fan's slow spin. She attempted to still her heart. The nightmare had taken her breath and left her unsure of what

The future held. All these years, prayer had become a habit. She wondered how long it had been since she felt the words. She pulled her tiny daughter close and tucked the thick quilt in around her neck. Before she met Britton, she had not one sensitive bone in her body. At least, not when it came to the spiritual world. Unlike Britton, who'd seen the dark ones and Light Warriors his whole life. She honestly chalked it up to God paying more attention to those who needed Him more.

Picking up her cell phone, it blinked 4:08 a.m. She relaxed her neck, adjusted the pillow, and mumbled, "It's just a nightmare; it doesn't mean anything!" She squeezed her eyes, and the images came back, causing her to open them fast, making sure she didn't fall back asleep. Spiritually sensitive or not, every alarm she had inside was going off. Her heart wouldn't stop pounding. If she fell asleep, the dream might return. So sleep was out of the question, at least for now.

Slipping out of bed, she wrapped Maddie in a cocoon of fluffy comforter and placed a pillow behind and in front. She moved into the kitchen, filling up the coffeepot. Standing at the kitchen counter, she ran her fingers through her auburn tangles, sighing so deeply it hurt. She listened for the coffee dripping into the cup, lifting the rich, sweet aroma of energy into the air.

She sat down abruptly, her arms loose between her knees like noodles. She had no strength left to encourage herself. Through the kitchen windows, the moonlight reached through the darkness of the clouds, making fingers of brushed light across the ground. Loneliness fell on her like a shroud. She stood to get a closer look. Lightning crackled across the sky, ending in a drum roll. Then the rain came, vibrating into her heart. It felt like the sky understood her sadness. Tears rolled down her neck, and the film of the horrible nightmare tried to resurface in her mind. An eddy of loss swam through her. Huddled in her robe, she lifted the freshly brewed coffee up to her nose, taking in the smell of hazelnut. She loved the smell of coffee. It was a calming ritual she was grateful for.

Across the sky the sunrise began to peek above the horizon, swallowing up the darkness of swollen clouds in nibbles. It felt like hope. She whispered, "The sun will always rise." The hope was almost painful. She wasn't sure she liked it. Rubbing her hand over her heart, she wished she could reach in and scoop out the knot of tangled emotions that lodged there.

Swept by a strong impulse, she picked up her cell phone and counted on her fingers. "It's got to be close to noon in Jerusalem." She tapped his name. "Britton, please pick up. I need to warn you." For a solid minute, all she could hear was the pounding rain. She watched the sky light up again and again, the white bones of light grabbed as much sky as it could reach. The thunder shook the house, and the coffee cup in her hand, it also shook her soul.

CHAPTER SEVEN

THE PRESENTATION

B ritton stood at the front of the large auditorium, hands sweaty, butterflies dancing in his gut. His presentation was well attended, which was amazing, but it also increased the pressure. He watched the hundreds of therapists flow through the back doors, filling the auditorium to standing room only. Their clinic was the first real branch to implement all the research that was being done right here in Jerusalem. Much controversy surrounded the techniques...but they added a great many of their own. Their success was no secret, and the waiting list to be accepted into their program was long. It wasn't that they were so professional, though they were. It wasn't that they tried harder than everyone else, but they did. They had something no one else had ever had...someone on the inside.

A person who had been autistic...and found his way out. Britton was that insider, that missing piece of the puzzle that every school, every therapist, every parent wished they had. He knew what it was like from the other side, and it was making all the difference for the success of his clients. He often felt like a sort of circus freak, a unicorn that you could see and touch. But he could live with that...as long as his clients benefited. He tried to calm his breathing, standing in the middle of an auditorium that seated three hundred.

"This video is one of my favorite moments at the center. We have used techniques you are all familiar with, uncommon theories it's true. Yet these techniques have brought to fruition an incredible group of young adults who are capable of communicating. Not only for basic needs, but because communication is an inherent need for all humans. To be able to share their hopes and dreams with those who endure the same difficulties. Most of you know my wife, Asha Donovan? She was Asha Levi when she trained here. She is the director and head over all management. Our number one speech pathologist, Jazlyn Berman, is also an alumna from the Jerusalem Center."

Britton moved away from the screen as the presentation began. He sat in a chair in the back of the room. He wanted to watch the reactions.

The screen opened to Britton standing behind several of their clients, his hands clasped tightly behind his back. The camera zoomed in on the speech pathologist, Jazlyn, working with a young man who had yet to type one single word. She sat beside him at a desk. He sat forward, facing an iPad. Britton stepped forward and began to explain the session. "Here we have a young man who has been with us for almost two years. We wanted to include him in our training videos because we had all but lost hope that he would communicate." Britton allowed the video to continue playing, as he described the scene. The normal progression of this type of communication often begins on a letter board." On the screen, the young man began independently picking letters from the alphabet, making one word, then two.

Britton appeared on the screen sitting at his desk. He was being interviewed in reference to the young man highlighted in the video. "Yes, Jeremy is such a hard worker. I have mad respect for this young man. His mother has brought him three days a week for the last two years." The camera made a fast change to a woman in her late sixties. Sitting across from Britton during an interview. The camera zoomed in close. "One day he will communicate what is in his heart, and he will be grateful that he had a mother who never stopped pushing!"

The camera lens enhanced the dark purple moons under her eyes. Her jaw clenched, the years of determination seeped through to the audience. They all hoped for what they knew would be a victory for this momma and her son. The woman looked down at her feet, as if they had listening ears. "Someday, somehow he will tell me what is in his heart. I will leave no stone unturned." The warrior spirit in the mom stepped aside as she sobbed from the years of relentless pursuit.

Her testimony was powerful and full of hope. She braced herself and stared directly into the camera. "I watched the videos of young adults at the Jerusalem Autism Center. They were communicating, some even beginning to speak. I want that for my son. I showed him the videos, it's why he tries so hard. We have been everywhere, we have tried everything... I could list our failures. It would take me days. He's seventeen years old. He is a brilliant young man, and yet, he is trapped. How do I let go of this possibility?" Britton handed her a tissue. She wiped at her eyes. "I contacted the Jerusalem Center. They told me about this facility. I don't believe in coincidence. I just knew this center would be the answer we've needed all along." She wiped her swollen eyes a second time. "If this is possible, then I can't stop trying until I can cross this off the list."

Britton remembered the interview like it was yesterday. She sat across from him, hands clenched, not one ounce of pretense left. Autism did that to parents. It is the gift and the curse. No time for pretending when your child's life is on the line. This mom's days were spent caring for her child, a child she loved with her actions. That saying, "not only in word, but in deed," applied to so many parents who walked this autism path.

Jazlyn was the best facilitator he'd ever trained. She knew when to push, and when to sit relaxed. She knew when the fury of one of the clients was a rage of frustration against his own inabilities...versus against her requests. She was worth three times what he could afford to pay her. One of the many reasons the center had grown so quickly. He could feel the calm and the peace in her directions. He knew firsthand how important that calm was to someone who struggled with so much inner turmoil.

"Okay, Jeremy. One more time, I know you have so much to say. I can't imagine how frightened you are to share your thoughts...but I know you wish to be heard." She pulled back on his forearm, she relaxed her body.

She let him feel the peace she maintained...then, just like that, the miracle happened. "I wish to be free. It's frightening to be heard, but more frightening to live forever in silence." The iPad voice rang the truth of it as everyone, including the clients, collectively held their breaths. Yes, it had happened with client after client. Never ever would it be less or more amazing than it was the first time. Every breakthrough, every possibility, was like a new birth. The words rang out like the first cries of a newborn. The joy was similar, and the path forward a new beginning.

Chapter Eight

SEPARATED

B ritton sat down on the bench with his sandwich in hand. The weather was perfect, so he closed his eyes for a moment, letting the sun warm his skin. Far off, just before the end of the horizon, he held his breath, staring at what must be the Dead Sea. The starkness of the sun overhead shone in lines over the water, thin clouds floated through the intensity, softening the harsh glare of light.

He still had butterflies from the magical presentation. The questions and answers could not have gone better. He had come here believing he would find so much information, only to realize that Adonai had been guiding him in a new direction. He began making a list of therapists that wanted to come and train with Asha, with him. It opened up a whole new world of possibilities and income that could be a boost for the center. His eyes teared up when he thought about all that might be possible.

How different his life was now. How long ago had it been, when he could not speak? Back then, every day was a struggle for purpose, for hope. When his biggest joy was being led outside to sit on a swing where he could close his eyes and let the sun beat on his skin, the wind whip through his hair. That sensation was so important to someone who had no real life outside himself. All those years, it was so lonely inside himself. There was no getting tangled up in relationships, in life.

Even then, when he felt the dark ones eating him alive, he could always find some good, somewhere. Some slippery hope that got him through each day. He winced, a stab of surprise that the darkness from the life before could so easily rise and start to howl. Tears burned in his throat, hot and dangerous, but he forced himself not to shed them. He resisted those old fears and smiled at everyone sitting at the table. Around him, people talked and greeted each other. Inside himself, he found a quiet corner where he felt peaceful. It left a large space for all that he dreamed of blossoming. He hoped to bring a better life to every one of his clients, and he hoped to reach as many of those labeled "Defective" as possible.

The group from the Jerusalem Autism Center was taking their first break of the day. The seminar began that morning. With the excitement of traveling and all the possibilities, Britton almost forgot all the concerns that he left behind. The wind lifted the paper that was around his sandwich, and he shivered, not because it was cold, but because he remembered. Pulling the phone out of his pocket, the vibration felt urgent. He held up his cell. "Excuse me, everybody. This is Asha." A few laughs at understanding. So many of them knew his wife. She was a star teacher for the years she was at the center. He smiled and moved away from the bench. He needed to hear her voice. She calmed him. She always had. Finding Asha was like finding some missing piece of his own soul. He had amazing news, and she was the one he most wanted to share it with.

"Hello, Asha?" He tried to slow his heartbeat, but he knew she wouldn't call to check up on him. Something was up. He turned his back on the people at the table, staring out over the ancient city.

"Britton, it's so good to hear your voice." Asha, relaxed, now she felt silly. Bothering Britton over a nightmare, she blushed, though he couldn't see her pink face. "I...I had a bad dream. I was just...I needed to hear your voice.

Britton chuckled with relief. "No worries, Ash, it's all good. I wish I was there to give you a hug and hold you." She nodded her agreement, wishing she had never agreed to any plan that put an ocean between them.

"Look, I'm okay. Just call me when you get finished today. I don't want to interrupt. I know how important this is." He saw the flare in those emerald eyes, her quick dismissal. The phone silence made them both tense, stretching the thousands of miles between them. The sensation was like someone snapping a rubber band across his forehead. It woke Britton to the anxiety that Asha tried not to express.

"Ash, I'm being as careful as anyone can be. It's not like they know how the virus spreads or even what kind of virus it is. We are washing our hands with some kind of special antiviral, and half the people in this city are wearing cotton masks...and before you ask, no, I'm not wearing one."

Asha shook her head. "I wouldn't have asked; I know how you are. You'd say it's useless, anyway. It's not really the virus itself that has me worried."

This time, he cocked his head and smirked. "But come on, you know I'm right." Asha laughed quietly. It still amazed her how easily *he calmed her fears*. Brave, that's what he always was and had been.

She admired a man who lived through the terrors of...of death itself and still joked and walked through life with less fear than most people did.

Britton walked away from the group, staring out at the mountains that appeared to stand guard over the majesty of the bustling city. A whole world swirled in front of him. "I guess you know how beautiful it is here. I'm just overwhelmed that Adonai actually lived here and walked here when he was flesh!" The air smelled of spring and new beginnings. Asha didn't reply, so he asked, "Are you there? Ash, did I lose you?"

She ran her fingers through her messy red curls and closed her sleepy eyes. "No, no Britton, you will never lose me. It's me losing you that I'm worried about. I did that once. I never want to do it again." The memory slammed her like a gust of wind. Tears welled up. The memory tried to smother her. Britton, blue with no heartbeat, it happened. It might've been years and years ago, but it was not something anyone could ever forget.

She always pushed the memory as far down as she could manage, and inhaled, and then sighed long and deep. "Just wash your hands a lot. Stick to the hotel and the school and stay to yourself! Maybe there's some protection in less contact." The tight, hard knot in her gut had not released since she opened her eyes. That violent day was gouging too deeply in her soul to erase. She wrapped both her arms around her middle and tried to stop her the trembling. She paused. Maybe her bravado had gotten her this far, but she didn't seem to have any left.

Britton smiled, a mirror image of her, running his fingers through his own curls. He needed a haircut, but there wasn't time before he left. The wind blew the long strands forward, and they hung in his eyes. This woman, her fierceness. She had a heart as kind as dawn, and he had grown to love her more and more as days went by. "I will be as careful as I know how to be, okay? I promise." He imagined the clean smell of her hair, the back of her neck, the touch of her skin against his own. He could never lose her. Asha was the anchor that kept him hoping before, and even now.

"I miss you, Britton. Please come back to me." He listened to her sadness, and it made his own heart heavier.

"I will, honey, I promise. I'd move heaven and earth to smell your cooking and hear you in the kitchen singing while you bake." He'd meant to lighten the mood, but somehow his heart just throbbed. "I miss you. The smell of your hair, the softness of your skin. Everything about you."

They were both overwhelmed. Being apart was not a good thing. They were one, they really were. He pulled the crisp air in and tried to break the spell. "I had such a great day today. The presentation was fantastic. This really could mean all the difference for the center." He waited. She didn't reply...because she was crying. "I love you more than my life, Ash. You know I do." The words seemed trite, but he meant them. He meant them with every fiber of his being.

His eyes grew serious. Staring out at the buildings and the homes, most of them made of ancient stone. The school was in the new part of Jerusalem. Though most of the apartments and a lot of the buildings blended in, there was more of an industrial feel this far out. His eyes shifted to the golden globe of the mosque. He could see from almost every location in the city. The old world, how things used to be, seeped into the surroundings of the new. Two very distinct worlds...architects had done a beautiful job of meshing both.

He was so much like this city. There was the "defective" Britton, the person he used to be... now overshadowed by this new person, this whole person. "Ya know Ash, off the subject, but this city, this old and new city...it's a lot like me." He smiled the brilliant Kool-Aid smile and wished with everything in him that she was standing beside him. Asha heard the astonished realization in his voice. She knew exactly how he looked standing there, remembering. "I wish we were together. It would calm my fears if I could hold on to you."

When Asha met him, he was severely autistic. He was suddenly snared by his past, by sharp, painful memories. He was "defective." He lived the life that their clients live now. He sometimes stepped into those memories when he was reaching for a client. They would be angry and cruel, and he would have trouble catching his breath.

Asha knew that his desire to reach those with autism, to help them, was not only about business, it was a mission. Twenty-five years, he was incapable of language. His body tensed with the memories. He broke the silence. "I just believe that Adonai would warn me, Ash. He would send a Light Warrior, or..." He stopped in the middle of the sentence. The dark presence on the plane when they prepared to land came back to his mind. He shakily considered whether he was ignoring its meaning. "I just know that Adonai would show up in some way, that's all."

Asha shivered. "I know...I know He would. Some days I remember it all, and if Adonai had not sent the Light Warrior...Well, there are things you just never get over." Her voice trembled, the memories emblazoned in her mind. Britton watched her on his screen. She closed her eyes for the space of a few breaths. "It's just that I could never forget when, when you died."

The night Britton's life was taken, his face blue, his body cold. A Light Warrior had come and changed everything. But almost without asking her, the memories tossed the miracle to the front of her mind. She remembered feeling the heat, reaching to touch the glowing birthmark on her arm. She never understood how she knew what to do...but she laid her forearm on his matching birthmark. Even though he was lifeless, his birthmark began to glow. Then...as if lightning had struck their bodies, Britton inhaled, energy refilling his empty shell.

Remembering the birthmark, she reached for it, felt its heat. She'd almost forgotten it was there, but something was happening, something was coming because the birthmark was burning and throbbing. "Britton? Britton, the birthmark!" She felt she had whispered it, almost afraid of what it could mean. Britton leaned his head against his shoulder, holding his phone tightly and pushed back his sleeve. "All these years...how long has it been?" The shock of it hadn't settled in just yet, but Asha grappled at the possible meaning.

Across an ocean, Britton stared at the birthmark while Asha stared at hers. The panic began to rise up in her throat. The birthmark had not lit up again since the day he died. She had felt its heat; it burned like fire when she gave birth. It was now more than ten years since she watched a miracle that even she found hard to believe. "Britton, Britton, my birthmark is glowing!"

He was nodding, watching his own birthmark turn the color of the blazing sun. "Asha, we need to stay calm. We can trust Adonai. He always protects us." He felt his heart skip a beat." If this is a warning, we'd better pray and keep our eyes open!"

She thought she heard his voice quiver, but maybe she was reading more into things. "Call me tonight! We should probably come up with a plan or something."

Neither of them said anything. Britton bit his lips. The sun beat down from the hot blue sky, melting the miles between them. "I love you, Asha."

She set her cell phone on the table and picked up her oversized coffee cup. It wasn't hot anymore, but she didn't mind, not really. The sweetness of the cream, and even the smell, was some comfort. She closed her eyes, allowing the last of the soothing brew to go down and work its magic. A tightly bound bundle of emotions rolled up in knots and smashed into her diaphragm. She had to work to breathe.

She heard the hum before she felt the warmth on her arm. Her eyes fluttered open to a massive shadow across the living room wall. She knew that shape; she recognized it. The light filtered through the massive wings, his presence more like sunshine than reality. Something you could run your fingers through and come up empty, though you felt its warmth. Still, it was real. There was no doubt she'd seen this Light Warrior before. Maybe this time he was a messenger, but he was definitely a warrior. A great warrior to a Great King, the only King. She had seen him on the best and the worst day of her life. Paralyzed by his presence, by what it might mean. Was it every day that great spiritual warriors interfered in the affairs of men?

All those years ago when Britton had been murdered, that was the last time, the only other time, she had seen him. A handful of others saw him that day, but most refused to admit it. She shakily decided to stand, slowly pushing back the chair and moving cautiously into the living area. Britton's resurrection was proof that Adonai could certainly be trusted, and this was His protection. She needed to remember that, now, as much as she did all those years ago when she watched Adonai's power bring Britton back to life. She put her hand on the birthmark and prayed, "Adonai, thank you for this protection, for Your presence. Help me hear, and more importantly, help me trust."

Chapter Nine

HISTORY

"Thank you for allowing me to be part of the workshop, Professor Benjamin. I've gathered an extraordinary amount of information." Britton tapped the large binder and smiled. The professor returned the smile but nervously fidgeted, then held back what he wanted to say. He stuck his hand out to shake Britton's hand and squeezed harder than was necessary.

"It was such an honor to meet you, Britton. I'm grateful you could attend. My heart is sad that your family could not join you. I was so looking forward to meeting...all of them." The professor gritted his teeth. He was afraid, not so much of the past... He'd chosen not to regret a long time ago. Life had come at him like a hurricane. He'd done what he believed was best. Good and bad, it was the choice he'd made. He knew, given the choice, he'd do the exact same thing again.

Britton blinked. The professor stared at him so directly. He couldn't be certain, but he thought he saw a flicker of grief. It felt confusing, so he asked, "Um, Professor, did you know my wife,

Asha Levi? She was a student here...oh, quite a few years ago. But I thought you were new here."

His suspicions had been rising since this professor, this red-headed, emerald-eyed man, showed up at the airport. He seemed so disappointed that Britton was alone. He watched him search all around, looking for his family that was originally scheduled to be with him. Britton squinted, trying to figure out why, why would any man desert his wife and child? But that was a crazy idea. Asha's father was presumed dead when Asha was only six, almost thirty years ago. But the hair color, more than that, his mannerisms. "I wish Asha were here to meet you. She's a redhead like you, a beautiful one." Britton poked him with the possibility, hoping for some type of exposure as to whom he thought he might be. The professor's face flickered with sorrow, or compassion. It was hard to decipher. If this man was...why would he just now appear out of nowhere? Thirty years after he'd gone missing. Why now?

"A redhead? Well, we gingers must stick together. I will look forward to meeting her at my earliest opportunity." Britton thought his eyes looked sad, oh so sad. Everything in him wanted to ask, say something, but maybe there was danger, or maybe he was just making the whole thing up in his head.

Britton picked up his luggage and was going to thank the man one more time when the professor added clarification, "I joined the staff here, only this past fall. I have been traveling up and down Europe for nearly thirty years."

Britton continued to stare. It was all so familiar, the way he ran his fingers through his hair, the broad easy smile. He felt a shiver from the possibility of it, then shook his head. "Well, I hope to bring the whole family back, maybe next year. The kids were so excited to come, but then the whole virus situation complicated things. Asha and I decided that it was safest for the family if only I came this time." The professor nodded, and Britton watched him grind his back molars, holding back what he wished to express. He thought he heard him speak, but his mouth wasn't moving. He'd swear there was a cry for help in his eyes. That's when Britton saw it. The darkness thickened, and an overwhelming sense of loss sank inside his gut. A shadow of inky blackness hovered behind the professor. Chains wrapped in loops around his neck. The shadow yanked him back. Britton blinked, steadying himself against the vision, or nightmare. It was hard to decide which one had claimed his mind. "Professor Benjamin!" Britton called after the man, but he had spun away quickly...mumbling, disoriented, especially for such a brilliant man. Britton could just make out the man's words.

"Why not add one more thing to the list I need to repent of?"

Britton frowned, then yelled after him, "Professor Benjamin, are you talking to me?" Britton's eagerness to ask him straight out grew hotter the longer he spent talking to the man. But it also increased his pain, his grief for all that his wife, and his children, had lost. But the professor never turned around. He continued to walk further and further away.

A tiny pool of regret swirled in his heart. Without warning, the professor turned around, lifted his hand and mouthed, "Farewell." It sounded final.

Watching him and all his strange behaviors, Britton made the decision not to tell Asha. There really was no need to say anything about a hunch. But he decided to ask around. His flight didn't leave for two more days. The conference was two weeks, not including the weekends. But the cheapest plane tickets were Sunday to Sunday. So he would be here, visiting with Asha's aunt and uncle for those two days. Her uncle knew everyone. Uncle Amos was a respected rabbi in the city, and if there was any way this was Asha's father, wouldn't Amos know? There were so many rabbis, and yet everyone seemed to know Amos. Maybe there would be an opportunity to fish for information.

****

Judah

A loud throat cleared...scattering Britton's thoughts. "Hello, my name is Judah Ben Jesse. I've wanted to meet the lucky man who stole my Asha's heart." The handsome man stuck out his hand and waited. It took Britton by surprise because his mind was so far away. It took a few seconds before he met the sincere brown eyes. He took the man's hand and squeezed it. "Your Asha, I'm afraid there must be some mistake." The man with the side curls and prayer box tied around his forehead laughed such a hearty chuckle with an appealing sound, it was impossible for Britton not to smile back.

"Yes, yes, I have misspoken. She was never my Asha, but if I had a child, I'd hope she'd be just like her." His eyes danced a self-assured taunting; Britton liked the man instantly. That kind of confident peace was not a common attribute among most men.

Britton lifted his eyebrows, pretending to be perturbed. "How is it that you know *my* Asha?" He smiled his Kool-Aid smile, returning his own confident peace. He would never have believed it possible to be intimidated by a man with side curls swinging beside his cheeks. But twelve days in Jerusalem taught him a respect that many of these brilliant men deserved. Orthodox Jews wore the prayer boxes, not only on their foreheads but also strapped on their arms. It was serious business with their God, and not to be taken lightly.

"I was Asha's 'tour guide,' so to speak. The first semester she arrived newly plucked out of America." He used his hands to illustrate picking something out of the sky. "Her Uncle...he is a friend, a colleague. I was, I am still teaching at the University, and of course, there was an ulterior motive." Judah's voice had a soothing cadence about it, like the gentle lapping of water.

Britton enjoyed the calm, his shoulders relaxed. He hadn't known how tense he felt talking to the professor, but here, there might be an opportunity. "An ulterior motive? Did it have to do with emerald eyes and scarlet curls?" Britton stopped walking and stood, accusatory, but one side of his mouth smiled.

The tall man snorted, bent forward, and that's when Britton realized he was laughing. It was a deep belly laugh, and though confused, Britton joined him, patting him on the back. "I fail to see the humor, though I would love to be invited to the inside joke."

The amused man stood back up, wiping his eyes and clearing his throat. "I knew Asha's father when I was a very young man. Just finding my way to Ha-Shem. He asked me to keep an eye on her, so I did." He grinned, straightening his tall black hat that slid forward from the intensity of his laughter.

Britton's heart beat faster. This man knew Asha's father... "Judah, I'd like to ask you about Asha's father; you knew him before his disappearance?"

The man's friendly face became serious. He stood up straighter, and Britton watched him swallow hard. His eyes darting around them. Clearing his throat, he made an attempt to explain. More of a lecture than information. "He was tzadik...um revered for his knowledge of the law. He was my teacher, and my friend." If it were possible, the six foot, four-inch man stood taller, looking down his nose. The friendly manner gone with the question. Tension pulled at them both, each holding an end of it, each refusing to let it go.

Britton thought of the acid odor of abandonment. His beautiful Asha so often burned from it, even after all these years. "As you may have guessed, *my* Asha grieves the loss every day. We both wish our children had known him."

This newly serious man nodded, tilting his black hat up and down, then took a few steps before he turned back to whisper, "I'm certain he wishes so too."

Watching him walk away, Britton realized he had managed to run off every personal encounter that morning. But then the rabbi seemed to rethink their conversation. Revolving around, he added, "I am a virologist at the lab on the other side of this campus. I'm certain you know of the most recent virus scare." It was Britton's turn to nod, wondering if he was about to get a lecture for not wearing the cotton mask, but the virologist was not wearing one either. "The virus is highly contagious. I'd recommend you not go into the areas where most tourists go. I'd not eat in restaurants unless absolutely necessary, and of course, I'd wash my hands several times per day. But more than those things...I'd pray to keep my heart pure."

For a moment it was only his breathing, the pounding in his skull, that he heard. A long moment of terror slowly released him. He remembered the feeling, the unnatural terror, the presence of something not of this world. Finally, he steadied himself and replied, "Is the threat so great, then?"

The dark eyes pierced Britton's. He stepped in closer and talked in hushed whispers. "I do realize that you are not the biggest fan of the pharmaceutical industry, and rightly so. Most everyone knows your story, your incredible story. But this...this is not the typical scare tactic issued by so many government health agencies to create fear. This is not to pad pockets of greedy politicians and an ever hungry population that begs for protection. We have never, no one has ever, seen anything to compare to what this is. There is not now, nor has there ever been, anything like it. Not the black plague, not even Ebola... This virus is believed to be an ancient one, dug up from mass graves that were unearthed on Mt. Ararat. We still aren't sure...the virus mutates, but the mutations are happening through DNA. The virus," he leaned in and placed his lips on Britton's ear, "under a microscope is shaped like a claw, and no one, not even the most skilled virologists in the world, have seen anything that compares."

He leaned back and continued staring, weighing out how much to divulge. Leaning back in, he exposed the impossible. "If we speak to it, the virus moves, responds, and often multiplies, reacting to our voices. I, I know your story, and I wondered if you might consider helping me in the lab."

Britton scrunched his nose up. "I fail to see how someone with my skill set could be of use."

The man leaned forward again. Britton watched his mind as he searched for words. "I believe that," he paused, choosing his words carefully. "I do not wish to offend you, Mr. Donovan." He stood back up, as if rethinking his request.

Britton had zero idea where this was leading. "Mr. ummm Ben Jesse, I would help if there was something I could do."

The man stared at Britton with unblinking eyes. The spiritual possibilities paraded through them. Britton held the fiery gaze, bloated with all he had inferred. "Take my card; meet me tomorrow morning at 8:00 a.m." The man quickly rotated away, leaving

Britton to stare at his back. Mr. Judah Ben Jesse had given him lots of information, so why did he feel like he had a thousand more questions?

Britton placed the strange man's card in his billfold. He didn't plan to go unless Asha thought it was a good idea. His teeth clenched against the unwelcome jealousy. He resented the man's words; he mumbled them through his teeth. "After all, he and Asha were such good friends."

CHAPTER TEN

NO HOPE

J azlyn watched the monitors to the left of Jeff's bed. Beeping out the same rhythm, the same monotonous sound for days. Her eyes were open, the eyelids hardly blinked, the lack of sleep pulled down on them, but the fear of what might be kept them firmly in place. She pulled the hospital blanket tighter around her body, knees tightly curled up to her chin, to keep the precious warmth.

There was no change, nothing to hope for, but panic was not her friend, and she held it down, refusing to let it make suggestions. It was almost humorous, the way her mind could talk to her about hope, then betray her the next moment, pushing her fears so hard that she struggled to pull back from the imagined terror.

Shivering, not only from the cold, but from the realm of delusion that her sleep starved brain conjured. She watched Jeff through the glass windows that surrounded him; the nurse that was here this week was a stickler for the rules. She refused to allow Jazlyn in more than the designated time. The nurses only went in twice, at the beginning and the end of their shifts. She sat outside the room staring, hour after hour. She twisted her hair; she tried to read a book. Her body was numb, her mind was on fire.

The elevator door swung open, and a group of sour-faced doctors hurried through. She wondered why they always seemed to be in such a hurry; it wasn't like Jeff was going anywhere. They were both here, until things got better, or they didn't. Wearing paper protection to keep them safe from the virus. The yellow paper hazmat suits they reminded her of paper goblins. The sign on Jeff's door read, "Quarantined, no visitors!" The paper clad doctors huddled up opposite Jazlyn. She thought she might smother. There were too many for the small area. Muffled through their masks, the doctor got right to business. "We've some information for you, Mrs. Cooper."

She never corrected them. She was his "in case of emergency person." No one loved him as much as she did; someday when this nightmare ended, he would do more than claim her as his own. She bit her lip, praying inside, "El, let there be a someday."

"There are some test results we need to discuss." Jazlyn put her feet down on the cold floor and stood, still holding the blanket tight.

"Any news seems like it might be better than knowing absolutely nothing." The doctor, who was obviously in charge, gave her a blank stare, totally void of emotion, not a clue in those icy blue eyes. He reminded her of an owl she'd seen as a child. Only his eyes were visible, huge behind the plastic shield.

"We've consulted with the top virologists in Jerusalem." He cleared his throat, as if to prepare her for the news. "Jerusalem is the location of the majority of the confirmed cases. Their researchers have had the most time to study exactly what we are dealing with." He locked eyes, the icy blue stare frozen, unblinking; they waited for her to nod.

"You understand that a virus can mutate. The virus replicates the DNA of the host it has infected. This leaves us with the possibilities of millions of mutations as it infects its host, person to person, replicating each person's DNA." Again the cold stare. Again Jazlyn nodded, curling her lips under, consciously not biting too hard. "So far, each case has progressed at varying speeds. In Jeff's case, we believe he was infected while in the hotspot area, perhaps during his time in the Middle East." This time, she just nodded, wanting him to continue, instead of waiting for his "student" to comprehend.

"The cases in Jerusalem have followed the same pattern: blindness is always first, followed by loss of hearing, and touch...affecting all five senses." She hadn't meant to cry. Fury laced with fear had turned her into someone she didn't recognize. She had to be the warrior this time; she had to be the one to fight for Jeff.

Tears rose in her throat, rushed through her, welled in her eyes, and then--she would not let them fall. She pushed the traitorous tears away. Knowing her voice sounded demanding, but it came out even harsher than she meant for it to. "I know this! Everyone with the ability to search the internet knows *all of this*." Her voice shook, and that made her angrier. She had to be strong. "You said you had some information. Is this it?" Someone else needed a turn to be in the hot seat, and Jazlyn enjoyed watching this researcher squirm. The small quiver in her spine might reveal she wasn't as brave as she was pretending, a total imposter. But she needed him to come out with it before she collapsed!

"This virus is not copying DNA. It is closer to an RNA virus. That means it is not as stable as a DNA virus...and it's not exactly an RNA virus either. It's a type of both. We all agree it is a sort of antigenic shift." He cleared his throat and blinked, keeping the icy eyes closed long enough for Jazlyn to realize he was yawning. Her eyes got larger, she pushed the fury she deeper. The doctor lifted a hand to cover his mouth, but the mask. His voice had no inflections, an uncaring monotone. "It's how viruses occur after mutating, replicating, and then combining DNA." Another yawn. "That's how we believe this new virus became something far more deadly and unknown." Jazlyn's quivering increased, causing her knees to buckle. She cautiously lowered herself back into the chair. She refused to collapse in their presence.

The icy owl eyes didn't spark any concern for her, never missing a beat, the researcher continued, "We are working on a vaccine, something specific to fight this most recent mutation, time is of the essence, it is mutating quickly." He abruptly stopped talking. The room echoed in silence.

Jazlyn felt her earlier determination, that fierceness of a lioness, drain. She squeaked more like a tiny mouse. "But a vaccine. Is that the only thing you're working on? What about treatment for Jeff now? What are you working on to help him right now?" She stood back up, her voice rising with her elevation, the lioness returning. "How does any of this help, Jeff? Will he get his sight back? Will he ever hear again?" Her face flamed, her tiny body shook. "Obviously, we are all at risk now! This very minute, shouldn't you be concerned with how to treat those *with the virus today*?"

She was talking with her hands, moving them up and down. She watched herself; she knew she was getting louder, and her hands were moving faster, but stopping wasn't an option. The panic she so carefully smothered roared, and she began to scream her questions hysterically. "You say he's in a coma? You say there is no hopeful prognosis! But Jeff needs your help! Right now! Help Jeff! Help my

Jeff! How will you give me back the man I love?" Her arms were flying up and down while she yelled her panic at them. She stood there waiting. "Yes! Yes, I expect some kind of answer!" The tension built when no one moved. No one spoke.

"Obviously, you are all stumped by my demand for treatment. What are you doing for the other patients? Something? Anything?" When they each began backing towards the door, Jazlyn realized they were "just researchers." Not doctors that were used to a lot of patient-doctor interaction. They lived in a lab, patients were numbers. Her fury rose in her throat. This lioness had only begun to roar. She intended to give them a crash course on the real live flesh and blood patient that was more than a number or a test tube.

The paper gowns rustled, and one of the "lesser" researchers spoke. "Mrs. Cooper, we have some therapeutics in the pipeline." He waited, the big brown eyes watched her. She guessed her heart tearing demands had reached at least one paper goblin. "We have learned that there is a small population that appears to be immune." Jazlyn watched one of the other doctors take the arm of the doctor, speaking, warning him. "It's not anything we are sure of, it's just some hope. I don't want you to leave believing that those with the virus are of no concern to us. Of course, we are doing everything we know to do, and some things are more guesswork than science."

Jazlyn was so desperate for any help, she responded to his limited kindness. At least he acknowledged that her loved one mattered. "Thank you, doctor. I appreciate even the possibility of help."

The goblins synchronized and turned to leave. She dropped back into her extremely uncomfortable chair, her perch. She called it her lifeguard stand. She would not leave Jeff, never. But the surge of emotions had drained her, and she was already drained dry. The world around her began to blacken, and she grabbed the air. She needed something, someone to throw her a rope, because the world all around her was falling apart.

****

Asha

Jazlyn hadn't seen Asha step out of the elevator. All the doctors and researchers blocked her view. But Asha could hear her friend's panic. Her shrill cry for help was not lost. Finished with whatever it was they were saying, Asha urgently pushed through the paper goblins. Jazlyn was her dearest friend, and her friend needed her. Before Jazlyn collapsed, Asha wrapped her in her arms. Hugging her tightly, she gently assured Jazlyn. "I've got you, sweet girl. I'm here. You are not alone."

Asha felt Jazlyn's full weight against her, and she clung tightly to hold them both up. The heaviness of all of it, of so much grief, caused her to slide to the floor. But she held Jazlyn in a bear hug, for strength, as she cried. Asha looked at the dark purple circles, the pale cheeks of her beautiful friend. She wiped her chocolate strands of hair out of her face, soothing her the best she could. "Adonai, please! Please help my sweet friend. I know that You are powerful and strong. I ask you for a miracle for Jeff and Jazlyn. You do amazing miracles. I've seen it with my own eyes!" The doctors excused themselves. This was not the type of medicine they knew how to administer. Several of them looked down their noses, but a few prayed with her.

****

Jeff

Jeff listened to all of it...well, he guessed he listened. His flesh ears didn't really work anymore, but somehow he could sense all that was going on around him. His body was numb, but his spirit was more alive than it had ever been. The wheels turned inside his brain, sharp and alert.

He laid trapped inside the deep stillness that had overtaken his physical senses. But this new sensitivity, maybe this was that sixth sense people talked about. He wanted to move. He wanted to assure his beautiful Jazlyn, but he couldn't move his physical body, at least not here.

He kept waking up somewhere else. He wasn't entirely sure which place was reality, this hospital room where his broken body refused his requests, or the valley where he kept finding himself standing. It was as if a veil between worlds had grown thin, and he was feeling too much of both.

The gentle wind blew across his face again. He opened his eyes to find himself in a field of white lilies. As far as his eyes could see, the lilies covered the ground. They would bend gently with the wind, creating the visual of a white ocean. They were his mother's favorite flower. He sure wished she could see what he was seeing.

Jagged mountains of towering stone stood watch on the horizon. The air smelled like a heavy rain had recently cleansed it, leaving behind the kind of day that graced postcards. Every green thing filled to bursting with all the water it could drink. The breeze lifted the perfume off the flowers, beckoning Jeff to brush his fingers across them, which only increased the fragrance. "It's so beautiful! My momma would've loved it here."

He joyfully spun around, trying to see if he remembered this place, or if he might recognize something, anything, anyone. That's when he saw Him. The shape of The Man raised His hand in acknowledgement. Jeff slowly lifted his own in reply. "Hey there!" The voice gave him chills, not because it was eerie, but because it was intensely familiar. He must know This Man, but from where? The chill shot cold and sharp, Jeff winced. He wasn't sure he wanted to remember.

CHAPTER ELEVEN

ACROSS THE VEIL

The Man was no longer just an image, now he was close enough for Jeff to see who He might be. Jeff squinted and mumbled, "Who else could be in this place?" The Man stepped forward, taking Jeff in a hug. Not just a "man hug," but a genuine, "I've truly missed you" kind of hug.

When he returned the hug, it felt like he hugged a brother, a soldier, a dear friend. "Have we met before? I feel like I should know You, but..." He squinted, and shook his head in confusion.

Jeff assessed The Man who stood before him. He was in His thirties, His hair was long, which wasn't military, but that was the latest style. Jeff didn't like it; he was strict military, had been for years. The Man before him was taller, but also much thinner, hardly any muscle on His frame. The Man's eyes twinkled when He stepped back. He didn't try to hide His grin. "So how do I measure up, Jeff? I've never been much to look at, not in the flesh." He laughed and clapped His hands, simultaneously thunder boomed through the air. Jeff was undone by The Man's presence. The air buzzed with energy. An electrical current of power. Jeff refused to acknowledge..."I think we may have met before, but I'm struggling to remember." Lifting a wall of forced ignorance, he continued resisting the truth that dug into him like sharp talons.

Standing up straighter, The Man became serious. "You're right about Me. You know we have met. You've chosen to forget Me." Jeff was sure The Man must be mistaking him for someone else, or maybe this illness was causing him vivid hallucinations? Whatever had happened to him, he was forgetting his real life, the life he used to have. It was fading away, and this new place was feeling more real every day.

"I apologize, I don't seem to remember..." Jeff squirmed. The admission made him uncomfortable, because it didn't feel true. But The Man made no comment, no sign that He was offended.

The memories tried to rise up to meet him. He shoved them down. Deciding instead to ask the question that was burning in his mind. "So, do You happen to know where we are? What is this place?" The beauty, the peace that hugged him like a down blanket, overcame Jeff's normal control. He couldn't help himself. He rotated in place with his arms out like he loved doing when he was a small child. He felt light, giddy, and then a question surfaced. "How did a soldier of fifteen years forget himself like this?"

Adonai watched Jeff; He loved him so much, and He was excited for this moment. He chuckled, deep in His throat. "The better question would be, who do you say I AM?" Jeff stopped in mid-turn and tilted his head. The flowered field began to fade away. They both stood in a small, weathered church.

"This looks exactly like where I went to church when I was a kid. My dad's church." He looked back and forth, remembering the wooden pews and the long hours he'd spent there. The bench pews stood in rows, old, with scratches that time forgot. He ran his hand along the back pew, checking for the carving of his initials.

The building was empty, except for a little boy who curled himself into a small ball as tiny as a child could. Wrapped like a snail, he hid under a pew, trembling. Jeff watched the child. The emotions of that day stabbed him. "I remember this, though I sure try not to." The child's nose was running, and he was still small enough to believe that if he couldn't see anyone, they couldn't see him either.

The child didn't open his eyes, but Jeff remembered what he said, "I'm afraid. I want my mommy. Where has my mommy gone?" Jeff gasped; how does a small child ever forget the loss of the one grown-up that loved and protected him?

The years of growing up without his mother, under the abusive religion of his father, forced him to grow up unshielded, and alone. He was about to turn away when he saw an image and did a double-take. A slight shift in the light, or maybe dust that floated on the sun's rays, but there seemed to be something...or someone standing over the boy. "Yes, yes, he is there, watching and protecting the child. You called out to Me. I answered, I always do." Jeff continued to stare at the image, the possibility that perhaps his prayers had been heard.

Before the truth could take hold, a large man came bursting through the double doors into the sanctuary. The smell of whisky assaulted Jeff's nose, he was still repulsed by it. The odor brought the ugly memories still punching his heart. His dad stood beside him, sweat on his brow, both hands balled into fists.

Jeff looked at him with the eyes of an adult, something he had refused to do. His dad's face was flushed, the eyes were worried. He watched him wring his hands and shake his head. "Jeff, for goodness' sake, Son, where are you? I don't need this tonight!" Jeff watched himself trembling, he watched his tiny self curl into the tightest ball, wishing with all his strength to be invisible. The image that hovered increased with the child's emotions, covering him, shielding him from his angry father's view. Jeff almost felt compassion for his father, almost.

He cringed, even now, all over again. The constant accusations screamed through his mind, the day after day cruelty of the words weaving knots into his gut. "Jeff! Stop Crying! Grow up, kid!" His dad's lack of patience for such a small child sent flames through him. He wanted to punch him, punch him hard, again and again. "Get up, kid! Think you can take me now? Man enough to take a swing at your father? I'm all you've got left, you little punk." He was fourteen when he answered his father's taunts. He took a swing at him; unfortunately, he missed. He paid for it too, in blood, humiliation, and endless fear. The softness of the voice broke through the ugly memories.

"Yes, I was there too. I know you blamed Me; your mom gone, and your dad, well,he was so angry with the whole world."

Jeff turned to look into the eyes of The One whom he held responsible. "You? You let my mother die!" It wasn't a question, it was an accusation. "You left me...You left a small boy in the care of an evil man. A vile, cruel monster. How could You do that?" The emotions spilled out of Jeff, uncharacteristic of the nerves of steel that earned him a Bronze Star and the Medal of Honor.

The moment froze, and again they stood together in a hospital room where Jeff saw his mother holding him only moments after birth. "Hush little baby, don't you cry." His mother held him, tears rolling down both cheeks. "Thank you so much, Adonai. Thank you for letting my boy live. Thank you for helping me be strong enough." Jeff turned to look into Adonai's eyes. "What? I don't understand, strong enough?" Jeff faced The Man. This Man knew things, but what and how? Adonai's eyes turned a darker blue, drawing Jeff in...heart first. He stared into their depths. As if all the answers he had ever needed would be found there.

"Melody, your mom, is such a beautiful soul. Her story is one of great faith. She enjoys telling it. Would you like to hear it?"

Jeff stood frozen, his limbs paralyzed, but his mind rolled, and his stomach flipped. He asked, "My mom...she died when I was a small child. How did You know her?" Adonai couldn't help Himself; He smiled, and His eyes filled with joy.

Jeff felt confusion. Fury curled his lips. He ground his back teeth, turning his grief to anger. That's what he'd always done. That grief wanted to wring the answers out of whomever he could reach. This Man...He laughed at his pain, and so Jeff wanted to hurt Him too. He wanted to hurt someone, anyone, anything that might make the pain stop. His jaw clenched, and he looked to The Man for answers. "I asked You, how did You know my mom?" He stared into The Man's face, the deep ocean blue of the eyes pierced him. His mind tumbled through broken promises, hours locked in a closet, the wooden arm of a chair his dad pulled off and beat him with, time after time. "Are You doing this? Are You showing me these memories? Stop it! Stop it, I don't care anymore!" Love covered him, held him, consoled him. He recognized it, this love. Like someone had thrown a bucket of ice over him to stop his rage. The love held him. He shivered, draining the fury.

He was wrung out, tired and defeated. All he had lived through it didn't matter anymore. There was no undoing any of it. His eyes met The Man's again. "Who are You? I don't know You and I don't understand any of this." His mind began to roll again. The nights he drank too much, there were endless numbers of those. The women he had taken home, too many to count. The anger, the lies, all the things he had given himself to; his body tensed. Jeff squeezed his hands into fists, reaching for the anger to smother his emotions...but the anger would not return. He spun to face The Man.

"Is this Your doing too? This, this peace I feel." Jeff felt shame the moment he accused The Man of giving him peace...as if that was unkind. Adonai's eyes twinkled, becoming brighter. Inside the deep irises, Jeff was sure he saw "acceptance." Shaking his head, he wanted to keep this feeling forever, but the shame he felt in front of The Man was unbearable. His soul calmed, and more peace than he could ever remember filled him. His gaze shifted up to meet The Man's. He didn't really understand why he said it, but he whispered, "I'm sorry." Adonai stepped forward, and Jeff lowered himself to his knees. "I do know You, we met once before." He curled his knees tighter, holding onto The Man's feet. "I'm sorry, truly I am."

Again they stood in a field. Jeff smelled the lilies before seeing them. "Lilies are my mother's fav..." A woman came walking towards him. She wasn't exactly walking, more like skipping as if she were a little girl. Stopping, she picked a bouquet and waved it, then hurried toward them. The sun shone on her face, her skin drank it, causing her to glow. Jeff squinted into the light that came from The Man. So bright it was like the rising sun piercing through the snow whiteness of puffy clouds.

The Man stood between them. Jeff wasn't positive, but he wondered if The Man had caused the sun to rise. He shrugged it off; it was such a strange thought.

"My friends call Me many names." Yes, Jeff thought he knew exactly who this was; they had met once. Jeff had given Him his word, and promptly broken it, again and again. The Man nodded. "Yes, but I forgave you." All the emotions swelled inside, Jeff thought his heart might burst. What would it feel like to be clean, to be forgiven? The Man stepped forward, the woman joined them; she stared lovingly at Jeff. The intensity of her gaze made him uncomfortable. He was about to ask who she was when Adonai placed the woman's hand in Jeff's. "Jeff Cooper, I'd like to introduce you to Melody, your mother."

Chapter Twelve

HOME

The airplane taxied like a bloated bird. Britton wondered if any amount of propulsion would be able to get it off the ground. The flight attendant had finally closed the outside doors, the whoosh so loud that passengers in the first rows wondered out loud if the doors *could* close.

Britton pulled his legs up close, trying to delay the cramping that was sure to set in. Long legs and coach class didn't make for comfortable flights. He turned to the passenger beside him and smiled while trying to make himself fit in the small space. "I sure hope half these passengers unload in Telavi, then we can stretch out on the next leg of this forever journey."

He raised his arms overhead and stretched till his hands touched the overhead bins. The lady in the window seat raised her eyebrows, her tiny frame curled tight. Pushing her dark hair out of her eyes, she smirked, doubt clouding her face. "Wishful thinking; Christmas is over, everyone is going home." She motioned toward the surrounding passengers. "And I do mean, everyone!" She pursed her lips when she looked at his cramped legs. "This is one time I'm grateful to be short." She pulled her feet up onto the seat and curled even tighter.

Britton looked at the woman's tiny form. "Lucky you."

Britton flexed his toes to keep the circulation, then took a deep breath. Pushing back into his seat, he tried to adjust the neck pillow Asha insisted he bring. "Britton! You will thank me later!" He sat it down on the sofa, left it in the car, did whatever he could not to have to carry anything else. It didn't help that it was a leopard print. But she chased him down, just inside the airport before he got too far, and placed it around his neck. Placing a big kiss on his face, she held the horseshoe shaped pillow on both sides. "I love you Britton! I know it's leopard print, but I promise you won't care when it holds your head up so you can sleep." He smiled at the memory of the sparkle in those emerald eyes. It felt so long ago, and really, it had only been two weeks. He hugged the ends of it, and he was pretty sure he could smell her shampoo on it. Man, he couldn't wait to get home.

The plane took off in a steep climb. There was the awkward silence that always accompanies a take off in rainy weather. The hushed pause made the cruising altitude seem higher than normal. But once there, the passengers settled in for the short flight to Telavi. Flight attendants began roaming the aisles, bringing a comfortable atmosphere as they busied themselves with menial tasks.

The bursting flight, a mere thirty-four minutes, stretched into an hour by the time everyone got off the plane. Britton headed to the new departure gate and was disappointed to find it looked like an anthill. So many people waiting...his final flight would be just as crowded. He mumbled to himself, "At least it's direct to Houston. But it still feels like an eternity till I get home." His phone buzzed, and he pulled it from his pocket. He saw her name, and his heart did a little flip; she still did that to him. "Asha, hey honey, I just landed in Telavi. I'm already at the departure gate with the rest of the world, apparently." His eyes took in the crowds of people. That meant the flight was overbooked. "I sure hope having a ticket guarantees me a seat."

Asha was trying hard to keep her anxiety subdued. She held her breath, wishing this was over and he was finally back home. She needed to see the blue of his eyes, smell the scent of his skin, touch him, know he was safe. But she couldn't say those things. She held them back. "Well, the good news is...in less than sixteen hours you'll be standing outside in the Texas air, wondering how you could be sweating in January!" It was as long as she could wait. "I miss you, Britton; oh please hurry home!" She wanted to lighten the mood. She tried to cover her fears. But her voice quivered, and he knew her too well.

"Ash, listen, I know this has been hard. I'm not sure I should've come. I hated leaving you and the kids." That was when he heard her sniffing. "Ash, don't cry; I miss you too."

The sniffing got louder, and he heard her trying to calm herself. "Britton, I've, I've seen some things. Some things I haven't seen since before, before you were healed."

The chills crawled up Britton's spine, and he battled the panic. "What kind of things, Asha? Just tell me straight out!" She began to cry, and Britton felt an even stronger urge to get home to protect his family. "Asha, tell me! I'm imagining the worst!"

She didn't mean to be so loud, but the emotions were raw, and she had been hanging to the edge, it felt like she was slipping... "I, I had only put the kids to bed and was sitting up reading for a bit. I heard a noise...at first."

Britton felt his body tremble. He couldn't believe the nightmares of his youth could ever return. "What did you hear exactly?"

Asha braced herself. She hadn't spoken to anyone about it. There was no way to tell this story without sounding crazy. "It was a scratching noise on the wall, at least I thought it was on the wall. But then...I heard my name, someone, or something, calling my name."

Britton bit both his lips under, trying to steady his breathing. "You said you've been seeing things; what sort of things?" Asha knew this wasn't going to be easy for Britton to hear. He suffered most of his life with "encounters" that few would believe, but she had seen some of those "spiritual beings" herself.

The years had passed so uneventfully; it didn't seem real anymore, but the last few weeks made a believer out of her all over again. "I thought it was a shadow...it was dark out in the hall and then it kind of slid into the room and across the floor. I wondered if the house was on fire because at first, I thought it was smoke. It was like a dark fog when I first really got a good look at it. But then it took the shape of a creature. Bulbous eyes that glowed red, fangs, and a long forked tongue that slipped in and out while it drooled." She began to talk faster, like getting it out in the open might rid her of the terror. "He called my name; he knew my name! He threatened me. I haven't slept!" The silence surprised her, the stress clenched in her stomach.

His voice was tense and sharp. "Asha, did he say his name? Did he talk about himself in third person?" He heard Asha gasp, now he was sure. "Asha, listen to me, honey. I'll be home in sixteen hours! I'm coming as fast as I can."

She sniffed, and she knew she sounded whiny, but she had to tell him. "He, the dark one, says you aren't coming home. He says 'they' have other plans for you."

Britton ground his teeth, flexing his jaws over and over with frustration. Under his breath, he cursed the all too familiar creature. "Oh, how I wish I was home now!" He ran his fingers through his thick hair, something he always did when he was nervous. " I'll do my best to get there as soon as possible. Pray for me, and I'll pray for you. Remember, speak Adonai's words to him. He hates that!" Britton was squeezing his hands into fists over and over. Speaking Adonai's words was no longer second nature, the way it used to be. The realization shamed him. The life he had lived before was a battle zone, and he had been ready to fight at a moment's notice. He'd grown soft, flabby in this easy life. His spiritual muscles needed to hit the gym.

When they called his row to board, he wanted to hurry, like it could get him to her faster. "I have to board now, Ash. Hang in there, for me; be brave. We'll be together soon!" He grabbed his backpack and tried not to swear, then remembered where his help came from. "Adonai, protect my family! We were friends, weren't we? Please be my friend. I need you to protect my family." He fought the fear that he had long buried, the fear that evil would always win. But he also knew well that evil was personal.

"Drystan!" He spit the word. How he loathed the creature. The troll he battled all those years, the troll that had taken his life, was back for another go at him. This time, he had a family. That made him a much bigger target. He held his backpack like he held one of the children, up close to his chest as he slowly shuffled behind the line of passengers trying to find their seats. The prayers tumbled through his mind. "Adonai, my family. That's all that matters to me." He continued to bite his lips under and felt his eyes try to fill. His mind toyed with the memories of all the years that the dark ones tormented him. He knew what the problem was. He was the one who got away. They weren't used to losing. Just like Adonai warned, they would be back to see if he still held his faith like a shield. Chills raced up his neck when all he could think of was how long it had been since he'd really talked to Adonai. Now that he needed Him, would He hold that against him?

Chapter Thirteen

THE LIGHT

J eff woke to the sterile smell of bleach and stale air, not a good combination. He could sense Jazlyn's presence, but still he couldn't see, and his ears felt full of cotton. There was no sound. Everything inside him was hushed. He moved his hands, bending his fingers and extending them. He lifted his arms and opened and closed his fingers. Jazlyn stood outside the room, pointing and crying. Nurses didn't come instantly, so she rushed into the restricted area and grabbed his hands. Inside his mind, he imagined her reaction. Why his hands moved was impossible to say. But Jeff was certain it had something to do with the dreams, the place he had been, the man he met.

Jazlyn jumped at Jeff's movement, grabbing his hands and still screaming for the nurse. This was some kind of miracle. Jeff was moving, he was not paralyzed as the doctors speculated. Better than that, Jeff was awake! The nurse rushed in expecting the worst and found Jazlyn crying with joy. "He's moving, moving his hands; he's waking up! Do you see it? Watch him!" The nurse gently tapped her patient's hand. She was startled when he took her hand in return. He began lifting his arm, reaching for anyone or anything. Jazlyn stood up and squealed, "Thank you, God!" The nurse held Jeff's hand, and he squeezed hers in acknowledgement. There was so much that was unknown about this virus, but this was definitely some kind of miracle; at least she hoped it was.

"Ms. Jazlyn, let me call the doctor and let him know what's happening. He apparently still isn't hearing or seeing, but this, this would certainly appear to be good news."

Jazlyn was nodding, but then Jeff began saying her name. It wasn't the way he used to say it, but he was definitely trying to call out to her. "Jazzzn? Jaz, I know ew are near."

She took his hand and laid her face on his chest, her body shaking from the intensity of her sobbing. "Jeff, my Jeff! I knew you'd come back to me. El, please help Jeff find his way back. We are both so lost." Her prayer and sobbing felt unheard. The words crawled under her skin and scratched at her heart. A sinister squeezing there whispered El's cruelty to her, and she shuddered, then squeezed Jeff tighter.

Jeff felt her sorrow, but he also felt the darkness chasing him. As much as he didn't want to leave Jazlyn, the better place beckoned, and it was the only light he could see. Squeezing Jazlyn's hand, he hoped when he left this time, he would find his way back to her. But since none of this made sense, there was no way he could be sure. He squeezed her hand one last time and headed toward the light; maybe The Man had the answers.

CHAPTER FOURTEEN
FIZZY WATER

This wasn't a place Jeff had been before. The sun pierced through the clouds, and he made a visor with his hand so he could see. The golden ball glowed differently than the sun he remembered...somehow brighter, or maybe happier? He laughed at the thought; it wasn't something he'd considered before, a happy sun. But he smiled and looked off toward the relentless ocean waves that splashed against the shore not far from where he stood.

Startled, he spun around to look behind, sure he heard someone calling his name. But seeing no one, he was excited to find himself at the very base of a volcano. The black rocks climbed higher and higher. They were full of holes in every size. He spoke to himself, "They must've tumbled into place and then the lava cooled. Those are big enough to make giant sized stepping stones." He wished to climb them. The urge for adventure tugged, a longing that he hadn't remembered since he was a teenager.

He'd left home the day he turned eighteen. He decided to travel the world with nothing but a backpack and twelve hundred and forty-two dollars. He'd worked all summer for it. He knew how to make it last. He didn't need much.

The adrenaline surged, and he spoke to himself like an old friend. "An adventure; Jeff Cooper on an adventure of your own choosing!" The thought of it both surprised and delighted him. He stood there, letting the wild fill him up. It eased his spine and made him forget all the wounds and sorrows of life. "When did I forget that nature heals the soul?"

Without a conscious decision, he headed up the ebony rocks. In only a few steps, he could see a bubbling river running down through the rocky slope into the ocean below. The water hummed as it moved; it sang as it splashed and trickled, racing toward the ocean. Jeff laughed at what seemed like a song coming from the gushing and churning. He felt happy, so happy, not an emotion that came to him easily, or often. Leaning down, he scooped the aquamarine liquid in a handful and splashed his face. "You think you're alive, do you?" He would've sworn that the water answered when a big splash hit him in the face, and he had the overwhelming desire to reach in and "play" with it. "You feeling a little rowdy today? You want someone to wrestle with?"

Without one thought, not one care, nothing held him. With no reasons why not to, he jumped. Landing near the middle of the river, a splash went over his head, soaking him completely. The water ran off his hair and into his face. It was cold, really cold. It was more refreshing than any water he remembered showering in. Without thinking, he scooped up a handful and swallowed down a big gulp. "Is this sparkling water? Are you carbonated?" It felt fizzy, light, it tickled the back of his throat; he chuckled in response. "I think I'll just walk right in this fizzy water."

Jeff began slogging through the water, but it was much lighter and there was far less drag against his body than any water he'd ever been in. "Hey, Fizzy Water! I've been in water all over the world. I'm a Navy SEAL, after all. So water is kinda my thing. But you, you might be my favorite water ever!" The water bubbled around his legs. If this whole thing wasn't a dream or vision, he'd believe that the water was part of the conversation.

It took far less effort to wade through, though the fizzy water was up to his waist. He followed the river with his eyes and found it plunging from a waterfall so far off that he was surprised he could see it from this distance. Staring, hand blocking the bright glare of the still golden sun, he blinked, almost certain someone had jumped from the top. Squinting, he stared harder, trying to make out any movement besides the water as it dove more than three hundred feet over the edge. "I must've been mistaken. No one could survive a fall like that! What do you think, Fizzy Water? Could you make that jump?" He dropped his hand and splashed his face again. Laughing as the water swirled around his hand, tickling his fingers. "Is that right? You already dove over that death-defying edge." Jeff bowed to the water. "You have all my respect!" He continued to laugh, more relaxed than he'd ever felt.

He continued his leisurely walk through the weightless stream. He enjoyed the spray; it was such a fine mist. Each time it sprayed him, he smiled; this water made him happy. "I'm going to see that waterfall you so bravely jumped off." He felt the need to address his listener. "Uh, Fizzy Water, I was thinking, since you've come from that very waterfall...I was wondering, did you jump or did you fall?" Then he laughed at himself.

He needed to visit the waterfall, stand under the fizzy water while it shoots out into nothingness. Like an expert cliff diver, the water spiraled into sheets of glass, a liquid mirror. He imagined it stinging his skin and waking him to this new world. For a split second, his mind wandered, and he remembered that his body laid in a sterile hospital room with tubes and machines that pumped and hissed, making sure that somehow life continued; if you could call that life. He could feel Jazlyn's weight on his chest and her tears of grief washing over his face.

He pushed the reality far, far down. It didn't take much determination to keep it there. He was in paradise. There were rainbow colored flowers the size of his hands and fizzy water so clear he could watch his feet walking through the black sand. He decided to embrace the happiness; joy was such a new experience. The serious, stern, forever soldier he had always been could rest in that other world.

The thought was sobering, and all of life's worries began to pile back on top of him. That's when he heard a voice."Jeff! Hey there, man, can I join you?" Spinning to the right and then the left, he looked for the source, which didn't take long because instantly he saw Him. Standing on top of a large chunk of black lava, waving both hands like He knew him, like they were old friends. Jeff stopped, the water seemed to gurgle and fizz, as if his liquid "friend" was welcoming this Man. He shuffled his feet in the water, a way of communicating to the water that it should calm down. Jeff looked up into the face of the Stranger, "Ummm, do I know You?"

Adonai smiled, jumping from the rock down into the water to land beside him. The fizzy water seemed to reach up and catch The Man. But then what seemed like a delayed splash hit only Jeff in both his eyes. He blinked, the water clinging to The Man a few moments longer than seemed normal. Tilting His head to one side, Adonai grinned; His eyes twinkled. He patted Jeff on the arm. "We've had this conversation before...recently, remember?" He didn't wait for Jeff to answer, but turned toward the waterfall and began pushing through the current. Adonai waved back at Jeff, bidding him to join Him. "Let's get to that waterfall!"

Jeff stood, watching The Man's back. He was waist deep, and Jeff watched the fizzy water bubble around Him. He leaned forward, wondering if the water giggled. Jeff began walking again, but his mind held back things that needed figuring out. It was as if it was always there. He *knew who this was*. But he let it idle beneath the surface, waiting for the smallest opportunity to burst through.

After maybe an hour, Jeff began to "chat" with the water again. "I suppose you know who it is we are following. I met Him once or twice, but I guess He's a friend of yours..." Running his fingers through it, splashing it, and taking an occasional slurp, Jeff almost forgot that someone else was there. Well, someone besides him and the fizzy water.

Adonai stayed just far enough ahead that Jeff could still see Him. They walked in silence while the sun fell lower and lower, the color of the light growing more and more saturated. It cast a golden glaze over everything, a soft ball of buttery light just above the darkness of the volcano. The current started running faster, and it would've been impossible for Jeff to keep walking against it, but the river was growing shallower; and now it was barely tickling his knees.

Jeff almost ran into the back of The Man. He looked up just in time to stop himself. The Man revolved around, His long hair swaying from the motion. "The waterfall is just around this next turn."

When Jeff didn't reply, The Man leisurely turned all the way around; their eyes caught and tangled for the most fleeting of seconds.

"Can you feel how excited Fizzy Water is that you're here?" Jeff opened his mouth to reply, then he closed it. What does anyone say to a question like that?

The Man did not wait for an answer. He pivoted around and kept walking. Fizzy Water...how did He know what Jeff had named it? Jeff leaned down and swatted the water. "That was supposed to be our secret."

As they made the last turn, The Man started running toward the pool. The pool was like a mirrored glass around the edges; it caught the light and reflected it back up onto the falls. It was moving even as it reflected everything around it. Jeff knew it was impossible, but it looked like the aqua pool reached "water hands" up to catch the falling water in its hands. When each drop hit the surface, it pierced the pool with sound, making a mesmerizing melody like "wind chimes...underwater"! He stopped to listen.

The Man was running and then He leapt up onto the side of the waterfall and began climbing to the top. Jeff blinked, tried to clear his vision. Just making that leap was impossible. To climb a wall so straight up would be an incredible feat. Jeff watched Him, it was like He was a spider with speed and agility. He got to the top and waved.

Jeff felt chills cover his body; this was The Man he had seen diving off. Before he could make much sense of it, The Man took a run and dove headfirst into the depths of deep blue. He disappeared underneath the bubbling sapphire ripples and then burst up through the mirrored water. He punched the air, cheering. There was so much exuberance, such joy that Jeff couldn't help himself. He laughed. The Man swam to the shore and climbed out. He shook his head, throwing water in a circle like a sprinkler. Then used his thumbs to wipe water out of his eyes. He stretched both His arms out to the side, and let His head fall back. With closed eyes, He smiled, and hummed. Jeff mumbled, "I guess he's enjoying the water and the sun."

The Man opened one eye. "I was thinking...beams of warmth that caress the skin." He dropped His arms and then shrugged. "But that's Me, I like words."

Jeff stood on the same rock beside The Man. It wasn't uncomfortable like it ought to be, being this close to a stranger. But maybe...maybe he did know Him. "Jeff, I'm thirsty; how about you?"

It was the strangest question Jeff could've imagined. They had walked in a river for hours. He had gulped and slurped the fizzy water the entire hike. But truth be told...he was a little thirsty. He tried to swallow and felt the dryness in his throat. "I'm a little thirsty; do you have something special to drink?"

It was The Man's turn to be amused. He stepped back down into his own reflection. The mirrored water seemed to hold him with care. He reclined back in the clear aqua pool and closed His eyes, chuckling. "Something special? Well, you *have* been enjoying the 'fizzy water' of GanEden." He lifted back up and looked at Jeff; this time Jeff didn't look away. "I really like calling it that. "Fizzy water." No one else ever has."

Jeff realized he was enjoying this conversation. Sitting on the edge of the turquoise pool, nothing to think about but whether he wanted to swim or not. Two old friends, talking about things that were unimportant, but fun. That's when The Man cut into his thoughts. "The water I was thinking of is living water. If you knew who I was...you'd ask me for a drink." The words stole Jeff's breath.

He remembered the words. Of course he did. He'd spent a lifetime forced to be in church every time the door was open, sometimes even when it wasn't. He frowned, balancing on the edge of confusion and frustration. Right this minute, he wasn't sure which direction he wanted to fall.

"Ya know, I'm not always in church every time the doors are open Myself. As a matter of fact, a lot of times I'm not even invited." He flipped off His back and swam in long strokes across the pond.

Jeff watched The Man swimming; he watched the "fizzy water" circle The Man like it was *alive.* Jeff stood back up; he felt afraid, and judged. Undone and guilty...completely broken all in one fell swoop. "Are You, are You..." He couldn't say it...it was too absurd...it was too unbelievable.

"I AM." Jeff heard himself gasp; his eyes filled with tears. "Listen to Me, Jeff. Listen for My words. I am Truth. You will recognize Truth when you *hear it.* You will recognize Me when you choose to. I am The One. I Am The Way."

Jeff stood there, his mouth agape...his thoughts flipped and flopped on his tongue. "What do I believe?" The weight of the question made it hard to breathe. "Who do I believe in?" After all this time, after all the missions where he risked his life... He still didn't know what he believed? The Man swam under the waterfall and disappeared. Jeff felt a pull on his heart. He had to figure out what was true and what had proven a lie. He'd always wanted to help change the world, make it a better place. Seems all he had really done was to spend his life trying to escape it.

He was cold, back in the hospital bed, listening to the monitors beep and Jazlyn whispering, "I love you, Jeff; come back to me. Oh please, come back! Adonai, I'm begging You to bring him back to me!"

Did it matter? Did he have a choice in any of this? People died every day...horrible deaths, he knew. He'd seen more deaths than most. But for The Man to tell him to listen. That had to be some kind of cruel joke. His surly musings stopped when he understood...HE COULD HEAR Jazlyn pleading! His hearing had returned! HE COULD HEAR! "The Fizzy water of GanEden!"

Chapter Fifteen

REMEMBERING

"Good afternoon, passengers. This is your captain speaking. We are enjoying a smooth flight to our final destination. The hot and humid metropolis of Houston, Texas is a sunny ninety-five degrees. We're getting close to the halfway mark, and our estimated arrival is sixteen minutes early." There was a pause, and the speakers buzzed before he added, "The flight attendants have informed me that there is a sick passenger in first class. If there happens to be a doctor onboard, we'd appreciate any assistance."

Britton was asleep when the announcement startled him from his dreams. He grumbled that he'd been awakened; it was hard to fall asleep when his legs were folded up like an origami bird. He pulled himself into a more upright position and wished for the thousandth time that he wasn't in the middle seat.

The tiny lady by the window was no problem, but the hefty man who insisted on raising his armrest and allowing his large derrière to extend well into Britton's seat was not helping. The man's lap was littered with empty Fritos bags and Snickers wrappers. He had squashed two soda cans, and those were stuck in the back pocket in front of him. Besides being wide, he was a big man. His head was way above his seat back, and he was snoring like a chainsaw. Britton kept trying to unbend his knees, even an inch, but since he was in the middle of this people sandwich, there really was no way to budge.

When his legs began to throb, he decided he would have to wake up the large aisle napper. He had to be able to unfold for a few minutes. He really needed to take a walk, get the circulation going again or end up with both legs in a charlie horse. "Excuse me, sir. I am going to have to make a trip to the bathroom." The man snorted so loudly it woke several sleepers in two rows in front and behind. Britton put his head down, trying hard to cover his laugh. The image of an angry walrus was not very kind. The man struggled until he was able to stand up and slide out into the aisle.

He mumbled, "I had only just fallen asleep. I'd appreciate it if we could coordinate when we all get up." Britton wasn't sure if the man had finished his sentence. He hoped it was because he realized it was not a reasonable request. Sliding out in front of the man, he moved slowly through the narrow aisle toward the bathrooms that were closer to the front.

Passengers slept in twisted states of discomfort. Britton wondered who the "experts" were that decided how much space was needed to fly for eight hours. When he got to the bathroom, there was a line. So he stood with his hands clasped behind him, waiting. He stretched a little, reaching up and leaning side to side.

The scream pierced through first class and quickly through the rest of the plane. It was Britton's turn to use the bathroom, but he stood there, frozen with gooseflesh still making its way in tiny shivers up his body. The first few moments no one moved, paralyzed by the shrieking.

About a half second later, passengers began standing and talking, all dealing with their own gooseflesh. "What's happening up there? Can someone please go find out?" That was the general consensus. A shrieking woman on any aircraft caused some level of panic; passengers needed information to remain calm.

Britton was still standing in front of the bathroom, so he took the initiative to walk toward the first class curtains. When he peeked through the curtains, he came face to face with a flight attendant whose eyes were yellow, the pupils the shape of diamonds.

He'd seen eyes just like them on a python in a Costa Rican jungle. It had been a solid twelve years since he'd seen a demon troll. All those years ago, when he was one of the "Defectives." Seeing the spiritual world was how he had lived his life.

He'd forgotten about the snake eyes, the gnarly fangs that dug into their victims' necks. This creature was bigger than a lot of the demon trolls he'd seen in the past. The weight of deception caused the woman's back to stoop forward. Digging his long, black, half moon claws into her shoulders made its perch easier to maintain.

It was hard to see the woman anymore. This creature had taken over most of who she had been, and there wasn't much of her left. It took a second or two before Britton could take his eyes off the yellow orbs and the black drool that the creature slurped in and out.

"You are not welcome here, son of Adonai!" The sinister voice took him by surprise. How did one hear evil? The voice was not human, certainly not of this world. Britton tried to move. He wanted to respond, but coming face to face with this creature after all these years was so unexpected, so wrong. The woman cleared her throat. The creature that had spoken through her seemed to retreat for a moment, and the woman's eyes cleared. "This is for first-class passengers only."

Britton was nodding, trying to gain some semblance of control, act normal. "Yes ma'am, I understand that; of course, we all do. But speaking for all of us, um...not in first class," he waved his arm at all the passengers standing and questioning, "there needs to be some kind of explanation for the screaming that's got the rest of the passengers on edge."

Her eyes narrowed. "You just get back to your seat; the Captain has this under control." She hissed several of the words, and the snake eyes returned, rolling from the back of her head.

Stunned, Britton almost missed the burning that finally got his attention. When he pivoted around to head back to his seat, he was holding his forearm. It was on fire, and then he remembered. He wanted to roll his sleeve up and look, but every passenger was making eye contact with eyebrows raised, asking the same question. "What's happening?" He shrugged, repeating the flight attendant's words. "The Captain will make an announcement."

Once he got back to his seat, the large man was gone, so he slid right in. He figured he was in the bathroom at the back. He flipped up the armrest and took up the full seat for a minute; he let the stressed air out of his lungs. The small woman, still curled tightly in the window seat, was shivering. Britton couldn't help notice her tremble as both their seats vibrated.

Britton's arm throbbed, and panic pressed in on all sides. Gently, he pushed his sleeve up. The birthmark was glowing brightly through his skin. It was the way the Great King empowered him with strength in his life before. He used to feel things, like when life was about to go south, or when the world was about to get darker.

That skill, that gift of discernment, had warned him and saved him more times than he could even count. He certainly wasn't the expert he used to be on following its lead. That thought caused him to shake his head in amazement. "Who would understand calling someone with autism an expert in spiritual warfare?" One thing was for sure, the confidence he used to depend on wavered. This was a warning, a "glowing" red flag, and he was out of practice understanding the signals.

He laid his head back on the seat and closed his eyes. He hadn't allowed himself to think about the changes that had come into his life since the Great King had healed him. He had been "defective." He had been incapable of speech; all his life, he'd lived in silence. Those were ugly, cruel memories that drained him, burned his soul so deeply he rarely left them to simmer long.

But today...today a new understanding was surfacing. It was tr ue...he had been treated cruelly; he had been rejected and despised before. Yes, his own family was good, but they weren't the norm. The truth of all of it was rolling through him, waves of realization and understanding that weren't his own. "Adonai, thank you; help me remember."

Agony dragged at his shoulders...an insatiable guilt he worried would consume him. Reaching up, he made sure the grief wasn't running down his face. The silence of those years had given him a type of sixth sense. He often lived outside his physical world; he lived...he swallowed, and whispered, "Across the veil. I spent so much time with my Maker...I understood back then...that was the better world." The truth of the words stole his breath, snatched them straight from his lungs. The thought that he was backslidden was hard to dismiss. There was a knot that sat against his heart; he didn't know how to dislodge it. How to atone and begin to make things right again. Shame burned him. Living in the physical world was what most Shadow Walkers did. Forgetting the world of their creator was easy, so easy to do when life had promise, meaning, purpose. "I've drifted so far, Adonai. Thank you for reminding me."

Even though he gave his life to those with autism now...loving them, encouraging them, he had forgotten the inky darkness of it. Forgotten the isolation, the constant misunderstandings. He had forgotten that they changed a person, changed the perception of the world around them. He had the luxury of burying that jagged, ugly, honest piece of his soul; now it was raw and bleeding. Britton shook his head from side to side, knowing. "It's not possible to understand any of this, not unless you were"defective." There was no escaping it completely. The memories of that life sometimes sent him screaming from his nightmares, sweating and panting. He knew he was being reminded for a reason; he also needed to remember the benefits that came with the silence. Yes, there *had* been benefits, and he had allowed even the good part of that life to fade with all he wanted to forget.

"Prayer is the way to find my way back...to hear Your voice in all this insanity." Britton placed his hand across the birthmark and began to petition for the discernment he knew could change this whole situation. The birthmark he was born with brought peace to others; it had a type of power, if you could call it that. But today, he placed his own hand on it, and that peace he had given to so many others soothed him. He recited Psalm 139, his mom's favorite. He had memorized it when he was...maybe twelve. He had used it to calm himself most of his life. He could say it in his sleep. He *did* say it in his sleep again and again all those years ago. How had he forgotten it? He began to whisper the words, drawing peace from knowing that Adonai's promises never fail, even if *we leave Him.* "Is there anyplace I can go to avoid Your Spirit? If I climb to the sky, You are there. If I flew on the morning's wings to the far horizon, You would find me in a minute."

He felt the hum of the aircraft and the warm air outside caressing his face. It grew quieter, his hair was blowing, his whole body relaxed. He understood he slept, but he wasn't in the chair; he was flying. Not on the plane, but outside of it.

CHAPTER SIXTEEN

FLYING

The air beat against his face; his whole body vibrated, his clothes whipping and flapping like a flag on a windy day. He looked around, trying to figure out what held him aloft. Britton yelled over the noise, "Maybe it's the strong wind currents?" He didn't expect an answer; he was still trying to accept what his eyes were seeing.

The reply was immediate. "Must be magic...there can't possibly be another explanation."

Britton twisted his head around, feeling like he was face to face with Adonai. He couldn't see Him, but His presence was so tangible, the energy palpable; he felt Him smile. Yelling over the wind again, Britton nervously smiled back. "This is amazing!" The air blew his hair straight and then into his eyes, making him look and feel wild. His unfettered mood matched the untamed presence that hovered beside him. He didn't need to SEE Him with his eyes to know He was there. Britton squeezed his eyes tight.

He needed to own his guilt; acknowledge the ugly distance and all the selfishness he had allowed to grow between them. It was thick, and it wouldn't go down, shouldn't go down. Having a wife and children, a strong sense of purpose, all things Adonai provided, he felt like a spoiled child that had been given his dream and then instantly forgot who gave it. The ghosts of their tight-knit friendship wound around him, reminding him of all Adonai had done, had been. He pursed his lips; he was guilty.

Clearing his throat, he began the awkward conversation. "It's been so long since I've seen You, my friend." There was nothing to do except own it. So Britton confessed. "I...I'm sorry, Adonai. I have no excuse; I owe you so much, everything. I know I let the distance grow...and I haven't been very grateful either." Adonai didn't reply immediately, but Britton felt His love and then he heard Him laughing. His voice bubbled with joy.

"Britton! You are flying, flying like an eagle, like a dragon, or a Pegasus!" He said the words with such intense excitement, Britton wished to see the look on Adonai's face. "Haven't you noticed this incredible place?" A whirlwind of light soared up with the sound of His laughter. Britton leaned toward the familiar voice; it was louder than the wind in his ears. "Come. Follow me!"

Britton certainly didn't miss the analogy in those well-known words. Leaning his body, he followed; what else could he do? Wasn't there a time when he would've followed Adonai anywhere? The cold air blew hard against his skin. He knew what he was seeing, experiencing, was some type of vision, but different from when he was a "Defective" and crossed the veil. Back then, he preferred to spend as much time across the veil as he could. This felt...what was a good word? Prophetic? Adonai was showing him what was, and yet what could only be seen with spiritual eyes. This is the way they had always communicated when he was autistic. It was such a gift to leave his impossible life back then. When he crossed the veil, he was whole; he was who he was created to be. He'd forgotten so much, so very much.

Squinting hard, he attempted to understand. There was an airplane, a big commercial aircraft. Adonai's voice was clear now. "It's a 757, says so right there on the side." The big metal bird was breaking through some thick cloud cover when Britton began to realize it was his own plane. He saw himself through the tiny window. The woman who curled in the window seat, her eyes wide open, stared at him. She lifted her hand and waved. The shock that she saw him was a surprise, but then this was a dream; it probably didn't mean anything. He was sitting straight up; the leopard print donut pillow held the weight of his head. His eyes closed, his eyelids twitched, he watched himself dreaming.

The vision moved in closer. Britton strained to see through the clouds blowing in thick pillows of wet mist. The jetstream expanded behind the back of the craft, and it soared into more cloud cover. He stayed beside it, waiting for the clouds to break again. "This is...insane!" He yelled it over the wind and the roar of the jet engines. Still, he could not see Adonai, but he could hear His voice clearly.

"Look closely, Britton. What do you see?" The dark ones crawled all over the aircraft like ants on a picnic table. It was near black with the carcasses of hundreds of them. On top of the dark ones that crawled, there were larger ones that flew. Their dark rubbery wings seemed to glide and then flap, reminding Britton of bats when flying out of a cave. Immeasurable numbers of moving darkness eclipsed the sun.

The creatures opened and closed their short snouts. Long fangs hung out three or four inches over their dark, thin lips. Yellow and black drool flapped out of their mouths, flying and splatting to the creatures that were behind. Their nostrils flared open and then closed, snake tongues darting in and out. Their loud hissing caused him to shudder.

So close to the aircraft, he could see every detail. The diamond shaped pupils, the bloodless yellow eyes that stared, empty of life, and yet cold and dark. Their claws curled under like a hawk after scooping up its prey. These creatures howled randomly, causing him to shiver from the sound. Some had a dark green lizard type skin and extra long claws. It was eerie...the way he could hear each screech over the sound of the jet engines. The sounds were not something you could hear outside the spirit, but even those deaf to it could feel the evil vibrating through them.

The smaller ones crawled on top of the fuselage, stopping when they found new souls.

Reaching through the aircraft, the dark creature would grab unsuspecting passengers, using front claws to wrap their necks and hold their heads in place. They would dredge through their memories, searching for forgotten sins, the big, or the little...either would do. All the sorrows that were kept safely buried, the shredded bits from childhood, the protected secrets they couldn't bear to think of. Britton stared, frozen in terror. He was hung inside, stolen by the impossibility of what he was seeing. The creature held each chosen soul's head. With pinpoint accuracy, he punched a long nail through the victim's eye, or ear. Some even punched the nails all the way through the top of their heads. Releasing their prey, claws dripping red, they would throw their heads back and shriek before moving on. Britton watched the passengers holding their heads in pain. Cold fear sank like an anchor into the pit of his stomach; for a moment he thought he might vomit. The vision focused on a woman. Somehow, he knew it was the woman that he had heard screaming from first class. He watched her screeching, grabbing for someone, anyone. "I can't see; oh my God, I can't see!" She stood from her seat and moved her hands out in front of her, trying to feel.

"You will need to fight them." Britton whipped his head around to find Adonai's hand resting on his shoulder. His eyes locked into the peace that always came with His presence. It wasn't the first time Adonai asked him for the impossible. If Adonai asked him, then it would be possible, somehow. The question was always the same for him. What would be the cost? But this..."How do I fight what no one else can see?"

Adonai dropped his head to one side in mock confusion, then he lifted one side of his mouth in a smile. "You know the answer to that question well, Britton. Aren't you experienced? You have fought many battles for truth...in the dark."

The airplane hit turbulence, and Britton woke to find himself covered in sweat, and freezing. The screaming from first class was obviously intensifying, and he didn't know if he had slept through any type of announcement. He looked at the large man, who obviously feigned sleep, then turned to find the tiny woman still curled tight, her feet on the seat, a book on her knees. She mumbled the psalm; the one he fell asleep reciting. "You know everything I'm going to say before I start the first sentence." She looked at Britton, and her eyes pierced him with the truth, as if she willed him to embrace it. Neither of them blinked; she kept speaking. "I look behind me and you're there, then up ahead and you're there, too. Your reassuring presence, coming and going." Unblinking, she reached to place her hand on Britton's birthmark. "Is there anyplace I can go to avoid your Spirit? To be out of your sight? If I climb to the sky, you are there. If I flew on the morning wings, you'd find me in a minute. You're already there waiting. He even sees you in the dark." Then she shut the book, squeezed his arm harder, and asked, "Are you ready? Evil flies with us."

He looked past her, out the window, and watched a cold moon burn through the wispy grey clouds. Like an evil omen, it was speaking the truth of what was to come; the whole world's truth written in the sky. There was a ravishing, insatiable evil that flew in this plane; it had the power to consume everyone and everything. The intensity of that truth tugged on Britton's shoulders. The weight of it was heavy. He tried to inhale to calm the fear, but it slithered, wrapping its ugly reality all the way up, choking him.. He held the birthmark and whispered what he knew was true. "Surely you will slay the wicked. Search me, Adonai, know my heart; try me, you know my thoughts: And see if there is any wicked way in me." His face blushed hot; he was once a young man who embraced blind trust in Adonai. He yielded himself to death. So confident in his God, he had not doubted when they took his life. He let go of his flesh cocoon and believed...but this time, he had so many reasons to live. Back then, he had nothing to lose, everything to gain. "Adonai, would you ask that of me again?" He wanted to squeeze the fear until it evaporated into nothing but smoke. Wasn't the problem that he knew he was different now? He hadn't realized how high the stakes had become for him. Through clenched teeth he seethed, "I remember the weight of death, how much heavier than I ever imagined. Death is harder with so much to lose."

Chapter Seventeen

HEARING

"Jeff, Jeff!" Jazlyn ran into the room, touching his face and dropping tears onto his chest. "Can you hear me, honey? Oh Jeff, you can hear me, can't you?" Jazlyn stood beside Jeff's hospital bed, her body trembling. She jumped up and down like a cheerleader after a touchdown! He called out to her, using his arms to try and find her. Holding both his hands, her face wet, she loved that he nodded his head again and again. He was responding to her voice. They could have a conversation...who needed anything more?

"Yes, I can hear you, baby! I can hear!" Jazlyn put her head on his chest and held on with all her strength. Deaf, blind, none of those things mattered; she loved this man more than her own life. She ran her fingers down the side of his face, across his jaw. He was handsome in such a rugged, no nonsense kind of way. He had a lot of scars from so many missions, but it was the scars on his heart that robbed her of peace.

He placed his hand on the side of her face and pressed her into his chest. "I love you, Jazlyn. I hope you know I've always loved you." The cherished words were a type of salve on her weary heart.

Emotions bubbled up and through her; she breathed through her nose, calming her ragged breathing. She couldn't speak words, no words would come. So she hugged him tighter, holding on like he might slip away again.

The nurse summoned the research team, who rushed in to see the "miracle" they said would never happen. Jazlyn could hear the doctor outside the door. "What is it that makes his wife believe he can hear?" Half-closed eyes, the doctor mumbled his annoyance. He was obviously asleep when he got the call. He showed up in less than thirty minutes, his hair slicked down like an ugly black helmet, stray wiry hairs rebelled and stuck straight up. There were wrinkles across one cheek that could only be sheet marks.

The doctor stumbled into the small room as he finished the condescending question. Jazlyn felt like sneering at his ridiculous comment, but to her delight, Jeff answered his question. "Because I can hear you and answer your question. It's as simple as that."

The silence lasted only a few seconds, then the doctor stepped forward. He certainly hadn't expected this kind of recovery. "How long have you been able to hear, Mr. Cooper? Have any of your other symptoms begun to ease?"

It was difficult to believe the doctor cared much. His eyes were half closed as he asked the question. He hadn't even waited for an answer to the first question before he asked the second one. Jeff respected authority even when he didn't feel it was earned, so he answered both questions. "I, I think I've been back here...I mean, awake for maybe half an hour, and as of this moment, my sight is nonexistent." He reached for Jazlyn's hand; he couldn't see, but he could sense her presence. He hated being totally at the mercy of these researchers. So far, they had done nothing, not even one thing, to actually treat him. In the beginning or his ordeal, Jeff couldn't hear or see...but somehow he had been an outside observer to all his flesh endured. Listening to the researchers stumble through his care...he didn't have much hope that any treatment would be found. His worst fears multiplied if he observed too long. The researchers were not shy about expecting his condition to worsen. Maybe they hoped his virus ridden body would be the perfect lab rat to give them the answers they needed. The only one who had helped him...was The Man, the one on the other side.

"Overall, Mr. Cooper, how would you say you are feeling?"

Jeff searched himself, mentally assessing his physical condition; it was something he'd been trained to do. "I'd say there is significant improvement. I am hungry, and I've been awake for nearly an hour. It's been what, two weeks since I've been awake this long?" Even though his eyes stared into darkness, he still lifted his eyebrows with his question. The researcher wrote feverishly on his chart. Jeff knew this because he could hear the pen scratching the paper. He also suspected the researcher nodded, but truly, it was only a guess. Jeff had a million questions. But the truth was, most of the questions he wanted to ask were not for this doctor. He wanted to ask The Man. So he opened his mouth, tried to think of something relevant, then closed it again. He heard the doctor stop writing and close his chart. Jeff hoped...so why not ask? "I realize that this is not a question you or anyone can answer, but I need to ask. Do you think my vision will return?"

Not being able to see gave a type of supersonic focus to what he could hear. He heard the man inhale and let it out slowly, so he knew the answer before the doctor replied. "It's not something we have statistics for, so...no one has really gone this way before you. The

Claw virus is new to the world as far as we know. I'm speculating when I tell you that some recent research is saying that it is actually a very ancient virus. Perhaps something mutated not long after man stood up to walk."

Jeff frowned. The information was not at all helpful, just strange. The doctor didn't wait for his response; he just kept speaking as if he were lecturing. "We have found a population that appears to be immune. That is the most encouraging development so far. You are the first to show improvement. That is also very encouraging." There were a few moments of silence, and Jazlyn wanted to reply for Jeff...though the researcher was nodding, Jeff couldn't see him. Jazlyn looked at Jeff and then looked back at the doctor.

"Jeff...the doctor is nodding." Her face burned hot, having to tell him. She didn't know if he would be embarrassed or frustrated that she stepped in. It wasn't as if the doctor was ignorant of Jeff's blindness. She reached over and took Jeff's hand and squeezed it. He squeezed hers back. No one said anything until Jeff turned to Jazlyn and chuckled.

"I suspect the researcher's people skills have been lacking his whole life." Jazlyn leaned over, with her face burning.

"Jeff, he's still in the room." She was so embarrassed, she squeezed her eyes for a moment. But Jeff chuckled.

"Hey this blind thing could get me in and out of a lot of trouble." Then he snorted, holding back another laugh. There was no more conversation...the researcher seemed at a loss for his faux pas.

"I'd like to draw more blood; I'd like to see what the virus is doing now. Is there any change? Has it mutated? Perhaps you are developing antibodies. There are many important questions."

Jeff laid there, his mind far away...thinking about the waterfall. How alive it was and how all he wanted was to go back there and take Jazlyn with him. He heard the doctor tapping his fingers impatiently, waiting for him to give his consent. "Oh, oh yes; by all means, draw blood." Jeff almost laughed, his consent was really a formality, wasn't it? It wasn't as if these researchers weren't prepared to demand through court orders, or any other means available to them, to get what they needed.

When he heard the doctor turn to go, he asked something he really wanted to know. "Hey, um, I was wondering. I'm having some astoundingly vivid dreams. Do you think that could be caused by the virus?" The researcher tapped his chart again, then shuffled his feet.

"Mr. Cooper, anything is possible. I know that those who are blind often dream in great color and detail. Perhaps it is associated with that part of the condition. It could also be hallucinations. I wouldn't be overly concerned with that symptom."

Jeff was nodding and squeezing Jazlyn's hand. "Well, thank you. I was only curious." The doctor began to flip pages and spoke to the nurse. "Let's get these test orders in quickly and then if things look as good as I expect, let's move him out of ICU." The doctor was gone quicker than he came, his footsteps already fading. Jazlyn placed her head back on Jeff's chest and breathed her relief.

"Jeff, oh Jeff, I am so grateful. I can't wait to tell Asha!" She sat up when the thought came. "I don't know if you know or not. Asha has been coming to see you...us, every day. We've been praying together. I felt so sure that her God was listening. Do you think He might have answered our prayers?"

Jeff allowed himself to remember the dream, if that's what it was. The Man was hiking in front of him for all those hours. Fizzy water came alive in The Man's presence. Everything felt alive in that world. No way was the other world he'd visited, nothing more than the wishful thinking of a blind man. These were visions or another dimension? They were full of meaning...more than he could fully grasp. Powerful encounters with someone he had refused to know, someone who continued to tap on his heart.

"I met Him, Jazlyn. I met Adonai." He didn't mean to say it out loud. He didn't mean to confess, but it was the most amazing encounter he had ever imagined. He met Him, not once...but twice now. Each time He had given Jeff something back, helped him heal.

Jazlyn's tears fell on his chest, and he slowly moved his hand to wipe the tears off her cheek with his thumb. "I think He is the King of the World. I think...I think He loves us." Then he choked on the emotion that rose; he didn't have the strength to hide it anymore.

Saying the words out loud made the truth of it take hold. The amazement stunned him. He had not been loved by someone who knew him, knew all of him. His momma loved him, and then Jazlyn. But this love it wasn't something he knew how to describe. "I see Him in my dreams, Jazlyn. He comes for me. He cares about everything that's happening to us." Jazlyn smiled, patting Jeff's hand and then squeezing her hands together. She was a Jew. She was raised to believe that this Adonai was not her messiah, not anyone's savior, for that matter. But today, He had saved her Jeff. Today she was willing to accept any messiah who would save this man, the love of her life. She sniffed, then without looking up, she confessed, "He's certainly the King of our world, isn't He?"

Chapter Eighteen

Last Leg Home

C aptain James cleared his throat, took a few deep breaths. It was time to inform the passengers. "We will be landing in Houston in approximately thirty-two minutes. The CDC and medical staff are waiting for all passengers and staff when we exit the aircraft. We will be moved into a quarantined area until each of us is assessed. Please keep family and friends alerted to the situation. No diagnosis will be official until each passenger is assessed, and a diagnosis confirmed."

The flight attendant knocked on the cabin door. She held onto the wall, handing the Captain a towel. He set the radio microphone back onto the holder, taking a towel to wipe sweat off his face.. The flight attendant stood there, not speaking, wavering. He looked up to see her ashen face. She blurted, "I can't see." She slumped to the floor and sat crying in a heap. He wiped the sweat off his forehead and the back of his neck with the towel. He noticed his hands trembling. He wasn't sure what to do about the flight attendant. He turned to ask for backup from his co-pilot when he noticed he'd uncharacteristically dozed off.

"Maddox! Hey Maddox, I might need some assistance here. I've placed this big bird on auto, but you know how it can be when there are cross winds this strong." Maddox never opened his eyes, never moved. James reached over and nudged the much younger man. They had flown together no less than twenty times. This was not like him. He was always eager, often landing every flight manually just because he enjoyed the challenge. They lifted weights together every chance they got, and Maddox was strong enough to pick up a small car.

"Maddox, hey man, I know none of us is feeling one hundred percent, but I'm gonna need a little help." When he nudged the big man the second time, he fell all the way to his side into the plane's wall. Hitting his head hard and slumping into the small space between his feet. James tried not to panic. He had flown as a top gun pilot in the sixties. Coming face to face with more than one MiG-27.

Usually James was as calm as the morning waves, but right now his vision was pretty sketchy and his hearing was in and out. He swallowed the spikey panic; this was either going to go without a hitch, or it was gonna be every pilot's worst nightmare. Well, maybe not the worst; the worst would be surviving if your passengers didn't.

James radioed the tower. He had advised Houston of the seriousness of the situation...but maybe he had downplayed his own symptoms. He lowered his head, remembering all the times his pastor had told him to call out to God. That last sermon played in his mind. "Don't let the enemy take you down without a fight! You stand up to him. You call on your creator for help. He has promised to send help when we are in a world of trouble." James slowly shook his head from side to side.

"Adonai, you know I am in a heap of trouble right now. I need some serious backup. If You can see Your way to it...I'd like You to take over this situation." He swallowed again and continued to blink away the darkness.

The Light Warrior was more than eager to answer the summons of the Great King. He swooped over the large aircraft, sword drawn, scattering dark creatures like cockroaches when you flip on the light. He pulled the seething demon troll off the Captain's head, pulling the claws out of his eyes and ears. Demon trolls left a trail of oozing black stench behind them. Captain James used the towel to wipe his eyes. His vision began to clear. Seeing again gave him the courage to ask for more. "Adonai, I'm seeing a little better. Could You make sure I get this bird on the ground? These folks are counting on me, and truth be told, we are all counting on You."

****

Home

Britton held onto his stomach. Ever since he had woken, his stomach flipped and flopped with butterflies doing a tango. He held his breath and prayed. "Adonai, You have shown me the spiritual truth of this...this unreal situation. I'm asking you to help the pilot get us home. Please touch those all around me that are panicked and terrified." Britton watched the large man beside him sob. He had lost his eyesight more than four hours earlier. Britton attempted to soothe the man, but what could he really say? No one knew what was happening; well, technically he did, but...who would believe him? He got bags and bags of chips and crackers out of the man's backpack and continued handing them to him.

He ate, and he sobbed. "Eating calms my nerves." He wiped his nose with his sleeve, leaving a trail of orange cheese dust across his check. Britton patted the man's arm; he was happy to do anything that helped.

The frazzled doctor that was onboard didn't have many encouraging words. He moved from row to row, assessing each patient. In the beginning, he had total compassion and attempted some "bedside manner." By the time he got to row L, that was long gone.

To his credit, he made it to the last row before he himself lost his vision. Finally, he crawled up the aisle, calling his wife's name. "Tina! Tina! Honey, help me!"

She could no longer see, but eventually he was close enough that she called back. "Baby, I'm here, right here. Follow my voice; you're getting closer." Eventually, she felt his hands on the seat beside her. She helped him climb back into his own seat. It was unnerving for all the passengers that could still see, watching the doctor's trembling form on hands and knees as if he were looking for something he had lost...moaning over and over, "We're all gonna die. Oh God, we are all gonna die!"

The tiny woman who sat in the window seat beside Britton looked out the window, hardly ever turning around. She seemed mesmerized by something that held her complete attention. He realized, as he watched her, that she was still mumbling...praying. He tapped her on the shoulder as lightly as he could; he needed to know. She turned about two inches, cutting her eyes at him, her mouth still moving. "I was wondering..." That's when Britton concluded...what he wanted to know...was truly an insane question. If he asked it straight out, he would sound like a madman. She squinted at him, but never gave him her full attention. Wrapping her green knitted shawl tighter around her shoulders, she continued to stare; her vigil undisturbed. Dark chocolate curls, tinged with silver, fell over her face to cover her eyes. He wondered if she could still see...could she see...the dark ones? He couldn't bring himself to ask her.

Most of those who had lost their vision had a white scale like substance that covered the lens of their eyes. Their pupils were no longer visible. It was hard not to imagine he was in a metal cylinder full of the damned...or the "undead" as Hollywood called them. The woman beside him was rocking back and forth. If he listened over all the sobbing around him, he could hear a chant to her prayers.

"Oh Great King, El, hear my prayers. You see the darkness around us. You are the great King of Light. Send Your Light Warriors to rescue Your people. Keep us safe in the midst of so much evil."

Britton tapped her shoulder again; he had to be sure. "Ma'am, ma'am, I was wondering, um, how are you doing? I don't mean to be rude, and it's none of business, but I was wondering if you could still..." She reached over with one hand and patted his leg. It frustrated him that she wouldn't turn around. From where he was sitting, he wondered if he was the only one left who could still see. He had never imagined the terror of nearly three hundred people in one place, all sobbing. All of them were too terrified to console each other.

He eventually gave up his quest to speak to his seatmate, then she slowly pivoted and addressed him. "I don't have time to talk about this...this battle. Can't you see we are at war?" Her cheeks were a bright shade of pink, and her eyes beamed with intensity. The dark pupils assured Britton that she could definitely still see. The peace that gave him was short-lived when she laid into him. " What's wrong with you? Pick up your sword! I can't do this by myself!"

For a moment, he sat stunned; the sting of truth in her words singed a tad, and he needed that split second to recover. She glared at him, her eyes locked on his. She slowly turned back to stare out the window...but she spoke to him. "It's you and me against that hoard out there! You used to be a warrior; you need to remember who you are!" She began rocking in rhythm with the chant...her prayer vigil intensified.

The plane seemed to groan as it broke through the cloud cover. Weighted by the terror that ravaged the passengers, Britton was relieved to see the runway.

He held his breath until the captain came on the speaker. "There she is folks. Houston, Texas. A balmy ninety degrees in January. Please don't be alarmed by the emergency vehicles; they have arrived to assist us with whatever condition we are struggling with. We will be moved into a private area, and each of us will be examined by a physician. Let's all take a deep breath. Our ordeal won't last much longer." He paused, then decided these folks needed some good news. "My vision has returned, and is now crystal clear. I hope that gives some of you encouragement." He stumbled over his words but finally suggested, "It wouldn't hurt if we all said some prayers. We will be safe on the ground in a few short moments."

CHAPTER NINETEEN

QUARANTINED

A flight attendant boarded the aircraft as soon as the door opened. None of the flight attendants on the plane could see or hear. She lifted the microphone up to her mouth, and in a far too cheery voice for passengers who had been through such an excruciating ordeal...she spoke as if their lives had not been altered at all.

"Please leave all carry-ons on the plane, just one personal item. Yes, that's right, follow the men you see in yellow through the stairways; they will direct you." The woman quickly realized the impossibility of the situation. They couldn't see the men in yellow...they couldn't see the stairs. She didn't know how to help, so she told them the only information she had. "Your carry-ons will be placed in a safe area. You will be able to pick them up later."

Being herded off a plane was something most passengers were accustomed to. But adding staff in paper hazmat suits...not that anyone could see them, but the sound. The paper suits were stiff, probably because they were new. Created more confusion, for folks that couldn't see. Being blind seemed to have already heightened the sense of sound for a few who could still hear. About a fifty-fifty ratio for those who had lost their hearing as well. No one spoke, only whimpering and sniffing; it gave a far more serious tone to the situation. So many held on to each other, less than half the passengers could see. Navigating all the stairs and the twists and turns was impossible...it was going to take a while to move almost three hundred people.

Britton began texting Asha even though he was certain it would be a good hour before he even got off the plane. "Plane has landed. It could be a few hours before I'm able to leave. I'll text again when I know something."

He was trying to assist the man who sat beside him, but he was struggling because he could no longer hear any instructions. The man ran into seats and passengers and refused to give up his carry-ons because, of course, he had not been able to hear the instructions. Britton slid his phone back into his pocket. He needed two hands on the man to be of any use.

The woman who sat beside him mysteriously disappeared shortly after landing. She was there and then she wasn't. He had no way to account for it, but he also didn't have time to think about it.

Two hours and twenty-two minutes later, Britton slowly ushered the large man into the folding chair where medical professionals were still assessing passengers. The distraught man had continued to sob and wipe his nose for the last hour. His comb-over was now hanging to the wrong side, and he shuffled his big feet because he couldn't see where he was going.

Britton could hardly blame him; he kept imagining how terrified he would be. The medical personnel turned to Britton."Can you give me this gentleman's name?" Britton looked into the intensity of the eyes that stared back at him through the mask. He was pretty sure it was a woman, but honestly, these people were covered head to toe.

"Ummm, he was sitting beside me on the plane. I don't know much about him...only that he can no longer hear or see." The hazmat suit nodded, scribbling down notes. It was the first time Britton understood what was taking so long. How do you ask someone his name if he can't hear? With a sudden inspiration, he picked up the man's hand and began writing letters into his palm. Seemed far fetched, but hey, who studied communication more than he did? He knew about Helen Keller, and this is how her incredibly gifted teacher had been able to help her learn to communicate.

The man stopped his sobbing long enough to focus. Then he bellowed out, "Paul McCormick. My name is Paul McCormick!" The person in the hazmat suit stood up and gasped. "That's awesome. Ummmm, could you help us? We could try this with all those who are traveling alone and have lost hearing. This is brilliant!"

Thinking and just wishing to get home, Britton scratched his head. "Of course. Yes, of course, I'll help. What else do you need to know?" He went through the list of questions, and to his credit, Paul calmed down immediately.Though his responses were somewhat slurred, or rather not as pronounced as if he could hear...he was communicating. Britton shook his head when another hazmat suit came to escort Paul to the quarantine area. Paul handed Britton his cell phone and asked him to text his wife. Britton happily obliged. The hours rolled by, and the number of passengers he attempted to help communicate rolled into the double digits and then the triple.

It was after passenger number one hundred and fifty that he remembered he had never texted Asha again. "I need to text my wife;

ummm, can you give me a minute?" The woman in the hazmat suit sat on her own metal chair and motioned him to proceed. She leaned back, stretching; it had been a long evening for her as well.

He picked up his phone to find twelve text messages. "Boy, am I in a world of trouble!" He began his text with "I'm so sorry..." but then his phone rang. "Asha, yes, yes, I'm fine. I am so sorry. I am in the quarantined area. I have no idea why my phone finally decided to ring."

Asha wiped the tears off her face. She had imagined every worst-case scenario; her mind could conjure. None of her thoughts had been good, because of the unrelenting bad dreams she'd had since Britton left. The horrible, dark creature who visited her every night had even worse ideas. "I took the children back home; your mom is with them. Will you be coming home?" Her voice broke and she could no longer hold on to her strong resolve. She bent over, shaking, one hand on her thigh to hold herself up. Sweat rolled down her ribs; the hours of waiting finally broke her, and she began to sob. "Hey, hey Asha. Honey, I'm here. I'm home!" She continued to sob. Two weeks of worry finally began to ease...she cried in relief.

"Asha, I need to explain what's been taking so long." It seemed lame as he tried to form the words. "I've been asked to help some passengers communicate. A great many of them have lost their sight, but they have also lost the ability to hear. I got this crazy idea that if I wrote in their palms... ya know, like Anne Sullivan did Helen Keller? I'd be able to help them at least answer the questions. We've been able to contact their loved ones..." He waited for her to calm down, for her to say something, anything. "Ash? Honey, I'm safe."

She tried hard to get a grip on her emotions, but after living in torment for two weeks,her emotions were seesawing. "That creature, that filthy spirit, tormented me, night after terrifying night. He'd wear me down, and I'd fall asleep from complete exhaustion, then he'd spin nightmares that rival a horror movie." She left out the part where she woke to his jagged claws on her head, the darkest of nightmares still spinning through her terrified mind.

"Britton, can you come home? I mean, will they let you leave?" Britton ran his exhausted fingers through his hair. He felt the sweat on his forehead, and he felt the weight of all he had lived through. Even his hair was tired.

"I'll ask, Asha. I'm not sure if there is a specific amount of time for quarantine; or since I have no symptoms if I can go. Hang on, and let me ask this woman in the hazmat suit."

Britton looked up to find the woman working with the next passenger. She was attempting the letters in the woman's palm, but the woman kept pulling away as if touching another person was painful. Watching the woman howl each time she was touched made him wonder. "Excuse me, excuse me...Dr. Joyce? Is it possible that touching her is hurting?"

The green eyes above the mask seemed to consider his thought process, then she replied,

"Maybe that's it. Perhaps it is a symptom that only a few are experiencing." Britton gently took the woman's small hand, sliding his phone back into his pocket. The tiny woman with the short grey bob and bright blue eyes...dulled by the white scale over her pupils, moaned when he touched her. Holding her hand, he barely applied any pressure. He wrote, "What is your name?" When she finally understood, she whispered, "Beverley Jackson, I am the mayor's wife." Britton looked at Dr. Joyce, whose eyes grew wide. No one seemed to know that she was among the passengers, and why, why hadn't the mayor informed them?

"Mrs. Jackson...oh wait." Britton realized he was talking...so he gently wrote the letters. "Do you need me to contact your husband for you?" The frail woman sat drooped in the chair, then she answered with a very fast... "No, no, no, he will not come. He is angry with me for going on this trip!" Then she dropped her head and began to sob. "He said he had a bad feeling about it, and I wouldn't listen."

Asha strained into her phone; she listened to all that was happening. Amazed at what Britton accomplished, and yet she knew his heart. Teaching others to communicate was his gift, his dream. Here he was, being used by Adonai to help in a horrible situation. He was making it so much better...he had truly done the impossible. She smiled to herself. She wanted to tell that evil creature who tormented her what Adonai had done. But just thinking of him gave her chills. It made her angry that she trembled. She heard Britton ask the doctor if he could leave.

"Dr. Joyce, I see we are coming down to the last few passengers. Since I have no symptoms, am I able to leave soon?" Asha couldn't hear the answer right away. There was some shuffling. Then she heard the doctor say she'd need to speak to someone from the CDC. That's when Britton's exhausted brain remembered Asha was on the phone. "Ash, Ash, I'm so sorry. I was trying to help and I..."

She interrupted his apology. "You are the most amazing man I have ever known. I am so proud of you."

CHAPTER TWENTY

DRYSTAN

Six days passed and still the passengers were quarantined in some obscure wing of the gigantic airport. Hospital beds in rows reminded Britton of a MASH unit he saw on television. It was definitely a makeshift holding area. He hoped that meant they didn't plan to keep him much longer. Hazmat suited medical professionals administered the only things they thought might be helpful...vitamin C and D. So far none of the virologists found anything that even touched the Claw virus. It was aptly named because of its shape, under a microscope. The virus looked like a vulture's talons. The only information he had came from watching the news.

Sitting on one of three metal chairs up against the far wall, Britton was now the only passenger unaffected. He watched the television, which made him feel guilty since he was the only passenger that could still see. The plane's captain had reported having symptoms, but recovered quickly. Britton watched him being interviewed on the news. The pilot said he had prayed, and his vision cleared. Britton asked about it...over and over he asked, but no one seemed to know why the pilot was allowed to leave, and he wasn't.

So Britton sat slumped in the cold metal chair, hour after hour. He slept on the floor, but no one seemed to notice. He hadn't showered, hadn't slept much. His body was stiff and sore from sitting and sitting and sitting. He stared at the television; he wished his phone wasn't dead. He wished any of the hazmat suits would tell him something, anything at all.

The news reported that the virus was still spreading even though most known cases were quarantined. The country was shut down; the world held its breath. How did masks and hand washing stave off a pandemic of such magnitude? The news was focused. They reported on nothing except the virus. It made everyone fearful and nervous. This virus was like a cruel terrorist holding the entire world captive. So many cases, it was hard to keep count. Every news outlet had different numbers; how many blind, how many deaf. Britton stared at the screen, listened to the updates, which were mostly the same, day after day...more cases, less understanding. He knew why; he'd seen it with his own eyes. This wasn't a virus that could be fought with science. This was a virus of the soul.

An airport employee came into the area and began dropping luggage in piles. When he saw his bag, he made a beeline for it. He got his phone charger out of the side pocket; finally, he'd been given a "line of hope." The zipper was broken on his bag, his dirty clothes hanging out the sides. But there was some clean underwear and a few shirts. He picked the bag up and carried it sideways all the way to the bathroom. He sat it on the counter and started digging for his razor. He looked like a homeless man, and he was certain he smelled like one too.

He flipped over the tag on the handle. "The CDC has inspected this bag. If you find anything missing, please contact us at this number."

Britton shook his head. "What in the world did they expect to find?" He continued shaking his head; his clothes were in a waded mess, but at least they smelled better than the ones he had worn for a week. He stripped down to his skivvies and began using paper towels, soap, and water to remove some of the body odor that hung in layers on his skin. He put on his t-shirt that read, "Just because I can't speak doesn't mean I have nothing to say." It was, and would always be, one of his favorite quotes that one of the kids with autism typed. It was powerful and made people think about the possibilities...at least he hoped it did.

He walked out of the bathroom, luggage in tow. The busted zipper, he repaired with his nail clippers and a safety pin. A full week had passed since he had spoken to Asha or the kids because his phone had died. Now he had his charger. As soon as his phone lit up, he tapped on Asha's name. She answered, out of breath. "Britton! Britton, is that really you? I didn't know what happened. I called and called. Oh my gosh, Britton. Are you okay?" Asha was choking on the panic, not waiting for him to answer. "I tried to get information, even visited the airport again and again; they always turned me away." Holding her purse, she was about to head back to the airport to try again; she tried every day. When she took a breath, he quickly spoke up.

"I'm so sorry, Ash! They finally let me have my luggage, and I plugged in my phone. I called as soon as it powered on."

He had battled the anxiety of not being able to talk with her for a week. He clenched and unclenched his fists, tried to find peace in her voice, but then she began to cry. "The kids wanted to talk to you tonight...no one has slept. I finally got them to sleep maybe ten minutes ago." She grasped for any control. "I'm so grateful you are okay. *You are okay*, aren't you?" She didn't wait for him to answer; she kept talking. "I didn't know, couldn't get anyone to tell me what had become of you. My imagination has been running wild!"

He couldn't see her, but in his mind, he watched her wild curls fall across her face as she dropped her head. That was what she did when she was overwhelmed. She used those massive curls to create a wall of protection between herself and the world. His whole body was tense. He tried to relax his shoulders, but this was such an awful situation. He didn't know what to say, so he cleared his throat. But then she asked him, "How are you feeling? Are you still well? I've worried about your vision and hearing." She waited. It seemed impossible. "Out of a plane of nearly three hundred, how can there be only one man that is not sick?" She thought about it and shook her head. "But you're special Britton! You've always been special."

He broke through her tangled thoughts. "I've not really heard anyone talk about when we might get out of here. I can't imagine that I need to stay any longer..." He looked around the frigid room. Hospital beds and medical staff in hazmat suits. He sighed, his heart felt like lead. "But no one seems to know what to do *about me*. I've watched a lot of news...too much news."

He sat back in his folding chair and braced himself. In case she had heard, or maybe even in case she hadn't, he wanted to talk to her about it. "Hey Ash, they are saying on the news that...none of the 'Defectives' have gotten this virus." He waited for a reply. "Ash?"

She heard him. She just didn't know what to say. He wasn't "defective" anymore...he wasn't! "Yes, Britton, I'm listening. I heard all about it." She felt like every parent mentioned it at the Center. She ran her fingers through her hair and squeezed her eyes. "It's amazing, and pretty strange all at the same time. The fact that you also don't have it...well, I'm unsure how I feel about it." She sat down in the kitchen chair. Placing her elbows on her knees, she tried to see the good in the situation. "Of course, I'm grateful. I just wonder if that means something, that's all."

He waited. He hoped she would embrace the news, be encouraged by it. This free-spirited, wild child that he had married, the picture of calm and sunniness had changed. He couldn't think on it too long. All that loving him had cost her. It was more than he deserved. It was like he walked a tightrope, unsure of which way he would fall. Would he cling to the truth he was born knowing? That Adonai was in control; that nothing happened without His knowing. Or would he cling to fear, unclench his hand from the truth, letting faith slip through his fingers...like sand? He went so far as to watch the sand pouring through his fingers in his mind's eye. He sat up straight and dismissed the possibility. Self pity was not an option, his whole family would slip with him.

He attempted to chuckle, to make light of the difficult situation, but his tongue tied itself into a knot. He didn't sound convincing when he tried to encourage her. "Well, I for one, am super excited about it. Maybe there is something more magical that Adonai is doing with all this." He struggled, searching for the right words. He needed to, even wanted to tell Asha about the vision on the plane, about the dark ones crawling all over it. But not now...not until he was home, and she felt safe again.

"Those of us who were damaged by the injection...Maybe Adonai changed us, made us stronger? Maybe He is using it for some greater good than we ever imagined." He felt ridiculous after he said it. Yes, that was the right word. Ridiculous. Even saying it to his closest friend, saying it here, here in this physical world...his face burned hot and red. Maybe it was farfetched in the physical world, but not when he crossed the veil. On the other side in that better world, it was easy to believe that Adonai would take every evil and make it into something good. Like a blacksmith, He would stick the iron into the fire and watch the dross burn out of it.

Wringing his hands, he waited for her to say something. A hazmat clad official walked by and stopped. "I need to find someone to ask; most of the people that come and go are hospital staff." The ghost in the yellow hazmat suit hovered beside Britton and then cleared his throat. Britton had grown so accustomed to being ignored, he didn't pay attention. A solid week had passed, and Britton had zero hope that today would be the day someone would notice he was still waiting...give him his walking papers.

Asha was asking what she could do to help when the hazmat suit tapped his shoulder. "Excuse me, sir. Were you on the plane?"

Britton stood up; rotating, he was level with the eyes behind the clear screen. "Yes, sir, I was on the plane." He still held the phone to his ear, but Asha stopped talking to listen.

"I am Dr. Hazmaraz. I am in charge of taking samples and analysing them back at the lab." He stared, and Britton was not sure if the paper clad man ever blinked.

"My name is Britton Donovan. I'm a speech therapist. I've just come back from Jerusalem with the rest of these unlucky folks. I need to get home to my wife and children." He stopped, reached up and pressed on his temples. He hadn't seen his family in over three weeks now; this was definitely not what any of them signed up for.

"It's as if no one listens to me when I tell them that I'm not sick. I'd like to go home. At what point am I no longer a threat? But no one seems to be too concerned with my situation."

Dr. Hazmaraz didn't reply, only stood there for a heartbeat. Then it was like he snapped back from some other place. "Yes, well, Mr. Donovan? I would love to be of some help to you. I could possibly get you cleared in the next few days."

Britton heard Asha gasp; he lowered the phone down by his side. "What needs to be done to make that happen?" The doctor tapped his gloved fingers on his leg, pondering; Britton wasn't sure if that was good news or bad.

"Why don't you get your luggage and come with me? I can draw some blood, figure out if you are indeed immune..." The doctor paused, seeming to mull that possibility around in his mind. Then he finished his thought. "What a gift that would be." Britton blinked, his heart started to race, he blinked again, something felt off. The yellow of the man's eyes, the way they rolled back, and then the way he licked his lips with a tongue much longer than it should be. Britton felt a strong warning. It was no small matter; this was not the right path.

Stepping back from the paper-clad man, the terror slithered through him, tangling up his ability to think. This was not the way out he had hoped for. Putting his fate in the hands of one of the snake eyes would never be a good choice. "Dr. Hazmaraz, I think I'll continue to wait until some of those in charge of...releasing all of us shows up." Britton began to stumble on his words. Everything inside him told him to run. Who would have more authority than this man? Who could he appeal to if this man made demands? He desperately grasped for any reasoning that would prevent this man from demanding he go with him. "Until things are calmer...I can wait. I can wait until you have taken care of those who are sick." Britton continued to step away; the back of his legs pushed against the metal chair. There was nowhere to run.

The doctor watched him, but appeared unaffected by his impossible attempts to escape. "Mr. Donovan, it would be faster if you accompanied me to the lab, gave me blood, waited for the results, and then we'll see from there."

His words sounded like metal scraping against stone. Britton watched the yellow eyes spin; he felt himself shiver. He could hear Asha screaming. "No, no, no!" Again and again she screamed, "No!" Then there was the sound of her muffled crying. "Drystan told me this would happen. Don't go, Britton. Don't go!" He watched the doctor motion for security, and two of them came instantly through the glass doors.

"Mr. Donovan will need to be accompanied to the lab; help him make the transition safely." Britton stood still, placing the phone up to his ear. He held one finger up, hoping they would give him a moment. But the snake eyes inside the hazmat suit lifted an arm, and security immediately pulled the phone from his hand. The doctor reached out for the phone, clicking the end button. The snake eyes burned into Britton's. "You really need to remember who you are dealing with...friend of Adonai."

The doctor motioned for security to wait, and he placed his face inches from Britton's. "Yes, we have met before; but this time, the situation is far more in my favor. We'll become friends again, Britton. Remember? The way you and I were friends all those years ago at the Gap Center? I've been telling her...your Asha, that you would

NOT be coming back home." Britton shook his head, straightening his stiff back.

Asha had listened to the conversation, or as much of it as she could, before his phone went dead again. Her heart shattered. The longing and the anger pressed down hard, the pieces choking and splintering inside her chest.

Dr. Schmitz turned around and began walking toward the rows of beds. Security held Britton's arms, though he tried to yank away. He walked slowly, resisting every chance he got. His mind was rolling through the memories. The life he had lived before. All the horrors of the Gap Center. The dark creature knew him, and he knew the creature's voice well...maybe it was the tone, but more likely it was the spirit. A voice from his other life, the life he lived as a "Defective."

His body began to shake because he understood. This kind of evil was not something he wanted near his family, near anyone he loved. The thing he knew for certain was...fighting this creature in the flesh never worked. He needed advice, and Adonai was the only one who knew how to defeat a monster that moved from one human host to the next. Drystan was back...and he had a grudge. Drystan had killed him once, a long time ago in that life he lived before. His resurrection infuriated the spirit. He was not used to losing.

Eternal beings have a forever memory...a forever vendetta. Britton had the audacity to refuse to stay dead. Now this creature would fight him, but not so much for his life; now he wanted his soul. Tears pooled in Britton's eyes, and he tried to bury the terror of what the demon troll had done before. This time he had a family, a wife, children. Chills crawled all over him, almost like the spiders that used to inhabit his mind. He remembered the hopelessness he felt for so many years. He had fought this creature before, and he had won...well, Adonai had won. He would cry out to Adonai, and Adonai would save him...it was the only hope. It had been years since he'd thought of the sword Adonai had given him. It was time he used it.

CHAPTER TWENTY-ONE

LAB RAT

In the back of the security vehicle, Britton began counting the rows upon rows of vehicles from the Gap Center. That was the Government Autism Project where he had been imprisoned. His testimony before Congress brought light to the corruption. It saved thousands of "Defectives" from the evil intentions of a group of powerful senators. They had been lured by lucrative campaign donations, but also by the power the pharmaceutical industry wielded. They had planned to make insane money by selling body parts to labs across the world. Those in charge of The Center had meant for Britton to be their first victim.

The exposure brought arrests and a great deal of shame to a country that had to admit it was willing to dispose of its weakest for money. The Center had closed down for several years, but eventually had revamped into work centers and group homes for those with defects. Staffed with quality caregivers who loved the people, and loved their jobs. It was truly beauty for ashes, good birthed straight out of evil. Britton was so humbled that Adonai chose him to help save others. But it made no sense...that any of the "Defective" would be at a research lab... Why were there so many of them? From the back seat, Britton stared at the back of the guards' heads. The vehicle pulled onto a railroad bridge, crossed it; on one side was a levee, built to keep the long fingers of the San Jacinto river in place.

Britton's anxiety was reaching a crescendo. This wasn't only about him; this was about all the "Defective!" "What's going on here? Can't you at least tell me why so many GAP vehicles are here at the Lab?" But neither guard was willing to speak. They looked at each other, then looked ahead as if he hadn't said a word.

It had been so many years since Britton had been treated like he didn't have a voice; it infuriated him. He would have answers, there would be repercussions for taking him against his will...somehow he would make sure. Every alarm inside him was going off. The night was calm; but just beyond the bright moonlight, a spirit of something dark lurked. He couldn't shake the sense that things were about to come undone.

The car pulled into the gravel parking lot, and they yanked him out, cuffing his hands behind his back as if he were some kind of criminal. "Hey guys, is this necessary? I haven't done anything. I'm not under arrest." Britton didn't fight them; he wasn't sure if he should. So little of life made sense lately. His protests were met with silence...silence was certainly something he understood. Since he'd spent the first twenty-five years of his life with all his words trapped inside his mind. Fury crawled up his neck; he clenched his teeth so he wouldn't say more. Sometimes words did more harm than good.

They walked him down a long hall where each door had a window. He tried to look through the windows; he needed to see what was going on. He could hear moaning and crying, and that certainly caused his heart to stop more than once. There were beds, well, really they were cots lined up in rows; all full of "'Defectives."

The fear surged through him, his heart beat so loudly in his ears he couldn't hear anything else. He began praying, beseeching, pleading. "I don't understand, Adonai. I know You are with me; I know You have a plan. But...this sure is a crazy, crazy plan. Please, I need Your strength. There is truth in all this darkness. If You will light my way, I will be able to see in the dark."

He tried not to shake. He tried not to panic. He felt betrayed by his own thoughts when he heard the handcuffs rattle from his trembling. They kept pushing him forward, through hall after hall. Fear walked beside him on one side, but he clung to who he knew Adonai was. "To be honest, Adonai, I'd appreciate it if You would silence the voice of all my fears." He hadn't realized he'd slowed down and stopped to stare through the tiny window where he heard the most noise. The guards were almost dragging him. He even lost his footing a time or two. He certainly wasn't anxious to get to wherever it was they had planned for him. Then his mind cleared, and he understood. "The 'Defective' are immune!" He said it out loud; it was an epiphany. He was certain the men dragging him already knew. It was the very reason he was being brought here.

He stared through the small windows of each room they passed. "Defectives! How many? I know these young men!" He called out to several of them. "Jake! Jeremy, I'll get you out; don't give up!" He locked eyes with one of the young men he worked with at the Center. He was typing, communicating...making so much progress. Britton couldn't imagine any scenario that would cause Jeremy's mother to grant permission for them to take him here. He wasn't even a student at the Gap Center. He pulled back even harder against his captors. Trying to make sure the young man heard him, he yelled as loudly as he could. "I'll be back to get you. Don't give up, Jeremy!"

The guards yanked him, and he landed on his knees. Looking up to see if either of them would look at him, he locked eyes with one. "Why are they here? These young people are here without permission; I know you know it. None of this can possibly be legal!" He stumbled to his feet. It was that or be dragged by his arms. Seeing Jeremy energized him. He would not be silent; he would scream for those who couldn't speak for themselves." Those 'Defectives' all have families. They would need to give permission for this! You don't want to be part of this, do you?" The guards ignored his pleas; they apparently had no concern for what was being done. *It was as if a cure for this virus alleviated all human decency.* If sacrificing a few "Defectives" saved the world, so be it.

The room they brought him to was stark white and smelled of cleaning chemicals. They uncuffed him and motioned for him to sit on the table. In his mind, he relived a great many unpleasant moments on similar tables. Sitting down to "relax" was out of the question. An exam table smack in the middle of a large room, white cabinets, stainless steel trays. He would guess it was a type of lab/surgery unit. The exam table had multiple leather restraining straps; they were the first thing he noticed. In that life before...leather straps were the last thing he remembered seeing...they held his wrists, his legs, his middle. Their "mercy" to him had been not to strap down his head. It wasn't a memory he liked to dwell on; usually if it came, he would remind himself that Adonai was with him.

He stood still, listening to the atmosphere in the room; it was how he used to live his life. He would listen for any hint of what happens in that place. Often the room would "tell" its secrets. This room was quiet. He squinted his eyes closed and heard the hushed whispers, but this room was not giving up its secrets. A shimmer of deep loss brushed his heart; time kept tugging him back to the days before. Spirits might not dwell here, but Britton was haunted plenty by his own ghosts.

He survived those ugly years by compartmentalizing his life. He lived across the veil; the flesh life wasn't his real life, it was a nightmare. He shook his head in a vain attempt at staying in the now. A guard stood on each side of both exits, making retreat impossible. It still didn't quiet the voice in his head screaming that he should run. Like a fly caught in some intricate spider web, he knew the harder he struggled, the more entangled he would become.

A man in a white lab coat came scurrying through a back door. He hurried toward Britton. He stuck his hand out stiffly. "Thank you for agreeing to meet with us, to give us samples." His eyebrows moved up and down to some unseen rhythm; it was hard for Britton not to imitate the movement.

His hair was thick, the color of sand. It was straight, like sticks of straw, and Britton's exhausted mind whispered," If he only had a brain." Britton chuckled weakly at his own Wizard of Oz reference. He wondered if the stress and fatigue had finally made him snap. He tried to assure himself, "That's hair, just hair, nothing more." He talking to himself the way he used to. When he was "defective," when his words were trapped inside his mind, bouncing off his skull and landing like metal spikes in his heart. How could he be here? "Get a grip, Britton; don't lose control. They do not have the right to do this." If he allowed any of his emotions a voice, the panic would overwhelm him. All the nights of almost no sleep were causing his weary mind to play tricks on him. Compacted by the fears that stroked him when he let his guard down. He was slipping, and he knew it.

The man in the lab coat barely touched Britton's fingers when he extended his hand in response; it was definitely not a handshake. He noticed the man's nostrils flare as if he had touched something dirty or vile. Once the unsavory niceties were out of the way, the man spun quickly and took steps toward the exam table. He turned halfway around, motioning, acting as if this was somehow Britton's choice. "Please be seated here. I'll need some blood samples and perhaps even a biopsy."

Britton's mind swam. The memories of all the things that had taken place before. He knew what it was to be a lab rat...a guinea pig. This was a tad too familiar: the smells of alcohol and bleach, the metal containers, the table, and, of course, the leather straps. This was a replica of the cell he spent his last moments in. He always thought of it as the life before, before his real life. The years, he was incapable of language; the years only Adonai heard his thoughts.

The chill chased its way up his back, and he couldn't stop the shiver from causing his shoulders to shake. "It's freezing in here. I remember...that labs are usually cold. I spent some time in one...a long time ago." The man was arrogant. He turned his face away as if Britton was not worth his notice. Britton considered bolting again, but there were two guards at each entrance, and he could see the shadows of the two that escorted him in through the one tiny window.

Britton knew he talked too much when he was nervous, but he began asking questions, anyway. "So, who are you exactly, and what is your name?" Britton casually sat down on the edge of the exam table, purposely sitting upright. He would not be strapped to a table ever again; a helpless man seemed too big a temptation for those without morals. The doctor visibly gritted his teeth, then his nostrils flared. "I am Dr. Luka Schmidt. I am head of this lab and the research that goes on here. I work with Dr. Hazmaraz. I hear you are acquaintances."

He casually tied a rubber strap around Britton's upper arm and began slapping the veins. He mumbled to himself, "I do important work here, very important." He then reached for the needle and roughly hit the vein on the first try.

"Hey, take it easy. I may look like a big tough guy, but seriously, I'm no fan of needles." Britton tried to push down the panic that flared with the pain. He wondered if this doctor was used to working on patients that couldn't feel...but that thought didn't lead anywhere he ought to go, he squashed it.

The doctor appeared to be lost in his thoughts. But after filling eight vials of blood, Britton was out of blood, and patience. "Okay, so...I'm gonna need you to leave me a little of that red stuff; I have a wife and two children to get home to." The doctor again did not respond. Britton's anger surged at the disrespect. If he was indeed here of his own volition, then this guy needed to work on his bedside manner.

The doctor finished with the tenth vial. That's when he met Britton's eyes. "That will be all I need for the next few hours. I will run these through immediately, and then I will know where to start." He nodded and then picked up the plastic container he had so carefully placed each vial. He shuffled back out from where he came, scurrying. He walked hunched down, closer to the floor. He reminded Britton of a fat rodent.

Britton watched him leave, wondering just how he had allowed himself to be trapped again. He slapped the table, hard; the sound echoed through the room. He slid off the table and began to pace. His temper flared, his eyes the color of the ocean when a storm brewed. As he paced, he attempted to find some understanding of the situation he found himself in. "I've been back in Houston for a week, or maybe two. I have not seen my family since before Christmas. I need to go home, be with my wife and my children. I have rights, and they cannot keep me here!" He walked in the direction the doctor had gone and found a large door. The guards were standing in front of the main entrance and exit. This door was sort of hidden, cut right into the wall. He tried the handle. "Locked...like I thought for one second it could be that easy!" He began pounding on the door, as loudly as he dared, and yelling. "Look, Dr. Schmidt, or Dr. Luka, or whatever I'm supposed to call you. I want to go home. Am I done for today?" He had not expected a reply, but the words were barely out of his mouth when the handle turned, and the doctor stuck his head out, barely cracking open the door.

He stood completely still, as if someone had stopped time. His eyes bugged, he appeared to stare through Britton. Even in the frigid air of the Lab, Britton felt the sweat roll down from his temple. The doctor stared, his eyes dead. Rage radiated from those dead eyes in red waves, heating the atmosphere. Britton whispered the word "dead" out loud, and his body shook without his permission. When the man finally looked at him, one thing Britton knew to be true was...no one would ever get used to the snake eyes in place of a human's. The way they rolled back in his head...but that was not the first thing he saw. It was the creature that clung to him.

A monkey, spider, gargoyle type creature clung to the man's back. Britton knew his eyes were wide when he whispered, "A demon troll." He choked out the revelation, mainly to himself. But when he said it, the demon lifted his mouth off the man's neck. Blood and black saliva dripping from its fangs. The creature glared at Britton, mouth wide open. If a demon could smile, Britton was sure that's what this creature was doing. He'd not seen one covered in scales before. This one had dark green scales that ran the length of its face. The same scales covered the man's neck, blending the two into one.

The doctor handed the creature a vial of blood, and he guzzled it. The snake eyes rolled back forward, and the man spoke the demon's thoughts. "Did you know that blood is spiritual? Your blood has lived many lives!" The demon smacked his lips; the long black tongue licked his face, cleaning away all the blood that splashed across his cheeks. "All blood brings life...or death. All blood tells a thousand stories to those who know how to taste it."

Britton had no reply; the creature was so vile, the information so...he couldn't come up with a word. He struggled to know whom to address. Did he speak to the man or the creature that hung on his back? "I...need to go home. If you have everything you need, I am ready to leave."

The creature jumped off the man's back, plopping to the floor like a fat frog. He began crawling up Britton's leg, using his long claws and stopping every few inches to sniff. Britton instinctively began kicking his leg to be rid of the creature. "Get off, get off of me!"

The troll was unaffected by his movements. "Drystan would taste more blood, taste more life." He licked Britton's face as he crawled up to his chest. "Drystan will bite the traitor, take the blood he wants."

Unsure of how to fight this creature, his mind was repulsed. Finally, the memory surfaced. Britton dropped to his knees and began calling out. "Adonai, I need You. I ask You to cover me in your protection. It is Your blood that washes away sins. I pray that Your blood covers me, protects me from this evil."

The creature recoiled in fury, landing hard on the floor and scurrying back up onto the doctor's back. "You can call on Your friend, Brit toon! But remember, we killed Him too! You are not going anywhere! We've waited years for jusssssstiicccce. Drystan is eager to give you a chance to right this great wrong."

The man, this creature, whichever, whatever he was, turned slowly, like he suddenly realized he was balancing the creature across his shoulders. Then he was gone, and the heavy door slammed. Britton struggled to calm his racing heart. He crawled to a stand and nervously ran his fingers through his hair over and over. What was he supposed to do? He had not seen another person except the guards. Now this doctor/demon person was heading somewhere else. There had to be a way to get out, or at least to get to a phone. He watched the two guards' shadows through the frosted glass and wondered if there was a way to get past them. He squeezed his hands together again and again. He questioned what his next step should be. Finally, he laid back on the table, pulled his knees to his chest, and began to pray. He was exhausted, more than exhausted. The excitement in Jerusalem, the stress of leaving his family behind...this virus that crawled out of a pit somewhere. All of it refused him peace. He sat up. "What if I fall asleep? I could find myself strapped down again."

He slid off the table. But since there were no chairs, he went to the only empty corner and slid down the wall onto the cold tile floor. Putting his head on both his knees, he wrapped his arms around them. "Adonai...I know You are not surprised about where I've found myself. I can't even believe the nightmare that's unfolding. It's taking every ounce of faith I've got to still the writhing inside my gut. I'm scared, so scared. How can a nightmare like this happen again and again? I've lived two lives worth of tragedies." He dropped his head and tried to take some deep breaths. "The problem I keep bumping up against is...I'm not who I used to be." He chuckled with the sad realization. "In so many ways, I was a better man back then."

Britton shook his head at the shameful truth of that prayer. "We both know I'm not the same person." He began rocking back and forth to the rhythm of his words. The conversation was beginning to feel more comfortable, more familiar. They were so close before, he and Adonai...more than friends. During his darkest days, Adonai had given him strength and courage. But he was the one that had let the business of life come between them. The guilty realization squeezed his heart. "I've missed You, Adonai. I hadn't noticed how far I'd let myself drift. But here I am, in a nightmare, and You are The One I turn to. You are the only One with answers."

The truth of all of it was starting to overwhelm him. He'd slept in a chair in the airport for the last six nights; no one seemed to notice he was not in a hospital bed like the rest of the passengers. The only time anyone noticed him was when he tried to leave the quarantined area; each time, a guard would escort him back in, explaining that no one left without approval. He was so tired, so very tired. Down to his bones...past that, his soul was weary. He whispered the rest of his prayer, "It's like I'm holding my breath...waiting for the worst thing I can imagine to happen." His head began to bob; he was nodding off. The stress had eaten away his peace. He had been on high alert for so many weeks. Now that he faced this nightmare, his body began to demand that he sleep. He tried to lift his heavy eyelids, finish the conversation.

"I'm trying not to worry, Adonai. My Asha is alone, the kids...protect my family." The worry had etched new lines across his face. He felt like he was being engulfed by the inevitability of the darkness. He couldn't fight sleep any longer. Sitting on the floor, his head on his knees, he slept.

The cold air grew colder, and he lifted his head. He looked up when he saw snowflakes drifting by, thick and sticking in his eyelashes. Every tree and blade of grass was crusted over with white frost. The road that was in the middle of the snow shone like a silver river. The silence of the place echoed in his ears. He didn't waste time looking at the landscape; he had somewhere to be. Where, he couldn't say, but Adonai beckoned, and he would follow.

CHAPTER TWENTY-TWO

ALONE

Asha flipped over onto her other side, throwing the fluffy comforter off...again. She punched the pillow, fussed at the voices of worry in her head. "How in the world am I supposed to sleep not knowing where they have taken Britton?" She sat up, first shaking her head and then holding it in both her hands. "It's been more than ten years! How can this be happening again? I never thought we would face this kind of danger ever, ever again." She felt like she was standing in the middle of the street, staring at oncoming headlights in the dark. Her thoughts came barreling straight at her, and she could not get out of the way in time.

The terrifying memories crashed into her mind over and over. All those years ago, she had snuck into the government facility and found Britton locked in a cell the size of her closet. His face was bloody, his eyes black; he was lying on an old beanbag in his own filth. Apparently, he was never allowed out. It was at that moment she had known he had a higher purpose. That somehow her purpose was intertwined with his.

She felt a gentle brush against her face and remembered how she had gotten into that high security facility. "Light Warriors!" Sitting up straighter, she remembered that day...the day they had escorted her through locked doors. They had guided her to where he was being held and had shielded her presence from those who would do her harm. She closed her eyes and squeezed them tight. She shivered ...maybe from the cold. The temperature had dipped into the forties last night...but the memories would make anyone shiver. Wrapping her arms around herself, she rocked with her words..."Where is he now, Adonai?"

Memories poured in as she prayed. All the late evenings and serious nights conspiring with Britton's family. They had to find a way to set him free...the government had taken possession of all the "Defective" in pretense of protecting them. But protection was far from the government's real motives. Those had been the darkest days of all their lives. Gooseflesh covered her arms. "I thought we were too late!" She squeezed around her stomach and rocked faster.

The memory of Britton stiff, and blue, resurfaced. He had been long gone to the other side when they found him. "That can't happen again, Adonai. Please!" She dropped her tired head into her hands. "I am old and worn out from so much worry." The memory caused her to rub her forearm... Talking to herself was something she was doing more often since Britton had been gone. Feeling a tingle under her fingers, she stopped. "The birthmark is still here."

It was a wild story, so unbelievable she kept it close to her heart. It wasn't a story she shared with many people...after all, who would believe it? Britton was born with the birthmark, but amazingly, magically...she had no idea how he had shared it with her. The birthmark tingled more intently, turning warmer the more she thought of all they had been through. It made her wonder if Britton's birthmark was doing the same. She leaned her head back, tears ran into her ears. "I sure need You to guide me to him again, Adonai."

Asha believed the birthmark was a type of compass...she knew it had guided her to find Britton that first time...and again on a hiking trip when they had become separated. Britton always told her it was more of a "moral, maybe spiritual," compass. A way to find your way back to Adonai." Yes, it was that for sure... It burned and tingled a lot more back then. For her, it was often a warning; sometimes it was more like a premonition. When Britton was "terminated" at the Government Autism Project, her birthmark had lit up like a beacon. When she'd finally found him, he had already passed to the other side. She sat in the back of that ambulance, the birthmark glowing...crying over his cold corpse. That's when his birthmark began to glow, and she had known somehow...somehow she had known that she needed to place her birthmark on his.

She had followed that "urging" and when she did...it was as if they were struck by lightning. Like someone yelled "all clear" and a defibrillator sent shock waves through them. Britton's body had arched, and his heart had pumped life-giving blood back through his blue corpse. The part of that story that caused so much of a stir...he wasn't only alive, he was healed. No longer a "Defective," he was free; finally he was whole. He was able to speak out loud the millions of thoughts that had been imprisoned inside his mind for twenty-five impossible years.

The memory was half terror and half magic for Asha. She sat on the edge of the bed, remembering. The birthmark warmed under her fingers; her mind recalled in perfect detail. The powerful Light Warrior hovered over the ambulance on that mystical day. The brightness of the light glared like the sun, but was diffused from the warrior's body. The way the power radiated from the wings, each individual feather moved with that power. He brought Adonai's presence, and with that presence came assurance, protection, and peace.

The memories sometimes made her happy, and other days they made her heart heavy. It wasn't many months after that she understood the heaviness that lingered was a call to prayer. "Adonai, please Adonai, I can't imagine that You would allow something even worse to happen to Britton...to us." Her voice was shaking from the fear she allowed to envelop her. She pulled her knees to her chest, wrapped her arms around them, and sobbed. A giant waterfall of tears dropped all over the purple cats that stared at her from her flannel pajamas. Her body vibrated with each sob, choking out the grief in her heart.

She curled back up into the softness of the bed, pulling the big green comforter back over herself. Under the blanket, the darkness felt like a protection. Swallowing, she tried to encourage herself. "I will not cry like a small child. Crying isn't going to save him. We better come up with a plan! Adonai? I need to know what Your plan is." She waited; yes, she expected an answer, or an idea, something. Adonai always came through. "Your love never fails!"

Cocooning her knees tighter, Asha thought of how blessed she was to have Britton. How he encouraged her... How he encouraged everyone. "Adonai, he is so special...he always has been. Please protect him, keep him safe from the dark ones." The thing that made him so special was that he never forgot what it was like to not be able to talk. It was more than that, though. It was that he knew what it was like when people talked about you like you weren't there. It was Britton's idea to open the center and teach those with autism to communicate. It had been the logical next step for both of them. It was a struggle, the hardest work she had ever done. But she would never trade it for any other life. All the breakthroughs and moments of joy were blessings that no compensation could come close to matching. Their clients were a family. Watching them blossom was the best feeling in the world. It wasn't a job, it was an honor.

She pulled the comforter around her neck, grateful that focusing on the good in their lives helped her stop crying. There were amazing memories of the past thirteen years. She needed to focus on those things. For months he had traveled the media circuits and spoken out about the cruelty of treating those who were considered "defective" as ignorant. He wanted the world to understand they were intelligent, witty...and that they often had funny personalities. Probably one of the most famous "autistics" loves to say, "I am different, not less."

Britton had been determined that the world would begin to wake up to the truth about those locked inside themselves. It had gone well until he began to speak out about how it had happened. That was not something the world was ready for. When he expressed that it was the Chosen Vaccine that had caused his issues...his voice was once again silenced. The requests to hear his story had dwindled, drying up completely in a matter of months. *The world didn't have the stomach for that much truth.*

But in the end, she had Britton, and that was all that mattered to her. He had wanted a college degree, maybe more than one. He needed something that proved he was intelligent. It was personal for him. She sure couldn't blame him for that, certainly not after the life he had lived. She had worked while he finished college, graduating top of his class. Their life seemed magical to her. They were in love. He was everything she could've ever wanted, and she was grateful that he never seemed to question that they were destined to be together.

When they first married, the nightmares had tormented her for some time. But when she became pregnant with their first, the enemy became ruthless. Stealing her sleep night after night until she was hospitalized and medicated. Even in her drugged sleep, the questions were fiery darts. "What if their son was a "Defective"? Britton slept in a chair beside her, praying till his eyes would no longer stay open. He prayed, and Adonai sent protection to shield her mind while she slept. The harsh dreams from the past faded away, and life slowly drifted into a more normal rhythm. She rarely thought about any of it anymore...till now. Laying here alone, her thoughts a mesh of tangles...there was no unscrambling her fears at two a.m.

She cried out to Adonai again, desperate. "I want him with me now, not later." The words stuck in her throat. Her knowledge that Adonai is never the instigator of evil stung her conscience. "I want this over so badly, before the worst happens...again. Please, Adonai!" She punched her pillow into a more comfortable shape, but the truth was...she was angry. Angry with herself for allowing the difficulty of the situation to squeeze out some ugly emotions. And then there were so many nights of no sleep, and days with no appetite, and two children constantly asking when their daddy would be home.

"I give up!" Throwing the covers off again, she headed into the den, tying her housecoat tighter against what was a cold night for Houston. Sleep was elusive, mostly just taunting her since Britton had left for the conference. She whispered ridiculous rantings that came from her sleep deprived emotions. "Maybe I'll get used to being up around the clock! Who needs sleep anyway? Sleep is for the weak!" She sighed hard at her insane declaration and headed for the recliner she'd been dozing in.

Grabbing the blanket off the top of the sofa, she disturbed the kitten that must've cunningly escaped both of the children. She scooped her up and laid her against her chest. The surprise Christmas gift from Britton...he was definitely overcompensating for not being able to be with his family.

A tiny siamese that looked so much like the cat Asha had before she married Britton. When Britton had shown her the pictures of this tiny kitten on his phone, she was secretly thrilled. "She looks exactly like a baby, Itty Bitty!" She hugged him, and she let a tear slide down her face. Itty Bitty was her closest companion all through her college years. Man, she still missed him. The first years of their marriage she had loved teasing Britton that he was jealous of Itty Bitty. "He was the first love of my life!" She giggled at the memory when the kitten began kneading dough on her shoulder, purring with closed eyes. "Seventeen years with the best cat ever! Okay, Jingle Bells, you have some serious paws to fill!" She scratched the kitten's head and laughed. "Bells, that really is a great name!"

Grateful for another cat, especially now, she truly had enjoyed the company while Britton was away. Of course, now that his ability to come home was delayed, Asha took to sitting in the recliner most nights; it was Britton's chair, and it made her feel closer to him. The weight of the kitten on her chest eased some twisted tension along her spine. She relaxed, standing there, wishing for sleep. But...if she closed her eyes, the dark presence would visit. The spirit had driven her out of her own bedroom and into complete exhaustion.

She sat back in the chair and let her eyes close. The kitten's warmth was welcome, and the vibration soothed her worries. She loved talking to the kitten, telling her grown up thoughts that she dare not speak to the children. "With all that is happening in the world, and Britton unable to come home, that evil presence is stealing not only my sleep, but my peace."

The kitten was so tiny, and yet, if the dark creature came too close, the hair would stand up on the kitten's back. She would hiss, her tiny back arched up like a Halloween cat. She would slap at the darkness, and the darkness would drift in retreat. When that happened, she felt safe to close her heavy eyelids. She wondered if the spirit knew she could see him. She rubbed the birthmark again. It had been burning for several hours; it was even hot to her touch. "Hey Bells, we need to pray for Britton; I can feel it. Can you feel it?"

She snuggled the kitten closer till Bells meowed in protest. Asha was grateful not to be alone. Lying back in the recliner, under the light of another enormous moon, Asha knew she would need to be brave again. It took enormous courage to live the life she had chosen. She'd rejected the easy life, marrying a former "Defective." Many of her friends had turned up their noses at her choice. She'd never second guessed it even once, and she wouldn't tonight either. He was the best part of her life, and she was his.

Chapter Twenty-Three

ADONAI

The hospital phone rang loudly and since it was an old rotary phone, it sounded more like a bomb alert. Jazlyn jumped up to a stand from a very deep sleep. She was lying in the bed beside Jeff; he was snoring again since a lot of the tubes had been removed. She was able to sleep beside him even if the hospital staff frowned on it. Blinking, it took a second for her to come back to a more conscious state. "The phone, Jaz!" She turned her head to look at Jeff and nodded in reply. Sleep had allowed her to forget for a few hours that he was blind. "Right. Yes, I've got it." She took the one step it took to get to the small table with the big, bulky phone.

"Jeff's room. This is Jazlyn!" She heard Jeff snicker, and that caused her to smile. "Jazlyn, I was wondering how things are going. I was feeling guilty for not checking on you guys for the last few days."

Jazlyn smiled and covered the phone... "It's Asha." He nodded, and she turned to sit down in the chair. "Hey Ash, we are good; Jeff is good." She paused, and her heart leapt; it was her first realization of how much gratitude filled her heart. Jeff was recovering; his hearing was just the beginning.

She refused to allow herself to dwell on how their life would have changed if he had remained blind. "There haven't been any other changes...but he's feeling pretty good; he's wanting to go home! Which, of course, they aren't about to allow. The virus is still spreading and since he's one of the first...to get it. Even though he's on the road to recovery, they are being cautious." Her voice faded when she heard sniffing. "Asha, are you okay?" Asha hadn't meant to cry; she hadn't even meant to share her situation with Jazlyn, but she was her dearest friend, and she felt so alone.

"Did I wake you up? I didn't realize it was so late. I...I don't sleep much without Britton." The last few words came out all choked, and she knew she betrayed herself.

"Ash? Britton isn't home?"

That was it, the dam that held back the flood of walled up emotions released. She sobbed into the phone, but all she could really croak out was... "I'm sorry. I'm so sorry. It's ridiculous that I would complain to you."

Jazlyn held the hospital phone close to her mouth, hoping that Jeff might go back to sleep. He needed all the sleep he could get, but Asha...Asha needed her right now. Jazlyn picked up the old phone and moved as far as the cord would allow. Muffling the receiver with her hand, she whispered, "Asha, let me call you back on my cell. Wait...let me make sure it's charged." She fumbled through her bag and found it. "Yes, yes, it's still got sixty percent. I'll call you back in one minute." Gently, she placed the receiver down and stood, looking at Jeff. All the swelling was out of his face. There was color in his cheeks, and it made her smile. Blind...it really didn't matter to her; they would adapt. He was the man of her dreams, and nothing would change that. She leaned over to tell him she was going out to call Asha, but his rhythmic breathing stopped her. She quietly slid on her shoes and tiptoed out.

She sat on the old brown sofa in the waiting area . It was the "best seat in the house" as far as she was concerned. "Asha, it's me. Hope that didn't take too long. Jeff was asleep, and I needed to find my shoes. I can talk out here without bothering anyone." She rolled her eyes and added, "By anyone, I mean old nurse Ratchet that hovers over us twenty-four seven." Asha snickered at her reference to "One Flew Over the Cuckoo's Nest." It was one of Britton's favorites; he said he had lived there many months in his other life and never intended to visit. That was a sobering thought. Where was he now? Where had they taken him?

Asha needed to tell someone."Jazlyn, I don't know what's happening. At first I understood Britton would be quarantined along with everyone else. But he has no symptoms, and still they won't let him come home." Jazlyn listened, her head full of cotton from being in such a deep sleep.

"Um, I'm sorry, Ash. I didn't know you were going through all this. I guess I'm kind of sequestered here, and the world just revolves around us." A few folks came into the waiting area, dropping into the empty metal chairs. She snuggled into the worn, leather sofa; pulling her knees up to her chest, she shivered. "It's a freezer in this hospital. I'm so cold. I've been cold for a solid three weeks!" Her teeth started to chatter, and her voice shuddered. "So what does Britton say? Is he bored out of his mind? Does he just play on his phone all day?"

Asha tried to reply. Tried to tell her, but...she cried instead. "I, I don't know what he's been doing. There was almost a week that his phone was dead, and he had to wait for access to his luggage to get his charger. Then, he thought he would be coming home the next week...but he was talking to me, and this doctor came and he wanted to know why Britton was the only one who wasn't sick...and...and his phone went dead. It's the last time I heard anything from him."

The story poured out...it was a raging river that pushed up through her heart. There were so many emotions brewing; there was nothing to be done but let it flow.

Jazlyn listened, but she didn't know how to help. "So this doctor, have you spoken to his office?" Asha tried to calm herself. The kids were asleep now, and it had taken a lot of convincing. She'd finally just thrown up her hands. "Britton BenDavid Donovan, I need you to stop asking me questions I can't answer!" He'd huffed his frustration at her and went into his room. She closed herself into the bathroom and locked the door; the last thing she needed was to wake up the kids.

"I don't know his name. I've called and called, and everyone seems to send me to someone else. Then that person doesn't know; and I've talked to so many people that I've lost track. It's like he's disappeared, like he's just gone. Oh my God, Jazlyn; it's like all those years ago when they took him!"

Asha slid down the wall, sitting next to the toilet. "I don't know what to do this time. Tell me what to do!" Jazlyn wiped the tears of empathy off her face and stared at the rain rolling down the windows to the outside world. She wanted to help her dearest friend, but searching her mind wasn't bringing any answers.

She stood and walked over to the windows, staring out at a world she had not been part of for weeks now. A violent, white moon sent rays of light through the dark clouds that hovered over the city in various shades of grey. She shivered again; this time more from the fear that seemed to be gripping everything and everyone. Jazlyn placed her fisted hand against her heart. "Help! Please help my friends, Adonai!" She swallowed the terror that was building.

"Asha, Asha, are you there? Are you listening?"

Asha croaked her sad, "Yes."

Jazlyn plunged ahead. "If I remember the story you told me, it was Adonai who helped you before. It was Adonai that saved Britton's life. Am I right, Asha?"

Asha whispered. "Yes, yes it was."

"Then you know what to do, Asha. Ask Him; ask your Adonai. He's definitely The One who has given me my Jeff, back."

CHAPTER TWENTY-FOUR

A MOMENT IN TIME

A sha pushed the end button on her cell. What else could she say? She felt so guilty for waking Jazlyn. Jazlyn was having such a rough go of it. It was selfish to bother her. Besides, someone needed to sleep, even if that wasn't her. She used the toilet to push herself up off the floor, opening the door as if a burglar might be waiting outside. She barely cracked it open when the tiny kitten shimmied herself inside and wiggled between Asha's feet. Looking up with her stark blue eyes, she protested. "Well, hello Bells! You certainly are better company than I expected." She scooped the kitten up and cuddled her back to her chest. "I'm wondering if you had any dinner, little one? My days have been running together...let's at least get you a snack." She buried her face into the kitten's neck and wrapped her, using the edge of her housecoat as a blanket. The kitten licked her with a sandpaper tongue, meowing more urgently.

She opened the freezer and spied a gold lid. "Blue Bell, the best ice cream in the country." Giggling, Asha pulled the round tub out and sat it on the island. "We'll just have a tiny bowl. No one will be the wiser." She pulled out two small bowls and juggled the kitten with one hand while she scooped the soft dessert. "Two scoops for the human...and one tiny scoop for the lucky kitten." She sat the kitten's bowl down and let Bells jump from her hands. She was licking the ice cream as if it were the only meal she'd ever had. "I don't blame you Bells, I am seriously addicted to this stuff."

Asha slowly ate a few bites, before she realized she hadn't tasted any of it. Her mind was wandering. She felt a chill chase its way up her neck, so she wrapped her housecoat tighter. "You about done there, Bells?" The kitten looked up with a milk mustache that was so large she was licking it off her nose. Asha giggled again and picked up the bowl, setting it in the sink beside her own ice cream. She'd lost her appetite. Her bowl was still full, barely touched. The kitten began purring and attempted to crawl up Asha's leg, so she lifted her back to her chest.

"Let's go see if we can catch a 'cat nap' in Britton's recliner." She smirked at her pun and then snuggled the kitten again, grateful for the company. "Let's see if we can get the sandman to show up and usher us into dreamland." The kitten looked into her eyes, and Asha felt she understood every word she spoke. Plopping into the recliner, she slid back, wrapping the lap blanket across her and the kitten. Bells crawled into the bend of her arm and began purring, asleep, before her tiny body stopped moving. "Oh, how I wish to sleep with the ease of a baby." That same chill chased its way up her back again and she shuddered hard. The movement startled the kitten, who opened one eye briefly.

Asha squeezed her eyes closed and pushed her head against the back of the chair. "Adonai! How can I rest when I don't know where

Britton is? I need to sleep, so I can have a clear mind. I have to help him. Remember when You helped me all those years ago? You sent Light Warriors, and they led me to where he was being held? I know You know these things. I just, I'm just so desperate to save him." She was crying again. All she did was cry once the kids went to sleep. She wiped the tears away in frustration. There was a tightness in her belly. It held a creeping sense of disappointment, but what was she disappointed in? She rolled to one side, trying to get comfortable in the recliner. She placed the back of her hands on her eyes, willing the worry to give her one night of peace. Her exhausted mind felt like a ruthless enemy that refused to stop torturing her even when she yielded.

The Light Warrior stood behind the recliner. Dispatched by Adonai Himself. His wings expanded so wide they stretched through the walls...the feathers fluttering with an unseen breeze. Asha shuddered one last time. She sighed heavily. Sleep rushed through her body so quickly she didn't have the strength to fight it.

She was asleep; she knew she was and yet... here she stood in front of a snowdrift. A lone figure trudged through powdery snow up to his knees. The icy wind lifted her hair, and sleet stung her face. The snow was stark, so bright it almost hurt her eyes. Vivid against the steely blue of a cloudless sky. "Britton?" The name came out almost as a croak...she was asleep, after all. She certainly hadn't expected to find him here, but here he was. She increased the volume, the urgency and near panic filtered through. "Britton, Britton wait!" When he didn't appear to hear her, she realized he was no longer alone. Adonai lifted His hand, waving His acknowledgement.

"I am with him, Asha. I have brought him to this moment..." She opened her mouth to speak, but she couldn't think of what to say.

Comforted by the peace of Adonai's presence and His assurances. His view of the world was never the same as hers, or anyone else's she knew. He already knew the end, from the beginning.

She slowly raised her hand, waving back, locking eyes with The One she knew was trustworthy. She whispered, "Watch over him, Adonai!" She knew she was asleep in the recliner. Bells was snuggled to her chest, the fire in the fireplace was warm. But she couldn't believe how alone she felt. She didn't give herself permission, but asked Him anyway. "Bring him back to me, Adonai. Please. Promise You will bring him back?" The words faded with the arrogance of the demand. The wind howled, lifting the snow flurries in front of her. The dream world closed.

She opened her eyes, the morning light filtered through the shutters, buttery and new. She stared at the stripes of golden sun on the wooden floor. She stretched to get more heat from the sun's rays to warm her feet. The movement caused Bells to stretch, arms straight up and back arched. Asha scratched the kitten's tiny belly and laughed, holding her up to her face to snuggle. She whispered, "you are so warm! How did it get this cold in our house? I'm freezing!" She remembered. "It was the snow!"

The dream floated across her mind, Adonai's words in her ears. "I have brought him to this moment." She sat up so fast the chair teetered forward and she squeezed the kitten a little too hard to keep from sending her flying. She gulped on the knot that refused to go down. "Where is he?" She didn't know where her husband was, but she *did know* that Adonai was with him. "Please, oh please, keep him safe." She closed her eyes and tried to control her panicked breathing. She would trust Adonai. That was the only plan she had.

"Let's go get our kids up, Bells...and not one word about that ice cream!"

Chapter Twenty-Five

THE SEED

"I wish you could've seen it the way I saw it, Jaz." Jeff stared at nothing, not only because he still couldn't see, but because the dream world he was describing was so vivid to him. Jazlyn laughed at Jeff's explanation, his detailed description of that other world he swore he'd been to.

"Jeff! I wish to see it the way you did. It sounds like a mystical world of paradise!" She laid her head on his shoulder again and squeezed him. He'd described it to her over and over.

"Jaz, I'm telling you, the water there...it's alive!" When he woke from the dream, he found his hearing restored. To hear him tell it, he had spent time in some magical water that had healing properties, or something. "It's not only about the water, Jaz. It is about The Man I met there."

Jaz nodded and then remembered he couldn't see her acknowledgement. Squeezing his biceps, she leaned in closer to him. "I love your dream, Jeff. But mostly I love you and how happy it makes you."

Jeff held her without holding back. He would swear that he could feel the love he had always felt for her leave his heart and sink into her. He really was done with protecting his heart and refusing to love. He loved this woman! She squeezed him tighter, smiling. He cleared his throat. "You know I love you too, don't you Jaz? You're the best thing that ever happened to me." She laughed at his confession; he sure wasn't a romantic man, but wow, that was far more than he'd ever been willing to expose.

Jazlyn paused, wondering if now was a good time to approach the subject of "The Man" he kept talking about. She was raised by a more relaxed family atmosphere than Jeff was. Sure, they celebrated the traditional Jewish holidays. But she never considered herself overly religious. Neither did she believe the legends of parting the Red Sea, or of a God who actually talked to His children from "a burning bush or otherwise." But she had a secret she hadn't shared with anyone. The prayers she had prayed over this past month...they had begun to be so important to her. Her times of speaking with the "unseen" mattered to her. Far more than she would have ever imagined.

Jeff squeezed her hand and lowered his voice. "Jazlyn, you know I am anything but religious. But this Man, this Man knows me. It's not like He's some far away, out there..." Jeff paused, and Jazlyn watched tears form in his unseeing eyes. She started to say something to comfort him, but then he finished. "He is my friend. He cares about me. He never judges my failures. He cares...."

Jazlyn squeezed his fingers and felt the tears pour down her cheeks and onto her neck. She was a little glad he couldn't see that she cried. "That's amazing, Jeff. I'm so excited that you have found peace in all this." She wanted to say, "In this nightmare." But that seemed harsh and judgmental.

She laid her cheek against his chest and continued to hold his hand. She felt the rhythm of his breathing in and out. It soothed the fears that rose like a tidal wave every time she closed her eyes. She wished to swallow all the voices of doubt and never listen to them again.

"Adonai...if You are listening, I beg You to show me who You are. I'm beginning to believe You are 'The Man' my Jeff is spending time with. The Man who healed his ears...I ask You to heal my Jeff's eyes..." She paused, she didn't want her tears to soak through and wake up Jeff. He was healing fast, but he was still so exhausted. She lifted her face and used her sleeve to wipe the tears. She gently laid her head back down and finished her prayer. "Please, Adonai, help us both see the truth of who You are."

The sound of the wind blowing through the trees was the first thing she noticed. Blinking, she found herself sitting with her back up against a large oak. The wind caught her long dark hair and whipped it across her eyes. She reached to move it, then realized she didn't know where she was.

Pushing herself off the ground, she stood to stretch. She watched the sun wake, peeking over the horizon of endless fields of grains and flowers. The rays of light shimmered, reaching long fingers through lavender clouds and turning the world gold. She knew that it was spring because new leaves were sprouting on every branch that reached above her. The grass shimmered with morning dew, like glass, as the early morning sun seemed to yawn and glisten across the chill of the ground.

Jazlyn took a few steps, the grass a cushion under her bare feet. Each step gave a bounce back to her weight with a push off the ground's energy. She breathed in the coolness of the air; it was sharp and cold in her nose and throat, causing gooseflesh to run up her arms. Shuddering, her shoulders shook; but she felt awake, so completely rested and awake.

"Hey there, I think you nodded off!" She saw The Man with a shovel; she squinted, trying to figure out if she knew Him.

She raised her hand slowly, felt timid, but she didn't think they had ever met. "Hey. Um, do I know You?"

The Man chuckled and kept digging. In a moment He sat His forearm on the top of the shovel and looked at her. "I seem to be getting that a lot lately. People forgetting who I am, and not recognizing Me." He chuckled. "I guess I just have one of those faces. Ya know? Faces that look like so many other people." He shook His head and went back to digging.

There were rows and rows ready for planting and even more rows in various stages of growth. She watched The Man digging with such diligence. Maybe the right word was "gusto." He stopped again, this time not really standing all the way up--the shovel still in the ground. "Gusto? I really like that word. It is the perfect description of how I relish this work."

Jazlyn was shaken. "I didn't say that out loud, did I?" He continued to chuckle as He dug, shaking His head and using His forearm to wipe the sweat off His brow. She inched closer, wishing to ask about the scars across His back. Instead, she said, "Is this Your farm?" She kept moving nearer, curiosity getting the better of her. She didn't know what He was planting, or if He was safe. She was pretty good at growing things, but this wasn't a plant she'd ever seen.

Only a few feet away from Him, the closeness made her squirm. He continued to read her thoughts. "You're good at growing things, just like I am. I love gardens; they're one of the best things I ever created." She nodded at Him even though He was staring at the dirt, intent on His work. She knew He was telling her something...it seemed the words held the answer, but she wasn't quite getting it. Like trying to catch a butterfly with a net full of holes.

She lost track of how long she watched Him. So she broke the silence. "I could help; do You have another shovel?" He stood up, pushing His hair out of his eyes. He looked at her; His eyes, a cerulean shade she kept trying to match to every ocean she had ever seen. She blurted out, "The sea!" The silence between them stretched to such an uncomfortable level... it made her voice seem louder.

He grinned at her outburst. "Come closer. I'd like you to see these seeds." She stepped in, only about a foot away, and saw that He had a pouch hanging on His side. He pulled out a seed. He gently dropped it into the dirt, covering it quickly in the rich darkness of the soil. "Look closer." He opened His hand so that she could see the seed that looked more like a tiny ball of light than any seed she had ever planted.

"It's beautiful. I've never seen a seed made of light before." He smiled, and she saw a thousand thoughts flicker behind those breathtaking eyes. He motioned toward her to take the seed. She lifted her hand, allowing the golden seed to gently drop into her palm. It was weightless, and yet she felt its energy. The life of it flowed through her hand. "Are these seeds alive?"

He nodded at her fascination. "These seeds contain the greatest Truths the world has ever known."

She lifted the seed to eye level, holding it like a priceless piece of porcelain. She saw movement in the light and then The Man, *inside the seed. She saw The Man* dying. He hung on a cross and cried out, "It is Finished!"

When she looked back at The Man; her eyes filled. The questions tumbled, and she tried to make her words gentle. Her heart swelled with so much pain that the seams of it felt like it would unravel. "Why? Why did this have to happen?"

His eyes held hers; she watched life glow like a warm fire inside them. "For you; I did it for you."

She dropped to the ground, her knees in the soft earth, still holding the seed close to her heart. The "Man" stepped closer and placed both His hands on her head. "You asked Me for the Truth. I have given you the seed." She felt the seed seep through her chest and magically drop into her heart. The thrill it caused made her smile even as tears ran down her face. She looked up at The Man, but the only words that came, she mouthed. "Thank you."

He nodded. "Guard the truth with diligence, child. It has begun to grow. But like any seed, it will need water and light. I am the living water...and the light of the world."

Light burst from her chest, and a beam the size of her fist shot up into the heavens. It brought such joy she could hardly contain the love the light held.

Reaching toward The Man, she asked Him... "Are you The One?" His whole face broke into a smile like the sun bursts into golden rays of warmth as it peeks over the horizon.

She blinked, and He answered her, "I am."

CHAPTER TWENTY-SIX

DEFECTIVE

B ritton didn't know how long he slept. He only knew his knees felt frozen in place, and it took a few minutes to unbend and straighten up. He no more than got to a stand when the doctor came bustling through the same back door, more test tubes, more paperwork. "I'm going to need more blood, a muscle biopsy, and several scans." He talked at Britton, but definitely not to him. "Please come and remain seated on the table."

Britton attempted to hold his anger in check, he watched the doctor place the items on the metal tray and pull more instruments out of drawers. But Britton did not sit on the table. He stood where he had been when the doctor came back in with his demands. Britton's fury threatened to swallow him if he let it loose, so he gritted his teeth and waited. Only a moment passed before the doctor looked up and motioned Britton over. "Please don't waste my time. I need this information for research to move forward." He impatiently cocked one eyebrow and waved his hand for Britton to hurry.

Britton watched the doctor's eyes squint with frustration and then he saw his jaw begin to clench. Britton suddenly had a foul taste in his mouth; this man was not someone he would ever respect no matter how smart he was. This man was demanding, stubborn; and he could tell that it was difficult for him to treat "his test subject" like he was anything more than a petulant child. His own teeth began to grind; he was not going to be bullied. He crossed his arms and refused to budge. "Before I agree to cooperate by donating more of my body fluids, I'd appreciate a little consideration about *my time and, of course, my freedom.* I need to go home and see my wife and my children."

Britton spoke as authoritatively as he dared while still projecting some level of respect. "Could you at least give me a time frame? The doctor at the airport, Hazmarazz, or something like that, promised this was another step to getting me home." The doctor stared at him like he was speaking another language. Britton threw both his arms up; the frustration and his stiff body were not helping him remain calm. "How about you return my cell phone? Seems like a small request. What kind of place takes a man's cell phone? Am I a prisoner?" The question hung in the air and stayed between them. The doctor bored into him with his glare. The temperature in the room dropped; he shivered.

"You will never leave this place. There is no way back." Britton leaned his ear toward the sound, unsure if the doctor had spoken the words, or if he was hearing things.

"Excuse me? Are you talking to me? What do you mean, I'll never leave this place?" The doctor's body stiffened; he continued to stare, saying he glowered would be a more accurate description.

"We have collected a wide range of those labeled 'Defective.' It is extremely helpful that you can give us feedback, unlike the others."

The man glared; his jowls hung, and the dark eyes drooped like an old basset hound.

Dr. Schmidt removed his protective gloves and angrily threw them in the trash. Without one word, he huffed back out the door he had just come through. Britton watched him go, head down, muttering to himself. He hollered after him. "Hey! I don't understand what it is you need from me. I need to go home, and I am considering leaving whether you want me to or not."

Britton dropped his hands again; placing them on his knees. He rubbed the front of his legs in an attempt to remain calm. Quiet only for a moment. The whispering started up again. "You thought you'd get away. But here you are, right back in my trap." Britton whirled around, looking for the source of the voices. It was beginning to feel far too familiar. There were things a person didn't get over. No amount of time, therapy, or rituals could take away the pain of some wounds. They lived on in lumpy scars across your heart, or maybe across your very soul. Breaking into his dark thoughts, the doctor came barging back in. He walked fast, leaning forward with determination, two security guards in tow.

Britton backed up to the locked doors, feeling the shock of what he couldn't believe was happening. "What's going on here, Dr. Schmidt? What gives you the right, the authority, to hold me against my will?" Britton heard the whispering in reply, the giggling, and he began to wonder if somehow he'd been drugged.

"Take him! Place him on the exam table and be sure and use the restraining straps!" The doctor pointed the guards in the right direction, and they followed his orders without question... taking Britton by his arms because he refused to walk. Britton planted his feet and resisted donkey-fashion. He dug his heels in and bent his back, making it as hard as possible to move him. Eventually, they just let his feet drag behind him.

"If this was how it was going to be," Britton decided he would fight with everything he had. The second they slammed him down on the table, he kicked one guard in the nose, sending blood shooting from his face and onto the floor. The other guard would not be bested, so he placed his forearm down on Britton's neck and began to choke him. The first guard recovered, blood covering his chin. He was more than happy to hold Britton's upper body while pulling the leather straps as tight as he could get them.

"I have rights! This is against the law. I did not agree to any of this. I have a wife, a family. You have no right to keep me here!" Britton's protests fell on ears full of cotton. The harder he fought, the more straps they used. Dr. Schmidt walked over without a word. He stared at the blood on the guard's shirt and looked down at Britton, disgust in his voice.

"Calm down, Mr. Donovan. Is this really how you want things managed here?" He waved his hand at the guards, and they slowly released their hold. The doctor stared through Britton. "Is this the omen on which we open a new chapter of our relationship, Brit tooonnnnn?" A wry smile, a little self deprecating, washed over his stony face. He watched Britton struggle. "Fair enough." Reaching for a large syringe, he plunged the long needle into Britton's shoulder.

The drug was strong, and almost instant. Britton dropped his head back onto the table. It was only seconds before the room spun. Dr. Scmidt watched him, smirking, nostrils flared. "We have an important future together, and it would be far more pleasant if you would just lie back and cooperate." Britton rolled his head from side to side, doing what he could to find his bearings. His speech was slurred. He couldn't believe this was really happening.

"Cooperate? Cooperate means we discuss things." The more the drug took hold, the less sure he was if he was saying the words out loud. "I have had no information, *no choice* in anything that has been decided here." The idea of cooperating with this evil, this bogey-man, was far from his mind at this point. The disabling panic was subsiding as the medication swirled through his brain, numbing the terror. Britton felt a strange sensation of confidence that he would get out of this somehow. His brain, though not clear, felt an almost endearing love--for himself. He began mumbling assurances. "We'll get out of this, you and me! Adonai will come."

The room began to darken, and the voices got louder, the light diminished. The voices whispered and hissed. "We've got you now. This is what you've always deserved. 'Defective,' you will always be 'defective!'"

The darkness felt thicker, so very heavy. From somewhere far away, Britton heard Dr. Schmidt talking. He wasn't sure if it was real anymore. "I will be administering a few tests while you are...more easily managed. If in the future you decide to cooperate, perhaps we can loosen some straps."

Britton fought the chemical concoction as it flowed deeper and deeper into his consciousness. It was rocking him, luring him not to fight, not to care. As the medication eased all his fears, his mind kept telling him he had every right to be afraid. Yet...somehow, the fears already slid away. He pressed against the restraints one last time. How had he allowed himself to get back in this situation? The room became a kaleidoscope of colors, and then he wondered why he cared.

The doctor pushed Britton's head to the side, feeling for the large vein that pulsed heavily. "Here is what I'm looking for." A needle sliced its way into his neck. Britton's drugged mind still cautioned him to hold as still as he could. "It'll only sting for a moment." The doctor dabbed the spot with cotton and began to hum as if he were only painting or cooking. "I'm so excited to work on a 'Defective' who can speak. That's what you really are, isn't it Mr. Donovan? A 'Defective' who speaks?" He giggled as if it were some type of joke, merrily placing another large needle into Britton's bicep.

"This takes only a teeny little bit of muscle tissue; you won't even miss it." He continued humming, almost giddy with his work. The pain was intense; the doctor had not bothered to use anything to numb him. Apparently, if a patient was too drugged to fight, he didn't bother. The voices that whispered in the background talked faster and faster. Britton felt the doctor lift his arm and let it fall. "I don't think you'll be fighting anyone anymore!" He chuckled and kept humming and muttering. "'Defectives' don't have rights in this country. I'm amazed that you have forgotten that. I have been testing and sampling as many of you as I can. We must find out why the virus doesn't infect you. Imagine, after being such a drain on society...to finally be of use."

Dr. Schmidt turned and addressed the security guards, perhaps justifying his statement. "None of them should have been born, but we can salvage this tragedy. I am using their bodies to find a cure. Isn't it exciting? A cure from something of no use, till now!" He turned back toward Britton and explained, as if he were coherent, and he had not drugged him into unconsciousness. "As a matter of fact, it is a great honor for someone like you. Now your life has purpose and meaning. I realize you are in no condition to thank me, but be assured I know we both are sacrificing for the greater good."

The words slurred in Britton's ears. He would've sworn the doctor moved in slow motion. He felt everything that tethered him to reality dissolving, sinking into some other dimension. "I am not 'defective.' I haven't been for years. I am not 'defective!'" He knew he mumbled it. He knew that the doctor didn't care whether he protested, but somewhere deep inside, he also knew that this was really happening. The reality of it began to move farther and farther from him. Had the government really taken him again? Was he here? Was this all a bad dream?

All those years ago, when he could not speak, when he couldn't fight with words... He'd always believed that if he could have talked, it would've changed everything. He wasn't sure if they meant for him to black out or if they meant for him to retain some level of consciousness. "Here I am, Adonai. I can talk, and I can speak, and yet...still this world takes me captive, calls me 'Defective.'" He chuckled as the drugs refused him any muscle control. "You know, Adonai, everyone is 'defective' in one way or another. But I guess You already knew that." The terror that he should've been feeling slithered its way up his back, circling his throat. His tongue was thick, his mouth useless. "Adonai! Adonai! Save me!" Tears ran down his face and into his hair. The whispering was louder and louder; and gradually, the room faded from his sight.

CHAPTER TWENTY-SEVEN

SIGHT

J eff found himself in a subway station. People coming and going. He struggled to remember where he was, or how he had gotten there. He looked around for a sign, a clue to what city he was in. He guessed London; but he hadn't been there since he backpacked the English countryside as a teenager. Finally, unsure of where he was or even how he had gotten there...he sat on a bench and watched people go by. He caught a few words as they bustled through, but he recognized no one. He was scratching his head when a group of young adults, all energy and chatter, got out of one of the cars. That's what initially drew his attention. But it was the tiny bursts of light that caught his eye. Every one of them seemed to have tiny lights attached. Some of them sat on their shoulders, some on their heads, their arms, their faces.

Jeff tried to make sense of anything he was seeing. Squinting, he leaned forward in an attempt to comprehend. Were the tiny lights creatures? If so, he'd never seen anything like them before. They appeared to be made of light. The light was the palest of all golds, like a setting sun off the Mediterranean Sea. If pressed, Jeff would've said the lights were in the shape of tiny doves, but even smaller. They lit on each person like butterflies on a flower. Some sparkled, and some hummed with sound. Not one person seemed to be aware of the magical creatures covering them.

Thinking it was exclusive to this crowd, Jeff looked up and saw that everyone, every single person he could see, had the lights. Some had fifty or even sixty. It was hard to see past all the lights that covered some people. Jeff stood up, drawn by an irresistible attraction to reach out and touch one. He moved toward the group, deciding he would take the simplest route and just ask what the lights were. He had been holding his breath in wonder. The lights not only burned, they beckoned. He felt a plethora of emotions... "Acceptance. Love! The lights called to him!"

A stringed sound of a guitar played; his attention shifted to a homeless man who sat on a bench a short way down from where he stood. Guitar in hand, case on the floor, hoping for donations, a much classier way than begging. Jeff was drawn to the music. He felt such an intense fascination for all the lights. But there were so many. He took only a few steps when he realized the homeless man was also covered. He wore a black beanie over his fuzzy brown hair. The tiny lights were thick around his face. But his velvet blue eyes seemed old for his age. When he opened his mouth, holding a long note, light danced its way on his very breath.

Cautiously, Jeff approached the man, listening with the small crowd that gathered. The song was magical. A melody of hope that clung to the listeners, causing the dove shaped lights to flutter. Standing behind the man, he looked around and gently lifted one finger. He touched one of the dove shaped orbs. With the sense that he had stepped across an invisible line, he stood mesmerized.

The light sparkled and shimmered on the homeless man's back, making a circle around Jeff's finger. The warmth of it penetrated through his hand, up his arm, and then he felt it travel through his whole being. Something like glitter burst in front of his eyes. His body vibrated; he heard the word "song." Jeff nodded. Maybe he was beginning to understand. So he touched another, and another... "Faith, compassion, dance, courage, strength, discipline..."

The truth of the gifts began to permeate into his spirit, and he thought maybe he understood. The "hope" was soft, a whisper in his mind. "Are you sure you've figured it out?" Jeff spun, Adonai stood beside him. Adonai's smile burst across His whole face. He took Jeff by the shoulders and hugged him for a brief second. "His voice, it is incredible, isn't it? I gifted it to him when he was created." Jeff swallowed, his breathing sped up. He wasn't sure if he was ready for all this. "I filled his mouth with laughter and his tongue with songs of joy!" Adonai dropped His head back and heartily laughed.

"You are ready, Jeff? That's why you're here." Jeff turned his head and looked into the pool of The Man's eyes. "You, You gifted it to him?" Adonai's eyes burned brighter; Jeff wondered if he was disappointed at the question.

Instead, He lifted His hand and tapped each light, calling out its name. "Amazing faith, mercy, enduring love, patience, dancer, wri ter...!" Adonai rotated in a blur, tapping the lights on each person. He laughed as he whirled around in a full circle. "Dance! Joy, mercy, compassion, honesty, integrity, and this one...hope." Jeff smiled at the joy inside The Man. All the goodness in all the world must dwell inside Him. Adonai asked, "Do you understand?"

Jeff slowly nodded. A thin prick of light slid into his spirit; he closed his eyes, absorbing the truth. Adonai playfully slapped him on the back. A vision of himself crouching at the edges of his own life crept through his mind. Adonai took Jeff by the arm and curled his arm through his. "Let's walk, and I'll explain."

Jeff couldn't imagine how he had garnered the attention of...of this Man. "Aren't You too busy for this, for me? I mean, don't you need to be saving people?"

Adonai squeezed his arm and smiled, chuckling under his breath. "I am always about my Father's business, Jeff. Right now, this is where I need to be." He squeezed Jeff's arm again and kept walking. "It's not that I'm only here. I am in many places."

Jeff nodded, but he couldn't say he understood...not really. Adonai began to explain, and Jeff expected he was simplifying. "I give every soul what they need to become all they were created for. They are born into this world with those gifts. Sometimes the gift sits there, dormant, for a time. Then the right moment comes, and I call it forth." The thrill Jeff felt was difficult to describe. It reminded him of jumping off an eighty-foot cliff when he was almost eighteen. Adonai stopped nodding. "Horseshoe Lake, I remember."

Jeff had been backpacking in Canada when he heard about Horseshoe Lake. It was inside Jasper National Park, and the locals raved about the courage it took. He was seventeen; he had to take that challenge. The thrill of jumping into nothing, his heart beating so hard and fast he could hear it. This was just like that. This, believing the truth, was like jumping off a cliff into nothing. Adonai stopped and smiled at him, squeezing both his arms. "It's not like jumping into nothing; you're jumping into the truths you can't see. A leap into My promises."

When Adonai spoke it, the lights that covered Jeff became visible to his eyes. Jeff saw his own lights, his own gifts. "I...I never would have believed You had given me gifts." He said it before he thought. His face burned hot with the admission. Adonai didn't acknowledge the comment, instead He reached out and allowed the dove that sat on Jeff's shoulder to float into His hand. "This is the gift of sight...to be able to see what others cannot."

Jeff nodded. He remembered all the missions when he could see the enemy, when he knew where the captives were held. He never knew how...it's where his nickname, "Hawk," had come from. Adonai nodded the truth to him, then He released the gift to float back onto Jeff's shoulder. "Now I return it to you, with the literal gift of sight."

Jeff stopped walking; he needed air; he was so overcome with all he was understanding... He put his hands on his knees and bent over to steady himself. "Your friend, our brother, is in need of your gifts. I have given you all you need to find him."

Adonai held Jeff's arm. Heat penetrated through him. He felt frozen there, unable to look away. Adonai squeezed both his shoulders one last time. "A man who has been in another world doesn't go back unchanged. It may be difficult to find your footing at first." Jeff held his breath; but his spirit soared, and he cried out from the love that surged and held his heart.

Sitting straight up in the hospital bed, his eyes were wide open and clear! He turned to stare at Jazlyn. His quick movement startled her awake, not to mention how loudly he called her name! "Jazlyn!"

"Jeff? What's wrong, honey?" She rubbed her eyes, trying to clear away the less than two hours' sleep; she'd been ordered out of the bed and back in the visitor's chair. He reached for her hands, and she placed them in his palms. "I can see, Jazlyn! Adonai has given me sight!"

The shock hung in the air; the miracle of Jeff's complete healing sizzled in the atmosphere. Jazlyn looked down to find a birthmark glowing on Jeff's arm. "That...that is the same birthmark that Asha and Britton have." She looked up into his eyes...his clear, SEEING EYES. She was going to ask, but then Jeff squeezed her hands with excitement. "Britton needs me! Adonai says I need to find him!"

Chapter Twenty-Eight

CREATURE

Britton could hear people talking; he wasn't sure who all the parties were, but he was sure they were speaking about him. He decided not to move, to lie still and listen. The drug was wearing off quickly, and he was beginning to make some sense of the conversations. "This man is clearly not 'defective,' Dr. Schmidt! He cannot be used like some of the inmates you acquire. Unlike a lot of prisoners, this man has family and friends. His family has been making inquiries, and this situation has become touchy rather quickly."

Britton was unsure whose voice of reason was fighting for his rights, but he hoped his point was well taken. Dr Schmidt came over to the table he was strapped to and began checking some of the medications that were now flowing into his arm. "If you believe there could be a problem, I suggest we get Mr. Donovan's consent."

The other voice sighed loudly. "And just how do you expect that to happen? You have already kept him here for far too long...against his will, I might add. He's not even conscious enough to make a decision."

Dr. Schmidt began to chuckle. "You worry too much. Finding a cure for this virus is far more important to the world than a hundred 'Defectives.'"

Britton heard sighing again. "That may be, but this man has a family that has relentlessly asked questions about where he is being held. I got a call from the police chief just this morning. They need answers, and this lab is not going to cover for you if you push this too far. I've cleaned up enough of your messes to last me a lifetime."

The doctor kept chuckling. "Then I don't expect you will want to share in the glory when we find the cure." He continued chuckling and made a motion toward Britton. "These otherwise useless beings. It would be amazing to find that this population had a purpose, after all." The man's voice had begun to rise, and though Britton had begun to hope... that maybe...but this Dr. Frankenstein seemed to have silenced the one voice of reason.

Britton felt the swoosh of a door opening and closing, footsteps came toward him. He tried with all he had to lift his thousand pound eyelids, but they would not budge. The voice, he knew that voice. It came from a faraway memory; a memory that he refused to allow to surface, but then his hands shook.

"Good, good, Mr. Donovan. So glad to see you are finally awake." Barely able to lift one eyelid, the exam lights were too bright and the drugs still lingered. Britton wanted to turn his head away from the darkness because that voice belonged to a woman from his past. At least it was attached to a human, but the human had given up control long ago. He tried to open his eyes again, but the strap on his forehead dug into his skin.

"Who are you? Don't I know you?"

The voice was female. The more his mind cleared, the more impossible it seemed. The spirit that had tortured him...that had taken his life, was here again. "I bet you didn't expect to meet me here, but I came immediately when I heard they had acquired a group of 'Defectives' for experimentation." She patted Britton's cheek, causing his whole body to pull away in revulsion. "Imagine my delight in finding one of the 'Defectives' was you. Who could've imagined we would get a second shot at this, Britton? It's delightful."

Without a conscious decision, Britton began to fight the restraints. He kicked and writhed. He screamed with an intensity he didn't know he was capable of. Because he knew, maybe they all knew, this was life and death. This woman, rather this dark spirit attached to the woman, would do all it could to see him dead. He knew this; and he knew it well. Even if these researchers had less sinister intentions, which probably wasn't the case. The truth was, this spirit had killed him before...and Adonai had raised him up. "Adonai!"

Britton strained to believe what he saw. A chain hung from a thick metal collar around the woman's neck. The spirit perched on her back, its claws embedded deep into her shoulders. The dark spirit held the end of the chain and yanked it when he required her obedience. He would've had a much stronger reaction to the vision, but he was heavily drugged.

The spirit locked eyes with him, a fierce penetrating blaze. The demon yanked the chain, then jabbed his long nail into the woman's neck. She winced, struggling against the control. Britton could see a tiny glimmer of who she once was. That "before" person still wanted to struggle. But the dark spirit dug into her old wounds, and she followed his directions. Britton knew she wouldn't resist him. She'd served him most of her life. Desperate, he continued to struggle and fight the restraints.

The woman howled a command at the security guards, then berated him through clenched teeth. "Someone get a stronger sedative! Calm down, Mr. Donovan! Are you a child or just incapable of understanding that the world needs a cure?" Britton's eyes locked on the creature; it seethed and gritted its teeth. Then laughed and snorted. "You could help us find a cure, son of Adonai. If you understood...you would lay down your life willingly." The woman patted his cheek again, condescendingly, and with far too much force.

The slap snapped his head to the side. She looked up at Dr. Schmidt to explain her lack of restraint. "Good advice is wasted on these 'Defectives,' Dr. Schmidt!" She sighed heavily; her eyes rolling back and then forward. The creature hissed and jabbed... her voice became squeaky, sappy sweet. "Doesn't that seem like a much higher purpose for your life, Brit tooon?" She looked at the others as she spoke to him, as if he were a child or...ignorant. "If only he were capable of understanding how important this is, we might convince him to agree."

He heard the door open again and the "voice of reason" walked back into the lab. It would be hard for Britton to explain how he knew that. A change in the atmosphere, or energy? Britton's heart pounded faster, and he lifted his eyelids into a tiny slit. "Is he awake yet? Look, I am going to need to confirm that Mr. Donovan is in our custody. His wife has contacted several senators. Now, I'm not saying that they aren't on our side with this thing, but it's going to take some fast talking for us to keep him here much longer."

Britton opened his mouth in an attempt to speak to the one voice that might save him. But the world swirled in colors, and his body felt heavy, so heavy. The sedatives hit him harder this time. Someone must've turned his IV lines wide open. He could hear the voices, but he wasn't sure if what he heard was real. The sounds magnified; he heard the IV drip, drip something into his arm; his heart pounded in his ears, someone, or perhaps something, breathed heavily. He felt their breath on his face. He heard the buzz of the lights; he felt the vibration of the spirits that hovered above him. He was tired, so very tired of this fight... Exhausted, he relaxed; there really was no hope of escape.

"There now, Britton." He tried to roll his head over and watch the dark creature yanking on the chain. Yank and then jab, yank and then jab. His long claw plunged into his victim's neck, bloody, dripping. He manipulated the woman's every thought; there would be no appealing to her humanity. She wasn't human any longer. His eyelids were like heavy wool sweaters soaked in rain, too thick, too heavy. Britton heard the slurping and though he swam in a chemical cocktail of darkness; he remembered...he had been here before.

The demon troll spoke to him. Britton tried to focus on its face. When he was only a child, he saw trolls on the backs of lots of people and watched them watch him. He was only a young teenager when he realized that no one else could see the trolls. Most of them were a sort of gargoyle with excessively long fangs and claws. The creatures could turn their heads at strange angles, giving them the ability to perch on a victim's back, stabbing the long claws into his shoulders. Then they would move their heads around their victim's necks and bite down. Sucking out any amount of hope, or faith...they drained humanity of any goodness. Once empty, the creatures could inject a type of venom. It infected not only the mind, but the soul.

Britton knew his mind was drifting; the world he saw was black, void of life. The creature whispered into the woman's ear, its snake-like tongue darting in and out. This was not the same flesh, not the same human he had battled so long ago. But it was the same spirit, which boiled down to the *exact same thing*. All the voices faded away, but in its place, another voice came.

****

Creature

This voice was welcome, so very welcome. He was his dearest friend before, before he decided he could do everything himself. "Take my hand, Britton. Let's try again!" Britton looked up into the eyes of green, or blue, or brown. It was hard to say. Colors swirled through his pupils; it was not color really, it was life. Adonai was creation itself. The very breath and energy that gave the jaguar his speed, and the volcano the power to erupt...all of that dwelt inside the Spirit that was Adonai. The air around him smelled of the sea and of possibilities. He found himself standing beside Adonai, on top of a cliff. The warm wind blew his hair and massaged his shoulders with its billows. Adonai closed his eyes and leaned into the strength of the gusts.

"I'm not a big fan of heights, Adonai. You know this." Adonai turned and smiled with mischief sparking in his eyes. Britton knew this would literally require a leap of faith.

"Haven't you always wanted to let go, Britton? Just leap into nothing and see where you might land?"

Britton put his fists on his hips and took a few baby steps closer to the edge. "It's not that I don't believe You will catch me, it's just that...I don't want to fall, even if I know You will."

Adonai pointed his finger straight at Britton, a giant smile on his face. "That's it. That is exactly the truth. You believe that your way is better. You believe that there is no way that falling could be the best choice for you!" The second Adonai said it, he ran off the cliff and yelled back, "JUMP!"

Britton stood, frozen. Trembling from the shock and the possibilities. He spoke in sort of a whisper, under his breath. "How? I can't do it, Adonai. There's a big part of me that wants to and yet..." He stood shaking his head and sighing when a creature of orange and black slithered up over the side of the cliff. It crawled in his direction, using its stubby paws it didn't seem to need. They would flip back against its body as the creature continued coming toward him, slithering on its belly.

The size of a large alligator, or maybe a small dragon. Its long tail swished back and forth, and the serrated back moved with it. The solid black eyes stared directly into his. The cavernous glare gave it an otherworldly feel; Britton's skin crawled.

The creature was mystical, not anything he had ever seen before, except perhaps in mythology. Across the veil...he had met a dragon once, in that other world, the world before. The distinction between natural and supernatural blurred. Sweat beaded on his temple and ran down the side of his jaw. It was in this moment that he understood the word "human" meant far more than he had ever realised. It was more than being made of flesh, more than the ability to rationalize...it was a commonality of warm blood and experience. But this creature shared none of those things.

If the creature had pupils, Britton couldn't make them out. He took a few steps back as the creature got closer. He had no weapons and didn't know how to fight a creature like this, even if he did. As it got closer, the creature reared up on its two back feet, like a dog begging for a treat. The body began to coil up as if to give support to its heavier upper body. The eyes rolled back into its skull, exposing the backside of its eyeballs, which were bloody and red. It took all Britton's will to stand his ground. The reality...there was nowhere to run.

"Have you decided not to jump, ffffriend of Adonai?" Britton was taken back by the creature's size and, most certainly, by his ability to speak. He attempted to reply, only to find himself opening and closing his mouth like a fish gasping for air. The creature closed its eyes, and Britton waited, counting up to thirty before the creature opened them again.

"Your heart knows the answer to this question, fffffriend of Adonai." When he said "friend," it was as if the "F" got stuck in his throat, and he needed an extra puff of air to finish the word. The black, snake-like tongue shot out and in between each phrase. The creature slung its head to one side. Whatever it was attempting to portray was completely lost on him. Maybe it was an attempt at what it perceived as compassion? But it was definitely lost in the translation, because mostly it just appeared more fierce. "Your heart feels fear because you should be afraid. How many times has your fffffriend led you to destruction?"

Britton had yet to say one word. Squinting, his mind reeled through the possibilities...perhaps this could be an illusion. He was strapped to a table, full of drugs they were pumping into him. Worse still, maybe he was going mad. Either way, neither category would release him from the terror he faced. So struck was he by the creature's words and abilities, he had not truly considered what the creature was saying to him. When the accusation finally sunk in,

Britton bristled, stood up straight and proceeded to argue. "Adonai is indeed my friend. He has saved me, again and again. I have no reason to distrust Him. He even brought me back...I died once, and He brought me back!" The obvious loophole in his argument gaped. A childish whining thought arose in his mind: "Why did I have to die?"

The creature hissed rather loudly, spraying his foul breath so far it caused Britton to turn his head. He gagged in spite of being someone who considered himself to be well mannered. "He led you to your deathhhhh? Is this something you can forgive?" The creature's tongue stuck straight out and the forked end of it trembled. Then it stretched out a small pair of reptilian wings and flapped them as if preparing for flight. "Maybe He has twisted your thinking, convincing you that your death was for your own good?" Then the creature laughed...a hissing sound, but the clownish smile was definitely an attempt at humor.

The creature's voice lifted; the tongue shot in and out. His eyes rolled back in his head, his long tail swished faster....the stubby black wings flapped. Britton suddenly noticed the length of the claws on the short little T-rex legs. They still folded down like a begging pup, but the ends of each of them were covered in blood...some new, and some old. The creature didn't give notice to Britton easing further away. He was caught up in his own oration. "Who needs a ffffriend like that? A ffffriend that always chooses what is best for Himselfffffff. You have lived the truth of how Adonai treats His ffffriends. But we can't always save everyone...sometimes fate is more like a snake, and it will take you no matter what you do to stop it." Britton continued moving backwards. He looked behind him;

there were no trees, nowhere to hide. The creature's eyes rolled back as soon as he finished his discourse.

The lizard eyes fluttered as if he hadn't noticed; there was a sudden realization that Britton had eased away. Dropping back down on his belly, his hissing grew louder. "You are a fffffool, ffffffriend of Adonai. He will only betray you again when He gets the chance. But I, I will tear your heart out ffffffirst!" His body pulled back, and he prepared to pounce. His tail pressed hard into the dirt, he readied to launch.

There was no way out, nowhere to run, and nothing to fight with. Britton's mind spiraled out of control. He began to wonder whose thoughts he was hearing. "Yes! The creature will shred you, ripping your innards, and it will not be a quick death. Friend of Adonai!"

Shaking the creature's voice out of his head, he called out, "Adonai!" Britton heard the familiar reply. "Jump! I will catch you!" He didn't think any further; he ran off the cliff.

CHAPTER TWENTY-NINE

WHERE IS BRITTON?

C limbing out of her heavy sleep, the first thing Asha felt was fear. She didn't immediately know where she was. An anxious tremble covered her body, and she tried to calm herself from the violence of the dream. The same dream she had dreamed every night for almost a month. She rolled onto her side and let the tears roll down her cheeks and land in polka dots on the sheets. "Britton! Oh Britton, where are you?"

A sense of loneliness smote her, and a feeling of angry frustration. She buried her face in the sheets and called out to the only help she knew of. "How long, Adonai? I need to find him. No one is listening. I call every single day and no one will talk to me. I trust You! I know You are with Britton. Please, make sure I do my part." Squeezing her eyes hard, she thought of the last time she had crossed the veil. "I have walked in the world with the Morning Star..." She choked on the sense of lost sweetness. It was almost unbearable.

The day before, she and the kids had gone to the police station and spoken to a sergeant. He assured her that if Britton was in "medical custody" there wasn't much that could be done on his end. "There are people from that aircraft that are still unconscious. Mrs. Donovan, your family, your husband...you are the lucky ones." He looked at the dark circles under her eyes and the strain of all this woman's vigil, and he tried to regroup. Be kinder. "You know the virus has killed more than half of those passengers your husband traveled with?" Asha frowned; the trembling returned, her frustration was coiling itself around her heart. If the police chief's words were supposed to soothe her frazzled nerves, it was not working.

"I, we, we need your help to find him." She dropped her head, refusing to cry in front of her children. Struggling to ask the right questions, she swallowed several times. She needed to gain control.

Britton Jr. surprised her by speaking in her place. He stood up in the sergeant's office, stretching to be as tall as his ten-year-old body could manage. "Excuse me, Sergeant, my name is Britton BenDavid Donovan. My family has not seen our daddy in almost a month. We don't know where he is, and they won't tell us. You say we are lucky, but we don't even know if he is alive, not really." He lifted his small arms from his sides and shook his head. Then he motioned to Maddie, who was sitting in Asha's lap, playing with her phone. "My sister is not much more than a baby. Don't you think she needs her daddy?"

Asha watched him be brave, resisting his soaring emotions. He clenched his jaw just like his daddy did. At ten, he was a replica of his daddy. The same sandy curls topped his head, the eyes the color of The Caribbean. The long lanky build. He placed his small hand on his hip, looking like a miniature grown up. "We have the right to know where our daddy is, don't we?" Asha watched her unusual child. He kept his emotions locked down tight, and rarely ever cried. But she could see his eyes filling with tears. His emotions were about to betray him. He blinked for a second while biting on his lips, then regained control. " If someone needs our daddy's assistance, we know he is brave; and he will help them. But we know with all our hearts that if our daddy is allowed to call home, he will pick up his phone and call us. Our daddy is a good man, a brave man! All this hiding and...pretending, it isn't a nice thing to do to a good daddy or his family." His blazing eyes flooded with tears; the pretense of adulthood cracked.

Asha reached over and held his hand. With a final summation that would've made his Aunt Kate proud, he stomped a foot. (She liked to help him pretend he was a famous trial lawyer.) "All this sneaking and pretending is why we are so mad." A tear rolled down one cheek. "Don't you think we have the right to at least know where our daddy is? To know that he is safe?"

Asha's heart leapt, listening to him speak. He was his daddy's son; thinking rationally and using his big words to get a point across was something he did beautifully. Asha picked Maddie up out of her lap so she could stand beside her brave boy.

The sergeant pursed his lips, his mind searching. His Adam's apple moved up and down as he swallowed a lifetime of too much reality. He inhaled and slowly stood up, meeting their desperation with honesty. He looked into the big blue eyes of the miniature adult...who was just a small child pleading for his help. "I will find out his location, young man. I will call you before I leave this evening. You are correct. You have the right to at least know where he is."

The sergeant reached across his desk, sticking his hand out, and Britton Jr. moved to shake it as if it were meant for him. "You are a brave young man. I'm certain your daddy would be proud of your determination." Britton Jr. pursed his lips in a thin line. Asha knew from the look on her son's face he wasn't finished. He screwed up his little boy face and shared his family's most important secret.

"My daddy used to be one of the 'Defectives.' Did you know he was healed by Adonai Himself? He is an important warrior for The Great King, Mr. Sergeant. Nothing will happen to my daddy without Adonai saying so." The sergeant's face broke into a smile. Asha couldn't help but wonder when the last time that old leathered face had stretched into anything but a frown.

The man's eyes glistened a little. "It was a great honor to meet you all. It's not everyday I get to meet a family that is so..." He paused, searching for the best description. "So determined to get their point across." One side of his mouth lifted. "Done very professionally by a ten-year-old spokesperson." Asha took Maddie by the hand and headed toward the door. Britton Jr. stopped just before leaving the office, spinning back around with a final thought. "Don't forget about us, Mr. Sergeant."

The sergeant nodded; his eyes filled with compassion. "Yes sir, young man. I will keep my word to you. And...it is highly unlikely that I will ever forget you."

Chapter Thirty

GLOW

The ride home was quiet except for Maddie singing the alphabet song. "Tell me what you think of me!" Then she would clap at the end and giggle. Asha's thoughts were a million miles from their serious situation. Strangely, she was remembering the day Britton proposed. The memories made her smile, something she hadn't done much since Britton left. The idea that she was having to remember her husband caused her heart to ache. She looked in the rearview mirror and caught Britton Jr. staring at her.

"What were you thinking about, Momma? Something made you smile." That boy, he didn't miss a thing. Asha shook her head and felt her heart warm; she loved her children more than her own life.

She smiled again. She had been rummaging through her memories, stuck in that one moment. "Mr. Britton, have I ever told you how your daddy proposed to me?"

Britton Jr., who was usually lost somewhere in a favorite book, was strangely attentive. "Ummmm, I don't think so, Momma. Tell me about it." She glimpsed at his face in the rearview mirror. He was smiling with his daddy's Kool-Aid smile; it caused her heart to skip a beat.

She resisted the fear that was haunting them all; the fear that they might never see Britton again. Then forced a smile across her face; she could be brave too. She opened the drawer of memory and took out one of her favorite pieces. There were always those pieces in everyone's life...the ones that changed everything. She pulled in a deep breath and let herself remember the beauty of the stars that night. The thought struck her...there was always light, no matter how much darkness.

"Let me start from the beginning. We had gone on this amazing hiking trip that was supposed to last for three solid weeks. It was your daddy's graduation present to himself." She giggled, remembering how excited Britton had been and how long he had planned the trip. "I agreed to go along with him. Hiking up in those mountains, we both loved the feeling of being alive under the sky. You can really leave all your troubles behind when you hike long enough. There's only room for wind and sun and rain." She lifted one side of her mouth in a smirk. "I loved hiking, till I did it every day for three weeks!"

She stopped and savored the precious memories. "I had blisters on top of my blisters; and so did your daddy, but he refused to complain." She smirked again. "Britton Jr., it was so funny watching your daddy take steps up that steep climb like he was stepping on fire. I'd ask if he was okay, but he would swear he was fine." She rolled her eyes, replicating the way she rolled them that day. "Still, it was one of the most fabulous trips we've ever been on."

Britton Jr. screwed up his nose. "I do like to hike, Momma, but I like to read more."

Asha laughed at his truthful admission. "You can always read by the campfire at night." He nodded, content with the idea.

"That summer, your daddy was determined to see as many waterfalls as he could. You know your daddy. He can hike for days; and I was just trying to keep up. It had been a good two hours since anyone had said a word, and I was starting to get hungry and tired. Our feet crunched over rocks. The sun was still hot on my head. We both had been sweating all day. The sun was dipping lower in the sky and I was starting to get cold. Your dad was determined to get to the camp before it got too dark to set up our tents. But between the blisters and his silence, I was done. I was just about to tell him how done I was when we came up over the top of a ridge, and there it was." Even as she remembered it, the excitement caused chills on her arms.

"Right there, sitting on top of a mountain, was the most beautiful lake I'd ever seen. It was spectacular!" She remembered that moment; she relished it. It was like a snapshot in her mind, and she pressed save. The detail was still vivid. "The mountains behind the lake sat in the shadows, and they looked purple with the sun behind them. Wispy clouds glowed a light shade of lavender, but they were pierced through with tiny beams of sunlight." She used her hands to show him, but, of course, the memory she held in her mind was beyond the words she had to paint with. "The lake sparkled a turquoise, like the color of the sky in the early morning. And the flowers, Britton Jr., every color you can imagine in patches; pink peonies in one spot, red pansies in another, and white daisies everywhere!"

She glanced at his face in the rearview mirror. His eyes were wide, he was hanging on her words. "We got to the very top, right when the clouds cleared, leaving behind a golden glaze as thick as honey. A large flock of butterflies sailed in around us, dancing and fluttering; their wings flashing blues and greens." The memory of their wings brushing her face and arms caused her to shiver. She hadn't thought about that magical moment in years.

"Your daddy got so excited, he started jumping up and down. He grabbed me and swung me in a circle."

Britton Jr. laughed and moved up and down on his seat, clapping. "Yay! I want to visit this magical place, Momma!"

Asha clapped too, loving the childlike joy coming out of her serious child. "We definitely need to go back there; maybe as soon as Maddie is a little older."

Maddie wrinkled her nose and added, "I'm already a big girl. I can do anything Britton Jr. can do." Britton Jr. scooted closer to the car seat and patted her arm. "Yes, you are, Maddie, but this is a grown up trip. Not for little girls!" Asha watched him mothering Maddie and just shook her head. He was such an old soul. Asha cleared her throat. "Hmmm, hmmm. Do you want to hear the rest of this story?" Britton Jr. and Maddie both nodded. "I don't even know where your daddy got the energy. Before he said anything, he started running even though we had several miles to go. I was so tired; we had hiked all day...over logs, through water. I didn't feel like running. I just kept on trudging along at my same slow pace. I waved to him to go on when he looked back."

She stopped talking; the memories rolling over her heart in waves. She didn't tell him how Britton had held her above his head, then slid her down so he could kiss her again and again. The memory was so vivid she thought she could smell the scent of the pines, the earthiness of the water...the masculine scent on his neck when she rested her head on his shoulder. She loved the scent of him, fresh cut grass, blown by the wind, all mixed with sunshine. That day he smelled of smoke from the campfire, with a hint of caramel from the snack they had eaten.

Britton Jr. waited, then he interrupted her nostalgia. "So what happened, Momma? Did you make it?"

She hadn't realized she'd stopped talking. "Oh, right? Yes, yes, we did. But your daddy sped up and was heading to the camp area. He moved so fast that I lost sight of him." Asha glimpsed at Britton Jr. in the mirror. He nodded at her to keep going. "Like I said, he ran ahead, and I was dragging my feet. By the time I made it to the campsite, he was nowhere. I called his name over and over. I walked for another hour trying to find him." She saw Britton's eyes wide; he was becoming anxious. "I decided the smartest thing to do was go back to the campsite. I mean, what else could I do?"

Britton Jr. was leaning forward, holding onto the seat in front of him. "Momma, where was he?" She laughed at how anxious her son was getting. "Britton, you know I found him!"

He frowned at her condescension. "I know; but still, this is a good story."

Shaking her head, Asha continued. "Turns out, he got too close to the edge on the back side of that lake, and he went sliding. I looked for almost two hours till it was too dark to see."

There was way more to his daddy's "accidental sliding" than Asha was willing to share with her ten-year-old. She skipped over the dark reality and saved it for when he was old enough to hear. She scratched her head and paused to consider what she could tell him. "I was sitting on my backpack and praying for Adonai to help me. About that time, my birthmark began to glow."

Britton scooted up as far as his seat belt would allow. "Show me your birthmark, Momma. I didn't know your birthmark could glow." She lifted her arm for him to take a look.

He screwed up his nose. "It looks like a regular birthmark to me. How does it glow?" She wasn't sure she had the answer; but before she could think of what to tell him, he begged, "Tell me how you found daddy, momma."

As grown up as he tried to be, he was only ten-years-old. This was one of the rare moments he allowed himself to be a child. Asha relished the moment, nodding her assurance.

"I was sitting on my backpack staring at the birthmark. I didn't know what to do. I was praying, and I knew the glow was an answer to my prayers. I stood up and started walking around the lake. I didn't know exactly what it would mean, but the birthmark grew brighter and hotter. Eventually, it was such a glow that I began to call your daddy's name. 'Britton, Britton.' I swear I held my breath when I heard a faint reply."

Britton Jr. began to clap. "Yay, Momma! You found him. You found him!" Asha held the feeling of that moment inside, and it made her gut roll and tumble. That feeling, the sound of his desperate cry, carved into her bones. She remembered thinking that finding him would require one bloody step at a time.

Britton Jr sat back, then realized his momma hadn't said where he was. He leaned forward to see her face. "So where was he, Momma?"

Asha shifted her eyes to the rearview mirror; she calmed herself from what really had happened that day. Smiling, the tears brimming in her eyes threatened to betray her. "He'd slid down the side of a steep cliff and was hanging on for dear life."

The reality of his encounter with the dark ones was far more sinister than an accidental misstep. A horde of them attacked him. He was so outnumbered. Britton had survived the attack, but not without some serious warfare. She had used every bandage and every butterfly stitch in their first-aid kit. His arms had been shredded with claw marks. The fangs left puncture wounds every few inches. She shook, remembering how torn up he was once he came up over the edge of that cliff. Blood oozing from his ears, his head, and all up and down his arms. He didn't tell her the whole story for months. When he did, she understood why...the dark ones didn't want to let go of him. They knew better than he did, Adonai had big plans for his future. They would always fight him; it was the reason he hadn't already proposed. He didn't want to drag anyone else into his personal war. But, as she often reminded him...she volunteered.

Those memories caused ugly chills to go creeping up and down her neck. Maybe their life had been sunny far too long? She shook off this sense of dread, this premonition of doom. But in her mind's eye, she saw him there again. Britton was hanging on the side of that cliff, most likely right now. Her mind traveled into that darkness, and she looked up to find Britton Jr. studying her. She ran one hand through her hair. "Sorry, Son. I was remembering lots of thing about that hike. Where was I?"

She inhaled, blowing out some of the tension. She needed to move on with the story. "I ran and got some of our repelling equipment, set an anchor, and lowered the rope. He said he knew I would find him; his birthmark was glowing. It got brighter the closer I got to him." She turned into the driveway and put the car in park. "Ahh, Maddie is sound asleep." The tiny five-year-old had her head turned, her face buried in a stuffed pink bunny. Asha's emotions were raw from the memories.

Her nose smelled the campfire; her skin shivered remembering the chill and the desperation of that night. She rotated around and looked at Britton Jr. "I don't have any idea how your daddy held on that long. His fingers were bloody from gripping the edge of barely two inches of rock. It was the only edge big enough for him to catch while sliding so fast. It was a real miracle that he caught hold of it. Ya know, the second he got to the top, both our birthmarks faded back to normal." She watched her son's eyes wide with wonder; he loved a good story.

"It took us a while to patch up all the scratches and cuts he had gotten sliding. And...it was pretty late, so we chewed jerky for dinner; we opted to get some sleep instead of cooking." She smiled and asked Britton Jr., "Do you like lightning bugs? Cause they were everywhere that night!" Britton Jr. bounced in his seat again.

"I love them, Momma; they are my favorite bugs!" They both laughed, and she wished she could describe the magical night when Britton was finally patched up and laying safely in his sleeping bag beside hers. "I remember it like it was yesterday. Lightning bugs everywhere, buzzing so close we could reach out and catch them if we wanted to. They looked like stars touching the ground. We put our sleeping bags outside because we never set up the tent. So we slept under about a million stars and a full moon that glowed as bright as a lamp. Your daddy said it was a lantern that Adonai had set in the sky just for us. The stars were so close it felt like I could touch them." She also remembered the gentle kisses that night. She knew she was madly in love with Britton. Even now, his fragrance filled her mind. He always smelled of the outdoors, a touch of musk danced on his skin. Asha blushed, suddenly self-conscious.

Britton Jr. was lost in her story. He pretended he could see the stars; so he reached up to pluck them out of the sky. Asha grinned at his playfulness. "I have never seen stars that big, or so many in all my life. It was like Adonai grabbed a handful and threw them into the heavens just for us on that special night." Britton Jr. allowed himself to laugh like a child. He mimicked throwing stars across the sky. "Look, Momma; He did it like this!" They both laughed as he pretended they burned his fingers.

"Anyway, I was staring at the stars and saying how amazing they were when I realized your daddy was holding a diamond ring in his fingers. He saw me looking, and my mouth dropped open. He held this beautiful ring up beside the brightest stars and asked me. "Which one do you think sparkles more?" Then he slid this ring, this one right here, onto my finger. I cried because I'd never been happier."

A tangled mass of sorrow, of fear, and love wound through her. Asha savored the memories of walking for miles, hand in hand. "We played board games, laughing till the sun told us it was morning. It was one of the most amazing trips we ever took." Asha suddenly gasped. "Britton Jr, I know why I remembered this story!" Her heart beat a fast rhythm, and she reached back and took hold of Britton Jr.'s hand. "Adonai! Can the birthmark help us find Britton? Will you show us where he is? He's lost, and we just know he might be in some trouble."

The birthmark began to warm; the glow of its soft light reaching inside her heart with hope. "Momma! Momma, your birthmark!"

Teardrops fell onto her face in giant streaks of hope. "Momma, Adonai answered our prayer!"

CHAPTER THIRTY-ONE

THE SEAL

A sha had no idea what she would say to Jeff...he was the one person who could help, if anyone could. The story Britton told of their first encounter gave her the courage she needed to tap his name on her phone. "Adonai, please help him hear me." The phone rang. Her heart thundered inside her throat with each ring. He answered in three rings. "Jeff?" She waited a second, then he croaked into the phone.

"Asha, hey there!" His voice was strong again, like the rest of him. He gave off that aura of "I've got this!" to everyone around him.

She took a breath. "I hear you made an escape from the hospital."

"Maybe there's a warrant out," he replied with a nervous chuckle. He hadn't yet come to terms with how he would explain his miraculous recovery to anyone but Jazlyn. "It's so great to hear your voice, and...I really don't think I'm as important to them since I'm basically recovered. It turns out, it's way better *not to be important.*" He smiled, and his eyes sparkled with the new vision. "Jazlyn told me you visited the hospital, but that was before, before I could hear, or see, for that matter. I wanted to thank you for coming and keeping Jazlyn company."

Asha patiently listened, but her mind was going in circles. "Yes, I came a few times. You were just so sick then; I didn't know if you remembered."

He was nodding while Jazlyn snuggled up next to him on the sofa. She refused to even have him out of her sight. She was so grateful to "The Man" that Jeff now talked about incessantly. Jazlyn piped in. "Hey Ash, I'm listening too."

Jeff hugged her up closer, if that was possible. "Yep, she's like a tiny koala cub stuck to my side since I got sick."

It helped...the kidding, the laughter. Life had not held much to laugh about in the last month. Asha couldn't recall very many easy moments for any of them since the Claw virus invaded the world. "Hey Jaz, I miss you. We have to plan to at least meet for coffee soon."

She heard Jazlyn yawn, then she replied, "Yes, absolutely; can Jeff come too? I plan to be by his side every second." They all laughed; Asha needed to laugh again. It was still a tad forced, but her life was so close to the edge. One slip and she'd lose her hold. The decisions she needed to make had grown sharp; mistakes weren't an option. The biggest problem was...who knew which moves were a mistake? This was gonna take blind faith.

"I called to talk to you, Jeff, about...Britton." She waited. She had no idea how much he knew. If Jaz had had a moment to fill him in on the situation at the airport. They both began talking at once, then Asha smiled. "Okay, you go first."

Jeff hesitated; he knew she would be glad he had met Adonai, but how did he tell anyone about all the things, all the adventures? "Let me begin by letting you know the best news of all." Inside his mind, he badgered himself; JUST SAY IT! "I met Him Asha; I met Adonai."

Asha sucked in air, her mind filled with piercing curiosity. "You met Him? How?"

Jeff began chuckling again. "Well now, that's the wildest piece of my story." Her heart fluttered, she felt chills, and she saw His face; the face of The One who saved her again and again. "Please tell me; I can't wait to hear."

Jeff loved telling the story to someone who would believe some of it. He had told it, and retold it to Jazlyn so many times that she knew every tiny detail. He wasn't sure what Jazlyn thought. As far as he knew, she had no real relationship with Adonai. She had asked him if he wondered if it was all the narcotics. He didn't tell her that the question burned. He knew it was near impossible to understand the adventures, the other world he had experienced, across the veil. But it happened, and he had no doubts.

Asha didn't interrupt the joy that poured out of Jeff; she knew about that joy. Spending time across the veil was a miraculous experience. She found it impossible to find words that others understood. Jeff, on the other hand, seemed to find the exact words. "Fizzy water?" Asha giggled; how incredible is that?"

Jeff hardly took a breath. "I know! But I'm telling you, Asha, it was not the drugs; it was not hallucinations. I was there; I walked in that healing water with The Man..." Jeff paused. It was no longer right to refer to Him as if he didn't know Him...not anymore. "I know His name. Adonai. Adonai is His name. I walked in the healing waters with the King of the World." A tear snuck out of the side of his eye, and he briskly wiped it away. He vowed not to cry anymore. He was not the crying kind. He didn't want to become a weepy mess of a man. He would never have believed that could happen to someone like him. Maybe it was a fitting punishment for all his sins...he shook his head, and let that thought fade.

Asha absorbed his joy, laughed with him and Jaz; and now they all embraced the tears of joy that came with the emotions of being loved by Adonai. "I, I really know what it's like to cross the veil, Jeff. Adonai has met me there. I crossed recently."

It took a minute for Jeff to absorb that news. "That is amazing, Asha! I feel so blessed that I am not alone. That...there are others. People I can share my story with that don't doubt me." There was excitement in that truth...that Adonai met other people across the veil. "Asha? Do you know why He does it? I mean, why would He choose you? And the bigger question... Why would He choose me?"

Asha was shaking her head. How did anyone answer that question? "Jeff, I truly believe you would need to ask Adonai that question. The only thing I know for sure is that...He comes for us when we need Him most."

It was Jeff's turn to nod. "Asha, I just never knew...this is not the Savior that my dad preached about. This Man, Adonai...He is brave and strong, and good. As small as that world used to be to me, now I know that Adonai is the King of that world. He is good; nothing else compares." They sat there in silence. What was there to say to that other than, "Amen."

"Do you want to tell me about it, Asha? I'd truly be interested to hear what it's like for you." Gathering her courage, she waited for Adonai to fill her with strength. She fought the tears; demanding that she hold it together. Not only for herself, but for her children ...for Britton.

"Jeff, this is really hard for me... I expect it may be difficult to believe my story. There's a lot, and I don't know what Britton has shared with you." She struggled for the words, for the right way to ask for "what?". She wasn't even sure what she needed, not really. She dove in, talking fast, trying to persuade, and for the millionth time she wished she was as good with words as Britton. The irony made her want to laugh and cry at the same time. "Jeff, I need to find Britton. He's being held somewhere. I feel strongly that it is against his will. Everything inside me..." she paused. She needed to just tell him and wait for his questions. "Okay, listen. You know that Britton and I have...the same birthmarks. I know you have seen them and probably wondered about something so bizarre. How in the world could two people have the same birthmark? But the thing is, we don't have time for all the explanations. What you need to know is that they are the mark that Adonai placed on us; a birthmark, a seal is maybe a better description. They are His way of claiming us. Britton says the best way to describe it is like being knighted. I'm probably not making any sense." She was shaking her head, the frustration rising.

The dam broke and Jeff became the weepy man he swore off. The birthmark, the same birthmark that marked Adonai's chosen, began to glow on his forearm. "Asha, I don't mean to interrupt, but I didn't tell you." He was choking on the truth she had just revealed. Asha listened harder; she was pretty sure Jeff was crying. She heard some deep moans, and she couldn't imagine what she had said to cause such intense emotions. "Ash, the thing is, I didn't say anything. I didn't know how. I have the same birthmark. I'm trying to say...I have been knighted. I wear Adonai's seal on my forearm."

He held his arm up, looking at the "birthmark" that appeared when he had been reborn. "Adonai placed it there the last time I crossed the veil."

Asha let out a gasp; it was louder than she realized. "You, are you saying that you, that you somehow, Adonai....?" Asha couldn't finish the sentence. She was overwhelmed by Adonai's goodness. Never in her wildest dreams had she considered the possibility. "Adonai has called you too, Jeff! I'm so relieved." She ran her fingers through her hair; she laughed through a barrage of tears. Then her birthmark began to glow. "Jeff, Jeff, is your birthmark warm? Is it glowing?"

Jeff was nodding. He finally realized he hadn't said it out loud. "Yes, Ash, the moment you began telling me about Britton. Another thing, Adonai told me I needed to go find him. We need to rescue him from the darkness."

CHAPTER THIRTY-TWO

WARRIORS

J eff crouched in the bushes, his legs still trembling. He'd been flat on his back for a month. He wasn't used to a body that wasn't in top condition. He looked up; a ripple of lightning edged along the horizon. He could smell the rain coming; a storm was brewing, and that was definitely in his favor. The noise he made, he could time with the thunder. So there was every chance that he would not be heard at all. He grinned. "Adonai, You're The Man!"

He was outside a government laboratory that served the whole city. He used every connection he'd ever had in an attempt to find the place. His military commander, all the way up to some general who knew where they took test subjects. Not one of them would give him a shred of information. In the end, he came to the conclusion that he'd used the wrong "connections." He knew someone in "high places." The highest place of all. Because of that connection, here he was.

"This is definitely the right place." He knew this was the place, because the birthmark led him. After Asha's phone call, he prayed, he considered and then he just waited. Asha called again. She felt they should circle the medical center just to see. If, like all those years ago, the birthmark led them to Britton. Sure enough, simultaneously their birthmarks began a sort of flashing. Jeff pulled his truck onto a dirt road and stopped at a cyclone fence that said, "Government Research Center." He insisted that Asha go home. After all, he would need to wait for the right amount of darkness to find his way inside.

****

Spiritual

Asha and Jeff sat looking at the large laboratory, lit up like Christmas, even in the wee hours. Britton was being held inside. She was sure of it, she could feel it. With the dark tension hovering around her, she couldn't help wondering how this whole situation would end. Asha was wringing her hands, trying to figure out what the next step should be. She swallowed, searching for a new topic, any topic to change the subject. She segued back to all Jeff had been through. "Jeff, tell me how you left the hospital so quickly. Jazlyn said it was against medical advice. I bet that caused no small amount of red tape."

Jeff chuckled; they eventually just let me go...I wasn't sick anymore. There were other virus patients back up in the ICU. I couldn't understand why they would still need me there. "I wouldn't be surprised if this lab, right here, was the next location they had in mind for me." He hesitated; he wanted to tell someone the virus was spiritual. That he knew it deep down in his soul. But who was going to listen to that kind of crazy talk? There was zero doubt in his mind that all the blindness, deafness, and numbness were physical manifestations of something no doctor could cure. Nope, he couldn't go there, at least not yet. Right now, he needed to take Asha home, come back...and find Britton.

Jeff didn't have a clue what was happening inside that lab. But whatever it was, it wasn't good. He had a direct order to follow; he could do that, he was good at following orders. Where exactly Britton was being held in that fifteen story building...he couldn't say. What he was supposed to do next? That was the hard part of this mission. On one hand, he was flying blind, on the other, he had a direct communication link to the King of the World.

****

Undercover Enemies

The journey back to the Lab had been riddled with fears he couldn't account for. Mental gymnastics weren't something he was accustomed to. Seal training kept him from overthinking a mission. Fear was a companion he learned to dismiss early in his training. But the questions beat at his consciousness till he began repeating the questions, and then answering himself out loud. "Why should I risk so much to rescue Britton? Maybe he doesn't even need rescuing. Maybe he is a willing participant." The thought came, and the sheer absurdity of it made him angry. Training helped him focus on the task at hand. But no sooner had he shut down the thought...than a new one surfaced. In a whisper, the inner voice baited him.

"What if this is a trap? Britton tells some pretty tall tales about his life before. After all, this could be some elaborate scheme to get you to participate in the virus research." Jeff gritted his teeth. "That's it!" His voice raised far too loud for a man crouched in the bushes outside of a high security facility. Shaking his head,he knew these weren't his thoughts. He would never think those kinds of things about Britton.

"Britton is my friend, my best friend. Adonai has brought me here to find him." The moment the words were out of his mouth, the truth of it went through him from heart to head. Yes, that was the truth; but where were these voices coming from? They definitely weren't his.

His mouth was dry; the back of his neck soaked. He drew in air with the knowledge, the reality, that he had spent time with Adonai. But knowing that good existed made the fact that evil was also present...a stark new reality. Like the thrill that goes through you when you lose your grip on a steep climb, he realized that he had been doing battle from the moment he responded to the command to find Britton.

Lightning made webs across the dark skies, revealing the red eyes that were hidden once the darkness returned. Fifteen feet into the brush, they pierced him, stabbing at his soul. He heard the hissing; it was electric, causing the hair to stand up on his arms. Not because he was afraid of the creature, but because it was otherworldly. Not an animal that would bleed warm if he killed it. Heart and lungs, flesh and bone were something he was trained to kill...but this creature fought with different weapons. This creature was ancient, before time was. He felt its age the same way he sensed someone behind him; he couldn't see it, but it was absolutely there. The voice he had mistaken as his own spoke.

"We are strong; yes, ancient. There will be no more of our kind. We, too, were created by the one you call great."

The fear that crawled and scratched at him was otherworldly. He had felt this fear once before; he recognized its stench. He was standing in an old silo in the middle of an Iraq wheat field. He had thought he was alone when he felt its presence. He had his weapon out a tiny window; the enemy in his scope. When he allowed himself to glance toward the sound, his heart stopped. There was not only one saw-scaled viper, there were so many he couldn't count. The silo was a nest of the most dangerous snake in that whole country. He had felt the drops of sweat running down his back at that moment...he was definitely in a nest of danger now. This lab, full of snakes...just a different breed. This wasn't the first enemy he couldn't see with his flesh eyes...so he did what he would do on any mission. He decided he needed backup. He reached to press the earpiece when he realized this mission had a different commander. "Adonai, I am on Your mission. You see me, and You know the plans of the enemy." He barely had the words out of his mouth when he swore he practically heard an audible voice tell him to "Move!"

Holding back the terror, he crawled in silence, making his way around to the farthest door. He listened; he wasn't sure if the dark creature had come behind him. Would he even hear it if it did?

"I have this! Move!" The instruction was an order; he recognized the voice of The One who had given it. He knew he was supposed to get into the building as fast as he could. The locks were an issue, but the three security cameras had to be managed first. The goal was to take them out without being seen. He hoped to leave the one stationary camera. Leaving one camera live just might keep security from investigating.

His black gear helped keep him hidden, but the cameras were high tech, swiveling toward the least movement or sound. Lightning feathered cracks in the night sky, then thunder boomed hard enough to shake the hospital's windows. The cameras moved back and forth, unable to locate the source. Jeff couldn't stop the smile that covered his face. He whispered his gratefulness, then pulled his 9mm SIG

Sauer P226 from his chest holster. He ran his fingers along the barrel; it was all in perfect order; he kept it that way. He screwed the suppressor to the end and waited. He wanted to hit the cameras when they were turned the other direction. He picked up a rock and threw it. Both cameras spun in sequence, following the sound. He took them out in less than a second. The glass and metal made more noise than he had planned for, so he finished the last camera just in case the debris was caught by the stationary lens. Thunder sounded simultaneously, and he felt amazement over who was in charge of this mission.

In his mind, the words, "every mission," caused him to nod. He was about to move when he felt the presence move closer to his back, causing the hair to stand on his neck as if the lightning had struck within feet of him. He inhaled till his lungs felt stretched, then blew it out slowly; it helped him control his breathing. Eyes wide open, he decided that he needed confirmation from command, and today that meant prayer. "Adonai, I'm new to this type of combat. I'm gonna need some guidance if you can see Your way clear." He waited; he knew the presence was waiting too. He felt it plotting. He wasn't sure if he had the tools to outsmart a two thousand-year-old creature that crawled out of a pit.

A memory seemed to come from out of nowhere. He was maybe sixteen or seventeen, sitting in church *again*. He was making spit balls and had a rather large plastic cup full. His dad was preaching as always, and he had long ago learned to drown out the monotonous lessons of everything he should **never** do. But this memory was vivid, and the words pierced through. "For the weapons of our warfare are not carnal..." His dad had hammered his fist into the pulpit, causing most of the congregation to wake up out of their

Sunday evening stupor. He remembered Old Man Jacobs snorting awake to the hilarity of all the youth on the back row. It was such a shame because the plan to shoot spitballs through a straw and into the old man's open mouth was foiled.

Huddled tight, his knees were starting to complain; he decided he'd just ask. "Adonai, is this memory from You?" That's when he remembered that his dad's mention of weapons had garnered his attention. He was a teenage boy on the brink of manhood. Guns were a new fascination. He thought the sermon would never end. When he finally got home, he pulled out his small black Bible, probably the only time he ever cracked it open. Found the passage and memorized it. "For the weapons that we fight with are not the weapons of the world. But they are powerful through God for the demolishing of strongholds." Jeff chuckled at the absurdity that he knew any scripture. He was just a kid, fascinated by anything that put a weapon in his hand. Now he needed that weapon, the only one he wasn't trained to use. He rubbed his chin, listening. Still unsure, he whispered, "I'm guessing You're trying to tell me what to do, Adonai. So, I'm going to follow my instincts; it's all I know."

It was the thing he wanted to do the second the red eyes made themselves visible. He wasn't sure; it seemed like madness, but it's all he had, so he went with it. Jaw locked, and teeth gritted, he spoke to it. "Creature from the pit! I am a soldier of Adonai." The sweat was beading up on his forehead, and he used his forearm to wipe it off before it blocked his vision. He continued speaking to the spirit through clenched teeth. What he wanted to do was stand up and challenge it. That was his nature, and his training. "I am on a mission, and I may not know much, but one thing I remember is that you can't stop me. I am His now, and you...you are nothing."

He wasn't sure what he'd expected, but the vacuum of darkness took his breath. He placed his hand on the ground and steadied himself. He sure wished he had a team or some kind of reconnaissance on the inside. "It's just You and me, Adonai. Let's go get our boy!"

When he got to the door and began to pull out instruments to jimmy the lock, there was a streak of light and then he saw him. It was the second time Raphael had shown himself...each time Britton was in trouble.

When Jeff had come to the rescue of "the speaker" at the university that day...it was this same warrior who stood over Britton. The Light Warrior had protected him from the angry crowd. Jeff knew exactly what he had seen that day, but wow, was he a sight to behold. The second he had walked up to see what was going on...light split the sky. He blinked. The warrior was hovering over Britton's crumpled form. If he had seen nothing else, the size of the sword that Light Warrior swung was awe-inspiring. He guessed it at ten feet, maybe even twelve feet. It vibrated, but not like a piano key, more like the sound and motion when you struck metal. It was not so loud as it was intense. You remembered he felt the vibrations through the ground.

The warrior hovered maybe two or three feet above Britton. The magnificent sword was drawn, and there was no question of how fierce he was. His body armor was made of something Jeff had never seen. He'd thought of it several times afterwards, wishing something like that existed in this world. "Sure would come in handy tonight, Adonai." He winked. It was such a new experience to know he was always heard and seen.

The one thing he knew...when he had stared at that warrior, was ...he was highly skilled in combat. It was difficult to explain to someone else, someone who was not seasoned in warfare. This creature, or spirit, or warrior of light...whatever was the correct terminology. Jeff had been grateful they were on the same side. It wasn't very often that he felt so outclassed, but he was not in this creature's league. There would be no contest.

The eyes that reflected the gold of the throne room where he received orders stared, and then he gave Jeff a slight nod. "Reconnaissance!" Jeff blinked, and he was gone. He let the shock of the moment settle. He tested the doors and found them open. He shook his head in amazement. "It's a little unnerving that You hear every word I speak." He took a deep breath, attempting to refocus on the mission in front of him. "But first, thanks Raphael, no telling how long that would've taken me."

He slid through the doors and then moved down the hall, attempting to stay clear of all the security cameras. When he got to the end of the first hall, he realized there were no lights, everything was now black. "No electricity. Raphael strikes again. Thanks man, we're a good team!" At least he would come in as a surprise, not the other way around. He pulled his flashlight from his utility belt and read the signs. The farthest one read, "Research," so he followed the arrow. After making two left turns, he heard voices. He crept up slowly, crouching so as not to be seen through the tiny window. He leaned his ear against the door. Maybe he could determine if Britton was in there.

Chapter Thirty-Three

RESCUE

'It was nearly impossible for Jeff to hear the conversation going on behind the closed door. It was muffled mostly, but he heard Britton's name solidly at least twice. A heated argument broke out and that helped him understand more words. One voice wanted to move ahead, and the other voice was dead set against it. "This is not going to happen. Do you hear me? 'Defective' or not, this is illegal. Besides, this man has a family!"

The other voice was just as adamant, pushing his opinion forward in no uncertain terms.

"Look, this isn't the same as working on... you or me. This man is one of the 'Defectives.' The fact that he was even born was a sheer accident. It's our good fortune that he's here and available. None of the 'Defectives,' not even one has caught this virus. Do you understand how important that is? If we can figure out why, we can save the world."

The first voice began to protest again, but was cut off by the stronger second voice. "The 'Defective' can finally have a purpose in this world besides just draining our resources. Maybe they were born for this reason...to save the rest of us!"

Jeff leaned one shoulder against the wall; he struggled to accept what he was hearing. "Save the world? Sacrifice one life for everyone else? That certainly sounded familiar." But... Britton was no longer "defective." How could they make such accusations? Besides, "defectives" were human beings, loved by their families. They taught the whole world a lot about love and patience. Their purpose was so often spiritual...and was the reason why those in darkness couldn't see it. This researcher was justifying his evil, and Jeff was here to help him see the light!

Jeff began whispering prayers. Becoming more comfortable that prayer was a conversation between a man and his God. He suddenly knew that Britton was not behind that door. Urgency pushed him to hurry. He looked down the hall and carefully made his way, reading the signs on each one as he passed.

He felt a nudge toward the next hall; he followed the "gut instinct" that was becoming more familiar. He stopped at double doors that read, "Surgery! Authorized Personnel Only." Jeff filtered all the possibilities. What was on the other side? Did he just slide through and hope there was another set of doors? Did he bust in and try to stop whatever butcheries or evil that these "researchers" were up to? He pressed his back against the wall and decided he better get some direction. One side of his mouth lifted in a grin when he began to reach for his communication device. He remembered again that he need only pray, and the "commander" would direct him in the way he should go.

"Adonai, I'm gonna need a little guidance here. Some kind of backup if I go running in with guns blazing." The sweat covered his face, his neck, and his hands were getting too wet inside his gloves. He had a carbine automatic M4A1 5.56 mm strapped to his utility belt. He hadn't loaded full gear; he couldn't imagine needing it. But here he was, wishing for a grenade or two. He shook the idea out of his head. This was not the Middle East, and he had no way of knowing who was behind any of these doors.

Jeff unhooked the carbine automatic and pulled it across his chest. If he needed to bust Britton out, he might have to use it. He really was long past the point of no return. If someone caught him outside the door, dressed in dark camo, carrying professional weapons, he was headed for a prison cell. Somehow, he hardly felt any uneasiness; he was following Adonai's orders. He had never disobeyed an order in his life.

A tiny shift in the light drew him from his thoughts. It reminded him of moonlight shining through a sheer curtain. With the light came the sound of a wind chime that was far away. He turned his head, trying to see better, but then he knew he "heard" directions. "Britton is behind this door...save him."

Jeff's body tensed; he pulled the weapon close, put his shoulder to the first double door, and burst through. The sight that met him was almost more than his mind could accept. Britton was strapped to a gurney, leather straps around his wrists, his ankles. A large strap held his head down, more straps around his chest and just below his knees. He wasn't going anywhere. His legs and arms had been carved on. Tiny pieces of flesh cut away, and horror of all horrors, Britton seemed to be conscious.

The sight sent fury through him, and then rage. Blood streaked down Britton's face, his eyes swollen shut. He wondered if the arms were even reparable. He could see bone on his right forearm. On the left, they had cut the birthmark completely off.

This was a terrifying moment; one of the doctors stood over Britton's head with a circular saw...the moment froze. Jeff stood only a few feet away in the shadows, but the cruelty of the situation sent unknown terror tingling along his spine. His mind tried to dismiss it as a bad dream of fantastic evil. But he was seeing this with his real eyes, with his flesh eyes. He had seen more than his fair share of horror. Mutilated children, mercy killings, the stuff of most people's nightmares. But this...the fear left him, and anger, a holy anger, rose to fill its place.

As the overwhelming fear faded, he became conscious of a new feeling, a sense of holy justice. The knowledge of Adonai's faithfulness overwhelmed the darkness, the veritable evil of the whole situation. Jeff stood in the most precarious moment, and yet the sound of the wind chime grew. With the sound, his shoulders relaxed, and the knowledge that he'd arrived in time helped him breathe.

Jeff let the doors close behind him with a silent swoosh. He aimed the rifle at the man holding the saw. "I'd put that down if I were you." The man stepped back slowly, eyes focused on the size of the rifle and the obvious experience of the soldier holding it. Jeff grinned. "I left my big gun at home; I only bring this one when it's a small party." The other two, in surgical gowns, stepped back slightly. "I suggest that no one in this room makes any movements without my permission. Are we clear?" Jeff knew Britton heard him, but his head was strapped down so tightly that he couldn't turn to see. "So who wants to be the hero and unstrap my friend on the table?"

He could tell one of the doctors was a woman. He watched her slide her hand toward the scalpels on the surgical tray. Jeff caught the slight movement. "So, you there...lady! You touch one instrument and this will not be the party any of us planned. So take that same hand...uh, uh, slowly and loosen every single strap you've got holding down your very unwilling victim." The woman hissed at him. Jeff blinked; he tried not to laugh, and yet the hiss sent shivers all over his arms. Britton slid off the table, but his legs wouldn't hold him. "Everybody move to the back wall...slow, real slow." He kept his eyes on the woman. The hiss, the willingness to pull a weapon on an armed man, told him that she was more than willing to take him on if she got an opportunity.

Britton pulled himself to a stand, using the table for assistance. Jeff moved in behind him. "You alright, my friend?" Britton only nodded. His breathing was ragged. Jeff stepped around him, aiming the rifle at the researchers. "Everyone have a seat on the floor, backs against the wall. Anyone moves too quickly, and there's gonna be an awful mess for the rest of you." They slowly slid to the tile floor; the woman hissed as she slid. "Now, Britton, my friend, can you take those wide leather straps and make good use of them? Dr. Kavorian and his roommates need to be taught a lesson. You in?" He turned and watched Britton struggling to put weight on his legs. He was wobbly, but he was able to use the leather straps to buckle the three researchers' hands behind their backs. "Pull them as tight as you can, Britton. We don't need anyone wiggling out before we're long gone!

Britton used the last of the straps to wrap their ankles. He had one arm that refused to work, but he used his teeth to pull it tighter. He looked up at the woman and patted her cheek, and winked; his Kool-aid smile causing her hissing to grow louder. "Britton, check every pocket for cell phones." Britton nodded, pulling cell phones from two different pockets. "Now, bring them with you."

Britton hesitated, and Jeff worried that he would finally pass out; but instead...he blew on the researchers. A thick purple mist covered them, and Jeff watched them inhale it in. Britton slowly stood up, still wobbly, but he moved his unwilling legs toward Jeff with serious effort.

Jeff opened his eyes, then closed them; he didn't know what he was seeing, but this was already one of the weirdest nights of his life. Britton stumbled toward Jeff, having no strength left in his Gumby legs. He tried to navigate the shifting room. When he got close enough, he fell to his knees. Jeff helped him back to a stand. All he could think about was how much blood Britton was losing. "Britton, put a hand on my left shoulder; I need a full view of those three." He never took his eyes off them. "One move, and I'll take you all out. If I kill one of you, I might as well finish you all. It's the same prison time." The woman hissed again, and her two conspirators' eyes grew colder.

Jeff stopped when his back hit the double doors. He added one more juicy bit for them to think on. "Being tied up with that female wild cat isn't quite as appealing as you thought it would be...is it, boys?" Britton's knees buckled again. Jeff noticed there was a trail of blood everywhere he walked. Man, he wanted to do more to make those three rethink ever doing something like this again. He reached inside a pocket and rolled a can of tear gas into the room. "Consider this our parting gift."

Jeff sure wished that he believed this kind of torture was not the norm in this facility. But this new connection he had with Adonai told him things. Their hearts had long since stopped feeling anything close to compassion. He shut the lights as he exited; the longer it took for them to be found, the better chance he and Britton had at getting far away. They hadn't gone ten feet when they heard screaming and screeching from all three doctors. Jeff stopped. "What could have happened? That can't be the tear gas."

Britton kept moving; he slowed down, then he looked at Jeff. "Maybe they are blind, and deaf; maybe they have the Claw virus."

They both stood there; Jeff didn't know what to say. "How?"

Britton looked intently at Jeff. "They pumped me full of it, trying to give me symptoms. So, I blew it on them. I thought it would take days if they got it, but maybe not."

Jeff had to admit, he would be surprised if they got out of the building without a battle. Britton needed assistance to stand, to walk, but he was thinking clearly enough that Jeff suggested they go back out the way he had come in. "No security cameras...just in case." Jeff held Britton around the waist with his left hand and kept his right hand on the rifle. He didn't plan to shoot unless he had to...but being surprised by security wasn't in his plans, either.

Britton suddenly stopped in view of the exit door. His mind cleared for a second, and he remembered he wasn't the only one.

"We can't leave them! There are so many 'Defectives' here." Jeff paused and tried to think it through. "Do you have any idea how many? Do you know exactly where they are?" Britton stood there, legs trembling, trying to remember the details of what he'd seen and what he'd overheard. "My guess would be fifty or sixty. I counted eight vans from GAP out front when I first got here...they hold about six to eight people. Then his legs buckled, and he was on his knees again.

Jeff grabbed around his back and lifted him up. "Bud, I know we gotta rescue them, but there's no way for us to get sixty 'Defectives' out, and not get caught."

Britton was nodding. "I understand. But leaving them would be a death sentence. We have to come back for them. We have to make sure their families know what's happening!" Britton fell again, and Jeff lifted Britton, and carried him out.

The panic of all the time they were taking was chasing him. "We have to go; we've got about ten minutes, at the most, before the Bride of Frankenstein wiggles herself out of those straps. I expect she's as stealthy as an alley cat."

Britton swallowed. He didn't want to do this. Leaving anyone to those three evil scientists was not something he'd do to an enemy. Britton knew he couldn't help them in his current condition. By blowing the virus on them...he had done what he could; if they were blind, if they were deaf...it was a game changer. "We have to come back for them all, Jeff. There's got to be a way."

They made it out the back, and Jeff felt the trembling in Britton's body slow down. Jeff stopped at the exit doors, giving Britton a moment to rest. Britton stared at the sky. "Wow, I don't even know what day it is, but what a beautiful sky." The golden glow of orange and pinks that painted the sky after the storm was a picture of freedom he longed for. He turned his head and looked at Jeff. "I am so grateful for your help, your rescue. Adonai told me you were coming, but I wasn't sure you would make it before they were holding my brain in their hands." Britton shuddered. "Old Dr. Frankenstein and his bride had some pretty gruesome plans for my brain." Jeff was listening; he knew Britton was attempting some comic relief...but it wasn't funny, and they were still in danger.

Jeff wished to give Britton a few minutes, but they had to hurry. "Hey Buddy, I know you are still floating in a cesspool of chemicals, and I can't even imagine the pain... But I want to get you out of here.

I expect they will call reinforcements in the next five minutes. My truck isn't far, but if you could manage maybe a mile of it...I could run the rest of the way and come back for you. Do you think that's possible?" Britton just nodded; he had no idea how his body would perform, but the further he got from this evil, the happier he would be.

The mile trek felt more like fifty. Britton's legs would collapse about every ten steps. This was not going well. He looked up at Jeff, who stayed focused on their surroundings. He was making sure they weren't being followed. Jeff felt Britton's eyes on him, and so he gave him a quick glance. "What's on your mind? Tell me, but keep moving." Britton smiled; he shook the wonder out of his head and kept pushing through the lightning sharp pain. "Those monsters were about to take my head off, literally." Maybe the medicine was wearing off, and he was struggling to believe that he was remembering clearly. "They were, weren't they?" Jeff felt the fury rising; he nodded while grinding his back molars, but he kept moving them both forward.

His mind went to the one time he'd been captured. Held by insurgents with a deep hatred for all things American. He'd spent three days hung from the ceiling by his ankles, an electrocution device as their play toy. It wasn't something he'd ever forget, even if he wanted to, and he sure wanted to.

"Dude, those three are more evil than any terrorist I've encountered, and I've seen more than my fair share. Let's get you home, some medical treatment, and we'll come up with a plan to spring everyone else."

Jeff finally sat Britton under some trees and ran the rest of the way to his truck. He placed his rifle on the seat, just in case. Britton wasn't conscious when he made his way back, and Jeff struggled to wake him. "Ah man, Britton. I don't want to risk taking you to a hospital, besides they're full of Claw virus patients." He put his hands on his thighs and tried to breathe. "Adonai, I don't know what to do; tell me what to do?" His cell phone vibrated, and he saw Asha's name. He smirked and looked at Britton. "The wifey is not very patient tonight." He scanned the area and hit the button. "I've got him; he's not in great shape. I'm trying to decide about the hospital."

Tears of relief poured down Asha's face; she'd been alternating between tears and prayers since Jeff dropped her off four hours ago. "Bring him home, Jeff. Just bring him home. I'll call his dad; he'll come right away."

Jeff nodded. "Roger, we're on our way." He clicked his cell off, shoved it back in his pocket. He bent over and tried to breathe against the pure searing pain that washed through him. He told himself he'd rescued a lot of soldiers in worse condition. But Britton was the closest friend he'd ever had. He didn't know how he could live if he had failed to get to him in time. He dropped his head and tears poured to the ground. "Do you see me here, Adonai? I've become the very mess of a man I could never have imagined. I'm begging You, please take care of him. Please, I really need him to make it. He's lived through more things than any of us can comprehend. How can I live with a failure like this?"

He looked at Britton, then apologized. "I'm going to take you to the truck. It won't be easy, and it's gonna hurt, dude; it's gonna hurt bad. I'm really sorry about that." He used his forearm to wipe the tears off his face, then he picked Britton up by his armpits and lifted him up over his shoulder. He stood for a second to be sure he could balance; it wasn't far to the truck from here. He opened the passenger door and laid Britton across the back seat. Running around to the other side, he opened that door and pulled him as carefully as he could by his brutalized arms till his legs were almost in. He placed Brittons's arms across his body, and swore when he saw the forearm bone poking through the skin, and then apologized again. He slammed that door, ran back around, put his feet in. He paused when he saw how much blood was pouring. He grabbed an old t-shirt he had in the back and wrapped the one leg that was bleeding the most.

Britton lifted his head. "Hey, where are we now?"

"This is Disneyland, bro, just go back to sleep." Britton gave him a thumbs up and was mercifully unconscious.

CHAPTER THIRTY-FOUR

MORE NIGHTMARES?

B ritton

As much as Jeff wanted to hurry, the last thing he needed was to draw anyone's attention. He finally drove over a small bridge and into Britton's neighborhood. The memories of all the injured men he'd carried on his back haunted him. He knew exactly how many lived and how many died. "Adonai, I pray You choose for Britton to survive. He's still needed here." He bit the inside of his cheek, wiped his face with his arm again, and noticed the birthmark. It still had a bit of warmth to it, but the flashing glow was long gone.

The low buttery light of early morning shaded the world as he slowly pulled into the driveway. He glanced up to find a worried Asha standing on the porch beside Britton's dad, Dr. Larry. He stepped out, splashing across the wet grass that made squishing sounds from so much rain. Asha was already opening the truck door; he heard her gasp. He hadn't warned her sufficiently; he just didn't know how. Larry was right beside her, trying to assess the situation. He nodded at Jeff and scooted a sobbing Asha out of the way. "I think Jeff and I can carry him."

Lights were still out in the Donovan house; Asha apparently didn't want to wake the children. But she had made out the sofa bed in the den with clean sheets. They sat him down as gently as they could. Jeff held his upper body, which was most the weight, but he figured Larry was probably used to picking up heavy patients and shifting them from stretcher to bed. They slid him onto the queen sized mattress, laying him sideways, giving Larry better access.

Britton moaned. The drugs and the unimaginable pain still held him. His mind floated; he heard his dad, at least he thought he did. He fought desperately to open the lead eyelids that came only to a slit...they searched for Asha's face. He wanted to touch her pretty red hair; he wanted to smell the lavender and soap of her skin. "Britton, Britton, you're really here!!" He heard her through the fog of pain. The weak smile he gave her shredded her heart into ten thousand pieces. Her thoughts skittered back to that dark day she had found him in the back of the ambulance. Britton saw the pain seep out of her pores, almost visible if you knew how to look. He wanted so much to spare her all that came with loving him. The pain made her neck tight and stiffened her jaw. He tried to lift his hand to touch her face, but the world kept spinning.

Asha realized how deeply they had both been wounded all those years ago. To repeat the nightmare was beyond imaginable. But they had grown strong at the site of those scars. She was married to the only man she could ever love. That alone was the greatest gift. He was like a creature from a dark legend, both cursed and blessed. She thought of their wedding day, the day they were finally one. They stayed up all night talking, eating giant pieces of wedding cake, and drinking coffee. They ate every single snack in the fancy basket in the bridal suite. He was touching his face, her tears dropping on his forehead. Britton groaned, startling Asha back to reality. She saw that the bone in his arm protruded. Her heart burned, filled with shards of glass, cutting away at her resolve that he would survive. "Larry, Dr. Larry!"

Britton watched her; not with his eyes, with his spirit. His eyes refused to open again. But he felt her presence. It gave him hope again...she always stood beside him. To him, she was like some warrior goddess! He tried to smile, but he could on feel one side of his mouth. He saw her, the way he always saw her. She stood with her hair hanging in long ropes of power, her eyes full of tears she willed not to fall. She was such a gift, and he would always be grateful. "Thank you, Adonai! Thank you for my beautiful warrior princess." Then all went black.

    ****

Darkness

Without warning, the door to the darkness of the last week swung wide open. At first, he couldn't see what was wrong in the dimness of light. Wind brushed over his face, cool and soft as breath. It rustled leaves in the trees above him, and he felt sweat run down his neck and across his back. He was in no hurry, and yet he didn't belong here in this place. Spiderwebs hung on lots of the branches, and he would swear he heard a raven call his name. It began to rain, and it didn't feel like it would ever stop. It fell in giant walls of water, and he was so hot and sweaty and the rain was cold, it was warm and thick.

He saw the demon troll, saw the creature's body hunched up on top of the woman's back. The eyes rolling like a slot machine and landing back on the snake eyes. A bright light swung back and forth over him as if someone had pushed it. Suddenly, he was freezing. His head would not move; it was strapped down. All he could do was cut his eyes to one side or the other. He mumbled, "A surgery center?" He couldn't see anyone, but the panic rose in his throat, and he began to yell. "Hey! Is anyone here? What is going on? Somebody come and let me loose!"

He was breathing hard and fast, trying not to pass over into delirium. It's not that he didn't know how dangerous the situation was, but he had escaped; he wasn't there anymore. "I'm not here; this is not real!" There was screaming...his voice.

He knew the human psyche could only bear so much and then it would divert the thoughts to prevent one from being overwhelmed. Maybe he had done that; maybe he was still strapped on the table? He pushed hard against the head restraint...there was a tray laden with surgical tools. "What in the name of all that is holy is that for?" He spied a saw with a type of circular blade, and he knew. Yes, he knew that it was used to remove the top of the skull during brain surgery...or autopsy. But the same minute the thought surfaced, it almost stopped him from breathing. "Jeff came; I'm not here!"

Dr. Schmidt appeared, moving back into Britton's peripheral vision. He floated by and then he was gone. He knew he should demand an explanation. Scream at the injustice of what was being done to him, but he felt the tears running down his neck and knew that he was sobbing. "Dr. Schmidt, I believe your 'Defective' is awake." Britton felt a cold, white fear that totally consumed his mind. There was fear, and there was nothing else. It possessed all his thinking: formless, infinite, and terrifying.

The creature appeared beside Dr. Schmidt and began making suggestions. "It might be good if your subject remained awake during the majority of the autopsy." The creature rolled its eyes and then the woman smirked and chuckled. "For however long, he would be able to be conscious. If we started in the middle and worked upward, he might be with us longer. At least till you reach the brain."

"No!" Britton screamed. He knew he said the words, but there was no sound. "No, I am alive. Can't you see I'm alive?" He pushed against the restraints with all the strength he had left. But neither doctor responded to his demands. He knew they could not hear him. "I must be dead. Am I dead?" He felt like he dwelt somewhere between here and there; he just didn't know where there was. If he was dead, why did he have to feel all this again? Britton dropped his head back down onto the table, wishing to lose consciousness...anything. The darkness of death or sleep, or maybe he could wake up. Was he lucid? He could hear the woman's cackling laugh. Why attempt to reason with these monsters? Then he joined her, laughing at the horror; it couldn't be real.

His mind was filtering through memories, some recent, some long ago. The lost memory of a condescending psychologist appeared in his mind. He made the comment that Britton, having been a "Defective," had learned the "self control of society" simply by observing. Britton frowned; he remembered how the man despised him. To him, "Defectives" were hardly human. His mind vividly recalled the man twisting his long mustache as he looked down his nose. "The high moral standards you strive for are nothing more than false ideals or hypocrisy at best." Britton thought him tainted at the time, perhaps even mentally twisted, but this experience made him reconsider the man's dark opinions. The memory floated away, and he saw only black for such a long time that he was amazed when someone spoke.

"Excuse me. Mr. Donovan?" Britton, having yielded to the belief that he was dead, took a moment to resurface. He tried to open his eyes, but the weight of them made it impossible; he begged them to open. When they finally did, Dr. Schmidt stood over him with a circular saw in both his hands. His eyes were the vertical slit of a snake. "I feel some obligation to give an explanation for your obligatory sacrifice." He paused, clearing his throat. The terror rose as Britton's eyes stared at the saw blade. He couldn't breathe; the terror took him to a place of unmitigated panic. If he were alive, he would hyperventilate. He wanted to pray; he wanted to scream; but there was no rescue possible. The doctor continued his explanation of how his sacrifice was necessary. "Unless you had a much higher IQ, I do not think I would be able to enlighten you to any level of real understanding. My defense is that your claims of individual rights must give way to the greater good. This is a great service you do for all mankind. Your...ummm, unusual condition...of being a 'Defective' and also immune to the virus, creates such a fascinating possibility. You will be a hero to the whole world. That alone should make you brave." Dr. Schmidt hit the power button on the saw.

Britton's mind spun, and he thought perhaps there was no other way. Maybe he was fated to die at the hands of this foul creature. Maybe there would be some good to come of it. Then he was falling fast, and he felt his stomach lurch. When he tried to grab something, anything to slow the fall, he opened his eyes to peek. The woman researcher leaned over him, too close to his face; he could smell blood, a metallic tang on her breath. She lifted his eyelids fully open to be sure he was conscious. She spoke as her snake-like tongue tickled his face, moving in and out.

"The rights of an individual or even of a thousand individuals could be easily sacrificed for a cure for the majority. You should be grateful." She hissed, and her tongue darted in and out like the common variety garter snake. Britton didn't see anything more, but he heard the voice taunting him in the back of his mind.

"Dr. Schmidt, this sacrifice is so small. A few 'Defectives,' is hardly more than nothing." Britton struggled to open his eyes to watch her. She stepped away from him, but she sneered. Then he saw him. Drystan looked back at him through the woman's eyes.

In his darkest dreams, this demon troll always came crawling out of every crack to taunt and condemn. The demon troll's voice, so familiar, scratched across his soul, and he shuddered with all the ugly memories. The chambers of his heart had been shredded by this creature. There had been the moment when the creature had held it in his hands, only to squeeze the life right out of him. A well of pain opened in his chest, draining all his hope, spilling into a pool of fear in his gut and then leaving him empty.

The raspy voice was jubilant. "It's time, Brit toooon! Restitution, that's what this is. It's time for you to give me the justice you took from me!" He removed his long claws from the woman's shoulders and jumped onto the table, landing on Britton's gut. The woman continued her dribble of justification for his murder, but without the troll, she wasn't as eloquent. "I truly would not have believed that even a 'Defective' could fail to be inspired by the opportunity to be a hero. Didn't your Adonai sacrifice Himself? That's what this is. We have at least fifty others waiting if we don't get answers from you. We hope to get all the information from one 'Defective.' You know you've always been my first choice."

Britton glared at the claws of the troll as he licked them. Instead of the torch of hatred he had always carried for the troll, he suddenly felt pity. He barely mumbled it. "I pity you." The troll didn't know what he said; or if he did, he didn't care. He hopped up onto Britton's chest, dragging the claws across his legs. Someone screamed, though he couldn't say who. It was far away, so far. The world would go dark and then Drystan would lift his head with Britton's blood dripping off his fangs, and the snake tongue would lick them. Finally the screaming stopped, poor soul in so much pain. Britton hoped someone saved him.

The creature began striking one leg and then the other leg and then he knew the screams came from his own throat. "I was brave once, Adonai. I mean to be brave, and yet I just want You to take me home; please take me home!"

For one long minute, Britton felt the two sides of his life in direct conflict. He wanted his life back, with his wife, his children...but the pain of the Shadowlands was overtaking him. Both worlds pounded in his heart, in his head, echoing against each other. The troll hopped back onto his chest, sharpening his claws as he slid them down Britton's face. Britton felt the blood bubble up, running down his cheeks. He didn't know what came over him, but he looked at the snake's eyes without blinking. The calm that he spoke the words with was chilling, and even the troll stopped to listen.

"I am not yours to take. My life is in the hands of the Great King. You killed me, He brought me back; you are not in control here. I am His, here and there." The darkness that pushed the troll boiled inside him. He shrieked in fury. There was a flash...he dug the claws through Britton's eyes. Britton felt the claws as they scratched through his mind. Like a piece of metal that had just come out of the fire, orange and red hot, so hot the metal was bending. There was *NO CHOICE* left; he would be going home. For a long moment, he hung between worlds...

CHAPTER THIRTY-FIVE

SONG

"**W**hen you walk through the waters, I will be with you. When you walk through the fire, you will not be burned." Britton opened his eyes to sunlight shining through the purple edged clouds. Holes of light punched through the puffy whiteness and landed in stars on the water that rippled beneath. He heard the soothing voice of Adonai. That other world, that flesh world, still pounded in his mind, but Britton refused it, resisted its lure. This was where he belonged; this was where he wanted to be. There was some pain; he'd never felt pain before, not here, not in this perfect place. But his legs burned, and he refused that too. He wouldn't allow it here; he was not flesh, not the cocoon that caused all the misery.

"Is that the truth, Britton? Is it the flesh that causes all the misery?" He stood on the edge of an aquamarine sea. It was blue and then it was green and then a wave rolled in, and it was another shade of turquoise. The waves pushed first powerful and then gentle, barely covering his feet. The King of the World held two fishing poles. Britton lifted his hands up in question; he wasn't far enough from all that he'd just lived through. He struggled to be in this better place. Never before had he struggled here. But it was as if a cable attached to his heart stretched back through the veil. He felt the strong pull of it. If he blinked, if he looked back one second too long, he would disappear into the dying cocoon.

He didn't know why, most likely because it was impossible to look Adonai in the face and not speak the truth. But his emotions surged and spewed out all he was feeling. "I miss my real life. I miss my wife. I miss my kids. I've disappeared back into the nightmare that You delivered me from. Did You forget me?"

The look of hurt passed through Adonai's eyes and then Britton knew who it was that had done the forgetting. A wave of deep regret rolled through him. "Adonai, I'm sorry. You gave me everything I ever wanted, then I hardly remembered You. Please forgive me for only remembering...in the darkness."

Adonai didn't respond to the accusation or the plea; He smiled a lonely smile. "I'd like to go fishing; would you like to join me?"

So many thoughts swirled through Britton's mind. "Adonai, I don't even know where I am. Am I still stuck on that table, being carved on by those monsters? Did Jeff really rescue me? Am I safe? I don't know which thing is a dream." The same fiery emotions, red and yellow sparks of passion, passed through Adonai's eyes. Britton thought He held a secret from him; but if he was honest, he wasn't sure he wanted to know what it was.

Adonai lifted up the fishing poles and his eyebrows, asking, "So what's your decision? Are you coming with me?"

It was so easy to forget the Shadowlands when he crossed the veil. To let go of all the tangles of love and loyalties that happened in that flesh world. Hanging on was like playing tug of war, but your rope is wet and slippery. Britton let go. He felt the weight of all that sat on him release, and suddenly he was as light as a balloon. "Of course, I'm coming. I'd go anywhere with You." Then he blushed because those words had been true...and then life got so good, and then he didn't even remember Adonai on his easy days.

There was a boat, well, more of a canoe, that sat on the shore, and Adonai climbed in and sat facing him. Britton took hold of the boat's edge and pushed out into the endless waves. He jumped in and groaned with the pain in his legs, but here they looked whole; it was in that other world where he struggled. He grabbed the oars and began rowing out into the unknown. He rowed till his shoulders burned. Adonai closed his eyes and enjoying the feeling of the sun warming His face or the rocking on the waves.

Britton's emotions rose and fell with the waves. He wondered if they might split the seams and come pouring out into the small canoe. He let the frustration build. "I guess I'll know when we get there." Adonai hadn't said where they were going, and He didn't respond, so Britton added, "You'll let me know if I go the wrong way, right?"

Without opening his eyes, Adonai commented on his murmuring. "I knew it wouldn't take long before you had to know."

Britton frowned. "Had to know where we are going? That would be helpful, wouldn't it?"

Adonai sat up; His eyes matched the cerulean blues and greens of the water that lapped around them. "I'm in the boat with you; what is there to fear?" There was no answer; well, there was no answer that Britton wanted to admit to. He knew Adonai's presence should bring him peace, but today his face grew hot, turned red, and he refused it. How could he fear when the King of the World rode with him? The lure of blame was not some light little stab; it had teeth and yanked at his conscience.

The air became heavy, turning the coolness of the day thicker. Purple rain clouds ambled in from the edge of the horizon, turning the mountains a deep, dark blue. The calm gentle waves grew choppier. Thunder boomed and lightning crackled across the already darkening sky. It made a cobweb pattern, and in an instant, a wall of rain began falling. The storm worked itself into a frenzy in seconds. Britton put his hand to his eyebrows, trying to see through the curtain of water. He opened his mouth to ask what was next when he realized he was alone.

The waves that were barely noticeable before now smacked the side of the small canoe with a vengeance. Britton looked to see if there was anything to bail with. He began to mumble through gritted teeth. "I know You are with me whether I can see You or not. I never forgot falling from that cliff; You will catch me." But if he knew it, he sure didn't act like it. His heart pounded against his ribs, and fear rose up through his throat. He continued "praying," if you could call it that. "It's not like I'd consider myself a godly man. I'm more like a wanderer who ran into You when I was lost. We locked arms, had a few laughs, and became friends. Sometimes I wonder what kind of friend You are." The accusation stung his own heart; he touched his chest, wondering if he was burned. Shame sizzled there.

The next set of waves took him up and over as if he were on an amusement park ride. The boat rotated in circles; the rain pummeled him, and the lightning flashed. When he began complaining again, a wave splashed over the side and smacked him right in his open mouth. The tiny canoe spun at just the right moment to give him a glimpse of the monster set of waves coming his way. There wasn't even a chance the tiny canoe would not fill up and flip on waves the size of mountains. He threw the oars into the boat and grabbed the sides. There was no use; the paddles were not controlling anything. Holding on, he ducked his head as the canoe rode up the wave like a rollercoaster cart. He held his breath, knowing that as soon as he began plummeting down the other side, it was game over.

The wave rose, and he climbed and climbed, but he never reached the top. As quickly as the storm had come, the waves subsided, setting him gently back down onto the peaceful ocean. Gentle ripples as far as his eyes could see. He was drenched and shaking. If he allowed his feelings out, the fury would burn his own skin. That thought broke through his pent up fervor. "Skin? I don't even have skin here!"

Suddenly the sun was brighter than before, the rays bathed him. He tried replicating Adonai by leaning his head back to absorb the warmth. When he opened his eyes, the canoe was bumping the shore, and Adonai held the tow rope. "Let's go; I'm planning on catching us some dinner!" Britton was soaked and trembling. He was so angry; why Adonai had left him...right when he needed Him most? Adonai pulled the rope, dragging the canoe onto the soft sand. Britton hopped out, trying to help. He was chewing on the anger of being deserted.

Adonai broke into his thoughts. "I deserted you?"

Britton's eyebrows pulled together. "I really hate when You do that; You should give me a chance to say it."

Adonai stood still. He dropped the rope. "To accuse me?"

Britton dropped his hands by his sides; he felt lost, confused, incapable. "Adonai, what is happening?"

Britton walked up out of the water and stood, head down, in front of Adonai. Truly, he wished that Adonai would assure him, comfort him; but instead of asking Him for what he wanted, he crossed his arms. "I just went through a storm that I can't believe I survived. You left me there; You could've changed everything. Instead, You just ignored my cries for help." Britton's eyes filled. The emotions of life, of all that troubled him, were building. A tsunami of fear screamed inside him; his physical body was broken, torn up. Evil was running rampant in the Shadowlands, "Defectives" were being held against their will again...he had accomplished nothing. He had failed completely.

Britton was so angry: at life, at himself, and most of all at Adonai. The moment the thought flickered to life, his eyes looked up to meet Adonai's. Their eyes locked...his heart skipped a beat. He had accused his Savior. He had failed Him and then blamed the King of the World for his own mistakes. His face flushed, he swallowed the rebellion that he had given so much room in his heart. Adonai held his gaze; He didn't speak, He just stood there piercing him with those dark eyes, now closer to the color of the ocean on that stormy sea. Without a word, Adonai turned and walked toward the treeline.

Britton was stung by Adonai's silence. A familiar knot tied itself in his gut. But rather than accept it, he toyed with it. Breathed some life into the ugly emotions. He wanted to defend himself, but how? He was guilty as charged; he knew it. It was how he changed when his life became so much easier, now that he was just like everyone else. He never saw his lackadaisical relationship with Adonai as a big deal. He had done worse than accept it. He had ignored it, never even acknowledging how he had turned his back.

Being a "Defective" was always living on the edge. Believing in the unseen was so much easier when it was all he had. He was soft now, his faith flabby. When he looked up Adonai had walked far ahead. He still held the fishing poles and was headed deeper, to some unknown place. Serving Adonai was not always safe...at least it didn't appear that way. He was the Son of El, the Great King. Though He had walked the Shadowlands, He was far more than just a Man. More than once He had appeared in Britton's visions as a massive mountain lion. Britton hesitated, but then he took off after Him; he loved Adonai, but did he trust Him?

Maybe a mile or so in, there was a creek running. It wasn't long before the creek became deeper and had several areas of bubbling rapids. Another mile or so and there was a waterfall pouring down into a small lake. The water bubbled and fizzed, barrelling over the falls and splashing at the bottom, causing a white spray they could feel while standing a good fifteen feet away.

"Do you feel the presence of the Great King in His creation?" Britton looked at Adonai and wondered why they had come here. He grudgingly found a spot and sat on the edge, feet dangling, fishing pole propped up between the rocks. Adonai joined him, laid back, hands behind his head for a pillow. He began to hum and soon Britton was drawn into the peace that surrounded Him. The sun, a glow of buttery softness, caressed his skin, and the warm sloshing of the water against his feet felt like heaven. The pain in his legs eased, and he finally let the knots in his shoulders relax.

He must've slept because he woke to the sound of singing. He sat up and rubbed sleep out of his eyes. The mist of the falls still bathed him, and the warmth of the sun glowed golden, warm enough to cause him to yawn. He kept looking for the source of the music, but unless his ears deceived him, it was the waterfall itself.

Adonai still slept, so he quietly slid off the rocks and into the lake, the coolness waking him completely. He swam as close to the falls as he could get, following the song.

He ducked his head, swimming under the powerful waterfall where the music echoed from the other side. Before he could find the source, Adonai swam underneath, and His head popped up beside his.

"Are you looking for the source of the music? It's amazing, isn't it?" Adonai placed His hand under the falls, then He put His whole head under it. He pulled back, shaking the water from His eyes, a gigantic smile on his face. "Wow, that's refreshing, and a great massage, too."

Britton reached out to the water; he felt the vibration in rhythm with the sound. "The music...it's the water, isn't it?" Adonai dove underneath the falls and stayed there. Britton wasn't sure if he should follow, but pretty soon he decided he would.

Underneath the white mass of bubbles, the music became deep, more like a base or a cello. The water bubbled around Adonai, caressing and hugging His skin. Britton surfaced, only because he had to. Adonai came up right behind him. Britton felt better invigorated. "The water is alive!" Britton was energized by the water...and the music. The song became louder, and the joy inside the sound reverberated through him. Adonai dove, and this time, Britton followed immediately. When he went under, he watched Adonai swimming deeper into the darkest blue depths of the lake. Britton followed Him, unsure, and yet if he was with Adonai, all was well.

CHAPTER THIRTY-SIX

SOURCE

It was only a minute when Adonai "fell" from his sight. Britton slowed his descent and paused. He looked through the darkness of the water. There had to be an air pocket of some kind. He put his hand through. It was definitely dry on the other side. He placed his feet down, hoping to land on them. He fell through fast onto dry ground, landing with a thud and rolling onto wet sand.

As he emerged, shaking water from his hair, he expected to find himself in a cave of sorts. He guessed right because it was a cave, at least on one side. But on the other side, it was open to the first fingers of sunlight tipping over the jagged grey and sapphire mountains. The light was a delicate pink, as if the rising sun blushed its way into the sacred place where he stood. He took a deep breath, feeling life pour into his lungs. He turned and found Adonai sitting on large black rocks, His feet in a pool of purple water. The water swirled in shades of purple and blue...he could see clearly through the water...because the pool was full of light.

Adonai looked up, undisturbed. "You came; I'm so glad." Britton got up, checking to make sure he hadn't hurt himself in the fall. He studied the ceiling of water. The waves moved in turquoise ripples above his head. It was hard to look away from such a miracle. He slowly walked over and sat down beside Adonai, placing his own feet into the mystical lavender depths.

A very soft breeze swirled around them, wisps of perfume in the air. It wrapped him for a quick second, a hug of such love; it took his breath. The glow of light in the purple waters reminded him of gold shimmers of light trying to wiggle between the cracks of black rock. If there was such a thing as water fairies...it looked like the water was set ablaze by some magical creature that held a lantern. He laughed at the image his mind conjured.

He truly wished for this moment to never end. The magical lights of the water, the caress of the breeze, the fire inside that made him feel ablaze. Sitting here beside Adonai, he could believe that the dark things, all the bad things...all the sadness in the world, could someday be washed clean. He looked at Adonai, the very essence of all that the word "Peace" conjured. Britton finally laid down all his defenses. He could just ask Him. He felt brave enough here to accept the answer. "Adonai, am I going back to the Shadowlands? Did they kill me?"

Adonai didn't look up; he seemed to be studying the lights in the purple tinged waves. When they finally locked eyes, a serious storm brewed in their depths. "Is that what you want? Do you want your test in the Shadowlands to be over?" Britton held the weight of the choices; as if he placed one outcome in one hand, and the other outcome in the other. With sincere curiosity, he asked, "I've never believed there was a choice. There isn't, is there? I have *No Choice* whether I live or die."

Adonai carefully lifted one foot out of the water. An unusual creature sat on His ankle. The mythical fairy...or perhaps miniature mermaid. somehow dwelt in this tiny creation. Her face was more human than fish, and yet it was covered in purple and aqua scales. The hands were webbed, but the legs were separate, though joined at the ankles, making a very large, very long, sweeping tail. More hairlike than a fish's tail. It trailed behind the lovely creature in long strands of purples, lavenders, and blues. The hair on her head, if indeed it was hair, seemed alive with movement. A deep plum color with streaks of silver and gold. Adonai smiled at the creature and held her up to meet Britton."This is Allura; she is a water sprite." Adonai laughed as the creature tilted its head back and released a soprano note that was flute-like. It bounced off the cave walls and echoed in their ears.

Britton was amazed that such a big sound came from the tiny creature. "The song...these creatures are the music in the waterfall!" Adonai lowered his foot back into the water, allowing the sprite to dive in the last few inches. The volume of the song increased, allowing a stereo effect.

Adonai clapped his hands. "Bravo, Allura!" He looked at Britton with such joy on His face. "These beings love the song they were created to sing. Their song pours life into the water and into all who bathe in it, or drink it."

Britton was mesmerized by the beauty of the tiny beings, and the magic of their song. "They are so mystical, Adonai. I am truly blessed. Thank you for showing them to me."

Adonai's eyes grew serious. "The tale of the water sprite is more magical, more mythical than you could imagine. They are spirit, and yet they cross over into the Shadowlands, where you see them as dolphins. There they sing a beautiful song of unity, expressing My joy by dancing and leaping on the waves. But to sing the most beautiful song, the song of sacrifice, they must choose to first dance in the waters of the Shadowlands."

Britton was amazed by this revelation, that the spiritual so often crossed the veil. Adonai moved his foot up and down, and a great many of the beautiful creatures leapt with each movement. "It's more magical than even the crossing between realms." Britton waited; he knew he needed to understand.

Adonai placed His hand out, and the sprite walked into His palm. "When the water sprite dies in the Shadowlands, it returns here, to this pool; and then the sprite has a song to sing." At that moment, one of the sprites leapt like a dolphin across the water, spinning and splashing. The colors of fire followed its leap, creating the light that lit up the violet water. The sound of the song was completely different from before. It pierced places in Britton's spirit that had never been touched. He felt the peace, the love of Adonai, vibrating through every cell of his being. The song was of Adonai's love, of His gifts, of His sacrifice.

Britton longed for this spirit life, to have never been tainted by flesh. But these sprites could only sing after their life in the Shadowlands. Britton reached up to wipe the tears off his face; he hadn't known that he cried. "I don't know what to choose. I miss my wife. I miss my children. Who will defend the 'Defectives'?" He ran his hand through his wet curls and frowned; his soul was torn.

Adonai touched his shoulder and squeezed. "As long as your spirit pulls you to the Shadowlands, could it be time to let go?" Britton's own heart leapt. He understood. He could choose to let go of that life, that flesh life. There would be heartache, there would be frustration and pain. That was the very nature of the Shadowlands. But if he chose to endure those things, when it was time to let go, he would have a new song.

CHAPTER THIRTY-SEVEN

EVIL PREVAILS

Jeff squinted, watching Dr. Larry work like a well-oiled machine. Going through the motions, assessing the damage and doing what he could do to manage all the bleeding. He hooked up an IV. Saline was running in less than a minute. He pumped pain meds and antibiotics to start. Once he had most of the bleeding under control, he slowed down a little. "This is going to need far more expertise than I have. He needs a surgeon for that arm. A plastic surgeon for his legs, and I have no idea what else. I need to know if there are internal injuries." The thin blade of loss and grief slid around his ribs. He tried to be professional because that's what was needed, but it was too much. Having done all he could as a physician, he dropped to his knees and gently placed his hands on Britton's middle...it was the only spot that wasn't injured. He prayed for his only son through heaving sobs.

Jeff stayed back, unsure if he should stay, in case he was needed, or get out of the way. When Dr. Larry had poured out all his loss in tears, he stood up and tried to gather himself. Jeff stepped to help him stand up. "Can I help you, sir? Is there anything I can get for you? Is there anything you need?" Larry was shaking his head from side to side. Grey moons hung under his eyes; the years of trying to save his son resurfaced again and again. Jeff placed his big hand on Britton's dad's back. He felt him trembling, so he kept his hand there, hoping to steady him.

Dr. Larry looked up at Jeff, trying to get back into doctor mode. "I think he will live. I don't know what kind of butchers can do something like this. I don't know how he endured it; how could anyone endure pain of such magnitude?"

Larry sat on the edge of the bed, his face in his hands. It was obvious that he was close to the breaking point. "My son, my son, has endured and fought evil since...well, since he was a small child." The tears poured from the man's face. Jeff looked around to find Asha sitting in a chair, her arms wrapped around her stomach. Her emerald eyes were on fire. Jeff could feel the heat from across the room. But her bottom lip quivered when she tried to speak. "Larry? Do we need to call an ambulance? I know we risk...losing him. But we risk losing him if we don't."

Larry stood up and began pacing. "I can't let them have him again. Last time, he was supposed to be in the hands of doctors I trusted. You know what happened after that? They let these same kinds of monsters have him. They killed him then, and they damn near killed him again this time. Britton moaned, a long, guttural groan. They all stopped to stare. He had been unconscious; Larry suspected he might even be in a coma. He spun on his heel as if an idea had come to him from out of nowhere.

Britton Jr. stood outside the den; he listened, and he watched. He was horrified at what he saw, but a dream had woken him, and he'd seen his dad sitting with his feet in a pool of purple water. Tiny fairies were in that magical place. They jumped and leapt, and his dad laughed at them. He wanted to let his momma know that his daddy was okay. He didn't know how to rectify the surety of the dream with his daddy's torn up body, but the childlike faith pushed him to walk over to his momma and hold her hands. "Momma?"

Asha stood up, shocked that he was awake and at what he had already seen. "Son, oh Son, let me walk you back to bed." She used her body to block his view of his daddy; horrified to think of what he might've already taken in.

"No, Momma, I came to tell you where Daddy is." The words, the shock. She slowly lowered herself into a squat, holding his hands. A thousand fearful thoughts surfaced, the possibilities of how this would affect him. She was unsure of what she needed to do, but her son needed to tell her this.

"Daddy is sitting beside a pool with water the color of plums. It's full of fiery lights, and you won't believe this, but the light is from the tails of these fairy mermaids." He smiled. Asha hoped he was still sort of in that place of being asleep and awake. He wasn't a child given to fantasy or any kind of make believe. He was serious, an old soul who refused even classic fairy tales. He was forever pointing out the impossibility of the mythical, rolling his eyes. Maybe she could walk him back to his bed, and he would forget the other things he had seen. But he refused her gentle nudge. "No, Momma, you're not believing me. Adonai told me to tell you. He said I needed to pray for Daddy's legs. When we pray, the mermaids are going to sing a song, and it is going to change everything. It's going to make Daddy well."

Asha looked up, meeting Jeff's eyes and then Larry's. Jeff's smile was bigger than the sunrise. "Hey, I've just lived through the biggest miracle of my life. I once was blind, but now I see."

Though tears rolled, and Asha couldn't hold back the sobs, she tried to prepare Britton Jr. for what his daddy looked like. "Son, Daddy is hurt really bad. There is a bone sticking out of his arm; his legs, well, there are pieces of skin and muscle missing. Baby, I just don't know if you should see it." She bit her thumbs hard, trying to decide what the right thing to do was.

Raphael watched this family, this warrior family. He was there to protect them from evil. The dark ones were outside, hordes of them, waiting for the death scream and the final bit of justice they felt they deserved. But he had orders, and he would not let one slimy creature near Britton. He planned to guard until the day Adonai called this Shadow Walker home. He locked eyes with Asha, and she sucked in air, shaking at the sight of the magnificent warrior. He tipped his head forward. It gave her the courage to walk her son to stand by his daddy's unconscious form.

Britton Jr. took in the sight, and his bottom lip stuck out and trembled. His face screwed up, and he tried his best not to cry. He looked up at his momma and then at Jeff. "I will be brave because I am a warrior, like my daddy." He placed his small hand on his daddy's arm, the one that Larry had pulled and reset the joint. He barely touched it, and he began to cry hard and then he prayed. "Adonai, I'm here. I told Momma everything You showed me. I think she believes me; You said she would." He stopped to sniff back the tears, but it was too late. His body began to vibrate with sobs. "I don't know what to do except ask You to make him better like You said You would. Please make my daddy better; heal his whole body."

CHAPTER THIRTY-EIGHT
PURPLE WATERS

B ritton lifted his legs up out of the amethyst waters; he moved slowly. Some of the water sprites leapt over his legs. They sang, not something he understood, but he knew he felt strengthened by their song. The translucence of the purple waters splashed on his aching legs, and he slid off the rock and into the warmth of the glowing waves. It was warm, but more like air than water...or a mix, if that was even possible. It was a spirit world where the souls of dolphins dwelt. Magical, mystical, and soothing.

Adonai joined in the song, adding light, hope, and possibilities. Britton laid his head back and let his broken body float. Adonai's deep voice joined the much higher-pitched voices. They sang in the language of the water sprite; inside the sound was the laughing squeal of the dolphin.

The tiny beings swam and sang, the pool churned in lights of lavender and stirred into deeper shades of plum. When the water sprites sang, the beauty of it lifted his soul; he felt his heart might burst out of his chest. He laughed at the joy that moved him to want to sing, to dance, to cry. Time passed, though he wasn't sure how much. He lifted his head; he knew it was time to go. He floated on his back and stared up at the ceiling of the ocean above him. "Will You go with me, Adonai? I never want to drift again."

He relaxed into the water that held him as if he had no weight at all. Though he no longer saw Adonai, he could hear His voice. Adonai spoke to his spirit. "You are a great warrior. You bear My mark. The Mark of Calling. There is much battle ahead, but I am sending reinforcements to rescue the others. We have come full circle, you and I. This is the place where life changes for the souls called 'Defective' in the Shadowlands. Run quickly to the battle-line; there is no time to second guess Me. Trust, no matter what you see; nothing can stop you. Raphael will go before you. This is the moment for which you were born."

****

Healing

Everyone had their eyes closed, praying. Britton opened his to find himself surrounded by his family. "Hey...family." When everyone's eyes popped open with a collective gasp, Britton tried to sit up. Larry was quick. "Lie back down, Son; you're just, just not strong enough." Britton grinned at his dad's caution. "I know, Dad. But I have been in the purple waters of GanEden. I am whole. Adonai... it's hard to explain, but he sang, and I'm healed."

Britton continued pushing himself to sit. He swung his legs around to place his feet on the floor. Larry bent down, gently lifting the bandages he'd applied with such care. He removed one and then another and then all of them. Larry began laughing through a deluge of tears. Then he stood and hugged Britton, refusing to let him go. Asha stood back, her fists at her mouth, afraid to breathe. She watched the great Light Warrior's wings spread. Spanning larger than the size of the room. It was always hard to breathe in the presence of someone who took orders from the King of the World.

But then she giggled at her thoughts; didn't all Shadow Walkers do the same? Well, perhaps they didn't, but yet that is what they were created to do. She waited. Britton stood up without even a wobble. Even the bruises on his face were gone; he was indeed, whole. She rushed over and reached for him. He took her in his arms, his nose smelling her skin, her hair, all that he missed. He would've cried, but he was too energized, too ready for battle to allow it.

"Hey, you guys are squishing me!" Britton Jr. was between them; he wiggled out, resuming his usual "old man" attitude. He ceremoniously wiped his hands and, with lifted eyebrows, said, "I see that my work is done."

The laughter rang out, and Britton grabbed his son and began tickling him. "Did you actually say something funny? What's happened to you since I've been gone?" They both laughed, and he tickled him till they were on the floor. When neither of them could take anymore they were lying on the floor side by side, staring up at the ceiling, breathing hard. Britton turned his head, wonder in his eyes. "All your life you've always been so honest, it shocks people. Please promise me you will never outgrow it."

CHAPTER THIRTY-NINE

THE PLAN

B ritton looked around his family's kitchen table; it had become a strategy room. Those called by Adonai to fight the impending battle stared up at him, serious faces. He relished the warmth of so much gratefulness; it melted inside his heart. Asha surveyed the few friends that Adonai called to stand with them. She nervously wrung her hands; she always needed to be doing something. "Who wants coffee? I've got cream, sugar...about anything you might want?"

The aroma was strong, and when she poured it, it was as dark as ink. But it smelled amazing. A sweet tinge of hazelnut hung in the air. Jeff mechanically reached for the first mug, his large biceps flexing, his mind already in battle mode. Britton's dad, his strong, courageous dad, tapped his pen over and over. Britton momentarily studied him. He was certain his dad felt all the same emotions from the night he had recklessly broken into a government facility to rescue him. He smiled when they locked eyes. Britton was so grateful for parents that didn't know how to give up.

Asha busied herself with refilling mugs and jokingly calling it liquid fortitude. She leaned down when she got to Britton and kissed his cheek. Sliding into his lap, she hugged him with tears washing her face. "I love you; you know that, right?" She pressed her exhausted face into the bend of his neck and smelled his musky skin, mixed with some type of flower. She pulled back and looked at him. "You smell like you...but with flowers?" She lifted her eyebrows and grinned, laying her head to one side with the question.

Britton's blue eyes filled; he rolled his lips under, holding back the emotion. "I swam in lavender waters...with the spirit of dolphins. I can't wait to share that experience with you."

It was only a few minutes since Jeff called her... that Jazlyn tiptoed through the front door. Her long dark hair the color of chocolate, her big eyes trying to take in the wild truths. She held Maddie in her arms when she came shuffling into the kitchen. The tiny child nuzzled into her, only half awake. Asha rushed over. "Let me take her." Jazlyn pushed a stray strand of hair out of Maddie's still sleeping eyes. "She came walking out of her room just as I walked in the front door." Asha lifted her. "Maddie is such a heavy sleeper; I guess excitement is in the air." She shrugged, squeezing her tighter. Jazlyn stood watching the beautiful child sleep. Longing tugged at her heart.

Britton watched her, her eyes desperately searched for Jeff. He smiled at Jazlyn when their eyes met. He nodded his head to the side, toward Jeff, wondering when Jeff would finally take the plunge. She was such a great girl, this woman truly loved his very best friend. He thought about how all their lives twisted and bent around themselves. You never knew where the connections were likely to be.

Jazlyn's shiny hair was not brushed; she'd definitely been awake through the night...probably wrestling with the darkness. The grey and purple circles under her eyes, the rumbled t-shirt...definite give-aways. Jazlyn waved her fingers at Britton, giving him a nervous smile. She scanned the table and found Jeff; his eyes were focused on her. He jumped up and took both her hands. "Before you sit down, I don't want to waste another minute." He dropped down on one knee and looked up, his eyes full of hope. "I know this might be a crazy minute to choose." He reached into his pocket and pulled out a ring box. Tears were already pouring down Jazlyn's face when she understood that this was the moment. "I've carried this into three countries. I always thought I'd ask you...always wanted to ask you." He choked on the heavy words, thick with emotion. He looked down, not wanting to spill tears. Jazlyn stepped in closer, hugging his head into her stomach. "Yes, Jeff. You know the answer is yes!"

Jeff stood and slid the ring onto her finger. She glanced at the antiqued design and looked back at him. The words felt stuck, but he finally choked them out. "It was my mother's; she wanted you to have it" Jazlyn wrapped herself around him, melted into his warmth; it was the place she was always safest. She looked up into the soft golden light in his eyes, her heart beating up in her throat. "I love you, Jeff Cooper. I think I always have."

Jazlyn's face turned a bright pink. She wasn't used to being so transparent. She always held back, just in case. Even now, as wonderful as it all was, it felt a tad dangerous. The onlookers began to applaud, smiles and tears. Asha came back from putting Maddie down. "What did I miss?" Jazlyn lifted her hand; the look of amazement still shined in her eyes. She wiggled her ring finger, and the light caught the diamond. Asha rushed over and hugged her; life just kept offering surprises. This surprise hadn't been expected...well at least not today. But it sure was a blessing.

******

The Plan

The wonder of it was overwhelming, and yet the nitty-gritty planning needed some focus. Britton was drawing a sort of map of the government lab he had been in. The truth was...he hadn't seen that much of it. The issue, the fifty "Defectives" locked inside. How did they rescue fifty people who didn't really follow directions? How many would be injured? He ran his fingers through his hair, then squeezed his eyes shut. "Adonai, guide me."

This was not possible, not with man, but with Adonai... Britton nervously laughed, looking around at his "team." "A team of scraggly, misfit amateurs breaking in and rescuing fifty, FIFTY young men and women that are difficult to keep calm." Britton squeezed his face between his palms. He looked up at each one of them, pondering what they brought to this mission. "Ultimately...we will need to convince the government that 'Defectives' have rights." He chewed on one side of his bottom lip and searched his spirit for details.

Jeff's eyes were lit. "I've been on a lot of impossible missions; when I rescued you, was the first time I experienced backup from Adonai. I have to confess, it's the best backup I've ever had." He sat up straighter, his faith so new, so on fire. "We got this; we will just follow Adonai's lead."

Britton shook away the dark thoughts that twisted his gut into ropes. He would take this one step at a time. He looked up to find everyone was staring at him. He tried to smile; he needed to remember his confidence was not in his own abilities. Adonai had promised victory. "Our goal is to rescue them, contact their families and then deal with the government once they are all safe."

Larry was feeling the intense déjà vu from the day that he had rescued Britton more than fifteen years ago. This was such an eerily similar situation. Just like before, the government had found a use for a population that few believed had any rights. If they believed that the "Defectives" might hold the cure to a deadly virus, would there be any stopping them from trampling the few rights they had left? Larry shook away the thoughts; he knew from experience...they would need to move cautiously, carefully. Adonai would need to orchestrate this plan.

Larry cleared his throat and then stood up to list all the reasons the government was going to fight them. The second he stood, his eyes were opened, and he saw a magnificent warrior. He knew him; he remembered him from the night that Britton's life had been taken. He slowly slid back into his chair. "Um, I think everyone should turn and see this."

Asha had not stopped staring; she struggled to breathe or even move. She knew he had been with them. They were under the protection of this great warrior. She noticed for the first time, however, the golden glow radiating from the key shape that appeared to be burned into his marbled arm. She should not have been shocked that he wore the mark of the Great King. That he, too, was chosen. They battled the same enemy.

Larry couldn't look away, but the others followed his eyes, and the shock and awe might've been comical if not for the fantastical being that stood among them. The gentle, buttery glow from the marbled figure was enough, and yet the wings...the wings looked to be ruffling in an unseen wind. The warrior had no true expression, but his energy was steady, strong. Light danced on the top of his head and along his brow, spilling along his high cheekbones. His pinions flexed like a large muscle; his hand rested on the scabbard at his hip. He was majestic. Jazlyn let her thoughts ease out when she whispered, "Not of this world." Britton blinked; the warrior was there, but then he wasn't. His presence dwelt between two worlds. Britton nodded, acknowledging the great protector. He used his hand in a salute. After all, they had known each other for such a long time. Adonai said there would be backup; knowing Raphael was that backup was a game changer. Britton's fears blew away on the unseen wind.

CHAPTER FORTY

LAB

In the Lab several of the "Defective" were sedated, laid out on stretchers. The researchers were conferring over slides of blood cells they had lined up from each "Defective." What they saw happening was not something they could grasp. The woman and the troll that sat on her shoulders hissed. "Dr. Schmidt, I have seen viruses attack cells, seen them insert their DNA. Viruses have always been my focus; they are aggressive. I admire them." The woman pulled the mask from her face; her snake eyes rolling forward and then back. She wiped the sweat off her forehead and sat down in the one chair that was up against the wall. She threw the mask down and looked up at all the researchers in the room. "Has anyone ever seen something like this before?"

The tension that hung in the air sizzled; the woman clasped her hands together and then unclasped them.. The creature that hung on her back hissed, and she winced as it dug its nails deeper around her shoulders. Her voice was almost a screech when she demanded, "Well? Someone speak up! We need to know what this means!" No one moved; no one dared. There was a deep moan, and they all looked at one of the young men strapped down on a stretcher. His body was seizing and no one even lifted an eyebrow. "Would someone add more sedation to 'Defective' number seven's medications? There is no need for us to be bothered with all that noise when we are trying to think."

"Defective" number seven, or rather Jeremy Blackwell, slid down a snow-covered mountain and was lying on his back laughing. Adonai slid down right next to him and joined in. He laughed till His sides hurt. They were both lying flat on their backs, exhausted from the fun. Jeremy turned his head, staring. "I'm pretty sure there is snow in my underwear; how about You?" Adonai stood and shook His whole body, attempting to empty His pants of snow. Jeremy crawled up next to him and stood, copying the movements. Jeremy pulled his hat off and shook his long blonde hair out, snow flying in all directions. Adonai dodged it, and that caused Him to laugh even harder.

"Hey, let's go back up and do that again. I'm pretty sure I could do that a hundred times before I got tired of it." Adonai was nodding.

"I have done it a hundred times, and nothing gives Me more pleasure than watching how much fun it is...for you." Jeremy stopped shaking the snow out of his hat to stare at Adonai. In the Shadowlands, he didn't really have anyone who cared for him anymore. His parents tried; they really did. But they were already old when he was born.

When the severity of his disability became apparent, his mom pushed and fought for him. His dad sat on the sidelines, almost like a disinterested observer. His mom had a stroke, and that was when his dad showed Jeremy how he really felt all these years. He didn't care that Jeremy had begun to type. He treated him as if he was a bad child, an ignorant child. He talked at him sometimes; but mostly it was more like his dad talked to himself. He confessed his guilt. "Your mom can't do these things for you anymore. You'll be better off where someone has training in the kind of care you need." He would nod to himself, but never look Jeremy in the eyes. "How am I supposed to manage you and your mother? We are old! I hope somehow in that broken mind of yours, you understand."

His mom had always done her best, better than her best. But when his dad had control, that was really the end of his contact with both of them. Their visits to see him had gotten fewer and fewer. His heart hurt from the loneliness. The guilt he carried because his dad said he was such a burden weighed him down. But he must still pay Jeremy's bills because he wasn't on the streets yet.

This past year, they hadn't even come on Christmas. He knew that his dad would've lied to himself to justify ignoring him. He would probably say that Jeremy didn't know what Christmas was. But, of course, he knew; all "Defectives" knew. Their broken bodies just betrayed them with unmanageable behaviors. No one could see past it, at least not enough to give them a real chance. He wondered everyday if his mom was getting better. But since his dad didn't come anymore, no one was going to tell him.

Adonai walked over and placed His hand on Jeremy's shoulder. "There's good news, back in the Shadowlands; your best day is fast approaching." Jeremy's big brown eyes grew larger; he raised his eyebrows and smiled.

"Do I get to know what's in store, or is this another one of Your trust-as-I-go kind of adventures?" Adonai laughed at the jab Jeremy made at the difficulty of walking by faith. He slapped him on the back, and snow flew into both their eyes.

Squeezing Jeremy's shoulder, His face turned serious. "I am so proud of you. You have never let go, never given up, loved in so much darkness." Adonai peered directly into Jeremy's eyes. "You have always trusted Me. Jeremy, I want you to know that I have heard your prayers for your mom. She is getting better, and you will see her soon."

Jeremy dropped to his knees in front of Adonai, placing both his hands on His feet. "Thank you for never leaving me alone. For letting me have the best mom in the world! For hearing my prayers for her. For always speaking to my heart when life becomes unbearable." He lifted up his wet face, looking into Adonai's eyes. Then he laughed, a moaning kind of laugh as tears ran. "Because my life has been almost unbearable every single day so far in the Shadowlands. But You, You make me brave!"

Adonai helped him to a stand and held onto his arms. "Where you are now is dark, so very dark. But when you wake up, you will find that your body is healing. The commands you think, your body will follow. The words you attempt will come out clearly. You will speak words of light into the darkness. The Truth will pierce the evil that has begun to smother that world. Some will hear Me when you speak, embracing Truth, and find their own way out of the darkness. But others will condemn you because they hate Me. Hold fast...I am with you always." When Jeremy stood, the mark of the Great King glowed on his forearm. Adonai hugged him. "I called you before you were born. Be strong, mighty warrior."

****

Jeremy

Jeremy's flesh, his cocoon, was heavily sedated. Larry watched the monitors; it was impossible to rouse the young man from sleep.

"We'll need to take him unconscious, Britton. Do we have a contingency plan for this?' Britton nodded as he spoke into his headset.

"Hey Jeff, I know it's a lot to ask, but we're gonna need an ambulance for at least two people, maybe three. Do we have enough drivers for five vans and an ambulance?" Sweat was pouring off Jeff's forehead. He wiped it with his forearm. He stood in the office of the Lab, having gotten all three of them past security cameras and four armed guards. Chances were that Britton's escape was the very reason extra guards were there. "There's good news, soldier; I've just found the mother load! Keys to every van out there!" Now radio our drivers; this is a go!"

The hair stood up on Britton's arms. Just being back in this lab was overwhelming. A young man was lying on the table...sweat held his dark hair to his head, bruises everywhere. Eyes swollen closed, bits of muscle missing on his shins. Britton shuddered. His anger hot as liquid magma pushed up from the center of his being. It geysered, spilling out his eyes in anger. Without warning, he realized he knew this young man. "This is Jeremy! This is our Jeremy!"

The swollen face, the bruises, everything had made him difficult to recognize. He was the young man from his presentation video. The young man whose mother had fought so hard for him! It was maybe three years ago when the video of his miraculous typing was made. Britton knew his mom was sick, but had been told that Jeremy was doing well. Something had obviously gone wrong, so very wrong.

All his attempts to contact Jeremy's family had been ignored. He leaned over the young man and wiped the sweat off his forehead. "What happened Jeremy? Where is your mom?" His mind searched through the last message he'd left. "Hello, Mrs. Blackwell. This is

Britton Donovan. I'm calling again to check on Jeremy, and you, of course. I just wonder if you need any help, or if there's something going on we could assist with? I guess I'll quit calling. I don't mean to be a pest." Britton shook his head, swallowed the regret of not just driving to the house to see what more he could've done. He turned to find his dad right by his side. "Dad, I know this young man; this is Jeremy. He used to come to the Center; he did so well there." His voice broke. This was unthinkable!

A type of holy fury pushed Britton. "How can one human do this to another? I just don't understand." Britton took his dad by the arm, pleading, "Can we move him, Dad? Can you tell me if it's safe?" Larry watched the monitors and began doing a more thorough physical assessment. When he flipped the young man's arm over, the mark flashed a warm light. The relief Britton felt ran through his whole body. Shaking his head, he smiled. He closed his eyes. "Adonai, thank you; thank you so much." Pressing the talk button on his headset, he was reminded who was in charge of this impossible mission. "It's a go. Adonai has been here before us."

Chapter Forty-One

BATTLE

Most of the "Defectives" were strapped on stretchers between two rooms that were side by side. Some were sedated; others were just so freaked out they wailed nonstop. Standing in the room with Jeff and his dad, it seemed an impossible task. His dad touched his shoulder; the look on his face said exactly what Britton was thinking. "How in the world did we think we could do this?"

It was as if warm water, full of light, began to cover him from the top of his head down to his feet. He didn't see anything, but he knew Adonai's presence; he recognized His voice. "I took over two million people across the Red Sea. Is this too hard for Me?" Britton was on his knees; he didn't remember getting there, but Adonai's presence did that to flesh. "I'll do anything You ask of me; please tell me how to accomplish this."

When he opened his eyes, an army...a spiritual army of Light Warriors was in control of the situation. They escorted each one of the "Defectives." Taking them by the hand, leading them out to the waiting vehicles. Britton shivered. Never would any Shadow Walker see into the spiritual realm and not be awed by it. Britton knew he was spirit first, all humans were. But once wrapped in a cocoon of flesh, the spirit world vanished from view. He whispered, "Of course, of course! This plan was so obvious now. "Defectives" could see in the spiritual...he suspected that most crossed the veil." His whole body shook, the evil was trying to smother him. But Adonai was in control. He steadied himself.

Britton was still on his knees when he saw his dad out of the corner of his eyes. Right beside him, on his knees, face wet, mouth wide open. He reached to give his dad a squeeze of assurance, but then he began to laugh. Britton tried to keep it quiet. He tried to remember the seriousness of the situation. But the laughter was pure joy bubbling up through him. There was no way he could contain it. Finally, he got control; crawled to a stand as the last "Defectives" were escorted to the waiting vans.

Britton stepped out into the hall, Raphael and three other Light Warriors were walking with Jeremy and the last three "Defectives." Four had been severely injured. Their eyes were open, but they didn't seem truly awake. He knew it was Adonai's protection. He hoped they would visit the purple waters before they woke.

Britton rushed ahead of them to see if Jeff had found keys to any of the ambulances that were out back. Jeff and Asha stood at the backdoor of an ambulance that was already running. Jeff's eyes were wide. Britton chuckled, thinking how he himself must look. It was not every day that you saw an army of Light Warriors. Jeff's eyes blazed, then he mumbled, "How, how is this happening?"

Britton still shook from Adonai's presence; he smiled a sort of crooked smile, then shrugged. "Adonai."

Asha looked in wonder at the Light Warriors and then back to Britton. "Everyone is loaded except these four..." She didn't get to finish her sentence; a dark shadow swooped down out of the black sky and knocked her to the ground. All the security lights went out, leaving only the headlights of the rescue vehicles peering into the inky darkness. The creature was so fast that no one really had time to react. Britton was looking up, searching the skies while running to scoop Asha off the ground.

From the opposite direction, there was a screech of intense pain that it turned their eyes on the creature that had attacked only moments before. His odor preceded him. As if they had opened a crypt or unearthed a dead animal, the rescuers gagged. The creature swooped again; the long claws running across Britton's back and then his head as he curled himself around Asha's still form. The creature landed in front of Britton. His fiery eyes peered through him, angry; a fury that Britton didn't truly understand. The creature's skin looked thick, scale-like, tough. When he landed, his muscled wings spread larger than a car, vibrating with strength. He held a sword...the right word is scimitar. It was curved and long. The hilt was longer than most, it curved to fit into his black palm. "It's been a long time, Britton." He spit the words. His long tongue slithered in and out of his thin lips.

Britton was still on his knees, shielding Asha. Gently, he whispered into her ear. "Asha, Asha honey, please talk to me." She opened one eye; her face was cut in jagged rows, each seeping blood. "I'm okay, Britton. I just hit my head." She struggled to get up, and he gently lifted her. When he did, their birthmarks began flashing in rhythm with their heartbeats. Jeff stepped up beside them, then Larry, then Jeremy. A bedraggled group of soldiers they stood facing an impossible enemy.

The creature threw his head back and laughed, at least it mimicked a laugh. It was a shrill howl, but then he ended it with a chuckle. "Do you no longer recognize Drystan, lover of Adonai?" He flexed his massive wings and swung his sword in a figure eight. It swooshed through the air, creating a ringing screech. The sound sent shivers through the tiny group, but they stood their ground, unmoved by the bravado.

"I would know you anywhere, Drystan. You can change your form, grow giant wings, and lift a sword. But the spirit of you, the ugly, nasty greed in you, will always be recognizable." The group felt solid behind him. Britton knew they were no match for this dark creature. He also knew that Light Warriors were close by. More than all that, he had Adonai's promise.

Almost as if Drystan had followed Britton's thoughts, hundreds of the dark ones appeared like a storm cloud covering the moon. With bat shrieks, they landed behind Drystan, all howling and slobbering. They itched for this battle. A battle where they were seen by the humans they do often humiliated, a battle of muscle, and blood.

It was Britton's turn to saber rattle. "Adonai, I know You are with me. I know this battle is Yours. I ask You to send Your strength, Your word, and Your hope. Rescue those You love." He felt the hilt of his sword before he finished the prayer. He braced himself. He knew the sword in hand meant he would need to fight this creature in the physical. He squeezed the hilt, flexing his arm muscles and gritting his teeth. He stepped forward. There was no mistake in his intention. He would challenge the creature. It caused all the shrieking and howling to drop into silence. Only the sound of the wind touched his ears.

Drystan slurped and rolled his curved sword around in his palm. Britton thought Drystan looked nervous; but why would he? Britton took another step forward, pulled his sword in front, and began making the figure eight Adonai had taught him so long ago. The first few swings he felt stiff, but by the third time, his shoulders relaxed. "What are you doing here, dark creature? What is it that you want?"

Drystan stood still; his sword hung loosely by his side like a gunslinger. The long tongue slithered in and out; he studied Britton. The thick cords flexed in his neck, and his eyes narrowed. "How dare you call me creature. I am a lord of the dark world. A formidable enemy of all who wear the mark of the King." Black spit came out with his words; he seethed in fury. "I want what is mine. What you took from me so long ago, Brit ttton! I want REVENGE!"

His sword began to spin faster and faster, and Britton didn't know what to do...he stood his ground. He heard Asha whimper behind him, but he couldn't turn to see why. Sweat rolled down his temples; he could hear his own heart beating in his ears. It was a whisper, but he understood it loud and clear. "The weapon that can hurt you has not been forged in this world. Trust Me! I will fight for you."

Britton wondered if time stood still. Then he saw the horde of darkness move. Drystan ran at him, curved sword raised, red eyes in fury. His wings, stretched into black pinions, were magnificent. If ravens were twelve feet tall...these would be the wings of the giant birds. Drystan's feet barely touched the ground as he flew at Britton in vengeance. His army of bat-like warriors screeching behind him. It all moved in slow motion in Britton's mind. He felt the sweat rolling down his face. His muscles tensed; he moved the sword around in his sweaty palm.

And then...Drystan was upon him.

Britton used both his hands to meet the dark blade. The sound of swords clashing was deafening. He could hear Adonai whispering, guiding him with each swing of the sword. The sound of Truth beating hard against the deception. Time passed, and they battled. Britton felt each slice of the cruel curved blade, but he also landed a great many blows himself.

Drystan began beating against Britton's resolve with words. It was the enemy's most effective battle strategy. "I know you fear me; you fear all the dark ones. You've always been a coward. I could've taken you out many times." He struck Britton again, slicing a small piece off his shoulder, then he cackled. "I just toy with you, friend of Adonai. I love watching Him fail you again and again." Britton could feel the sting of the words; they hurt him far more than his aching muscles. His arms became weaker, his strength draining out. He let his arms drop a few inches. And when he did, the scimitar swooshed above his head he barely ducked in time. The movement was so quick he was off balance and landed hard in the dirt. He rolled back up faster than he would've believed he could. Didn't seem to matter, Drystan was on top of him before he could blink. "You are nothing more than a worm to that king of yours. He left you to die! What kind of fool is left to die and yet still looooovvvves the one who failed him?"

The question took Britton by surprise. Yes, what kind of man dies for you and still loves you when you betray Him? He would've laughed, but Drystan had knocked him down to one knee. "Ya know, Drystan...you talk too much! Let me tell you what kind of man dies and still loves those who betray Him."

The fire increased in Drystan's eyes, but he refused to yield any power to this lesser creation. He swung his curved weapon, slicing a deep cut across Britton's chest. "I plan to kill you again, worm! But this time, I'll make sure you stay dead." Britton refused the darkness that attempted to cover him. The heat of anger would consume him if he let it. His mind perused the life before, the sorrow, and the cruelty. He still heard Drystan's taunts. His body fought...but he wasn't there.

He stood at the top of a mountain looking down on lush green fields. The slope of the mountain was an ocean of flowery waves in every imaginable color. The trees to breathe in and out, they were alive, and talking to each other. Britton smelled the salt of the ocean, the damp earth, and a mix of florals that lifted his spirit. His body began to ease. Adonai stood beside him; He didn't turn to look at Him, but Britton felt His presence; he knew. His eyes swept through the lands that were washed in a buttery yellow from the sun just barely lifting itself over the horizon. "What astounding beauty, Adonai. Do I know this place? It seems familiar."

Adonai lifted His long finger and pointed. "See the gate at the entrance? You've watched so many folks come through in victory!"

He turned to look Adonai in the eyes; he didn't know exactly what He was telling him. "Am I going home now? Is it time?"

Adonai wrapped his arm around Britton's shoulder. "No, there is much left for you to do yet."

Britton stared at the gate. A young man stumbled through. Cheers went up from a large crowd that gathered. Some jumped up and down...others broke out in praise to EL. He looked at Adonai, wondering why He had brought him here. "Because I wanted to remind you where this all began. You need to remember what you're fighting for. A great many souls hang in the balance. Your fight, your battle, will change the destination for thousands of souls." The truth of that rang through him; he shivered.

"I'm so humbled by Your trust in me. I don't deserve it. I've failed You..." Adonai squeezed his shoulder. "You have served Me. You are Mine. You have loved Me. You have given your life for Me."

Britton swung the sword with both hands; the strength of his whole body went into the motion. He began to fight with his mind. He could hear Adonai with each swing of his sword. "You are a great warrior; you are one of the mighty. Holiness, justice, faithfulness, and humility. These are your attributes. But above all...courage. Swing the sword of truth, exert justice for many." Drystan pulled back; he took a blow to the side of his head. The horde behind him shrieked, moving up and down like bats disturbed with light. Britton moved faster, taking advantage of the distraction. Adonai's voice empowered him, filled him with strength that was not his own.

"Lay your hands upon eternal life...this is your calling. Be of good courage, mighty warrior. The battle is Mine." His sword sliced through the thick dark skin in an angle from shoulder to hip. Drystan looked down as a dark black thickness oozed from the large wound.

The dark ones behind him took flight, leaving like a flock of disturbed ravens; black wings covered the sky. Drystan dropped to one knee, his scimitar falling with a loud clang.

Britton stood panting, sword still lifted; he refused to take his eyes off this old enemy.

With a brush of wings, Britton the darkness lifted. Raphael and two other warriors took Drystan under his arms and lifted him upwards. Their strong wings took him into the dark sky. Britton dropped to both his knees, using his hands to hold him up while still trying to get enough air in his lungs. Jeff slid forward, lifting Britton to his feet. "Let's take you home." After Jeff helped Britton into his truck, he noticed the ambulance was still sitting there.

"Is everyone safe? Where's Asha? What has happened?" Jeff hardly knew how to describe all that had gone on while Britton battled.

"Asha is safe. She has gone with the vehicles to the church. A big group of volunteers stepped forward to help with everything while each family is contacted." Jeff started the truck, but turned to stare at Britton.

"I've trained to be a warrior most of my life. I've fought a lot of evil, some pretty formidable enemies." Jeff shook his head. He didn't know how to see Britton, his friend, with these new eyes. "I,I don't know that I could've fought that battle, that enemy who stood before you tonight. I..." His eyes filled; he kept shaking his head. "It was the bravest damn thing I've ever seen."

Britton laughed a tired chuckle. "I didn't expect to have to fight. I really thought Adonai might show up in person."

Jeff was bombarded with so many emotions he couldn't find words. "When you took that first step forward, I knew you were a dead man."

Britton was nodding. "I knew I was a dead man, too." They both laughed. Britton laid his head back on the seat. "There's so much I want to tell you. So much that Adonai has planned. Jeff, this is the most exciting moment to be alive!"

Jeff's eyebrows squeezed tight. He didn't really know what Britton was referring to. "Okay, man, if you say so. He pulled out of the parking lot. "You got some serious sword skills! You've been holding out on me!"

Britton lifted one side of his mouth in a tired smile. "Adonai taught me a long time ago. I let myself get rusty." He didn't say it out loud, but he planned never to get rusty again.

Jeff gave him a wide-eyed side glance. "You just slaughtered some evil lord from the pit. You've got the mad sword skills of some samurai warrior. I gotta see what it looks like when your skills are sharp." Britton gave a slow nod. Britton continued staring out the window, feeling a strange, sad thing move through his soul. Jeff had always been the warrior; he'd never seen Britton in battle. Britton laid his head back again, squeezing his eyes.

There was so much battle ahead. But one thing he knew...Adonai would be with him. Adonai never left him; He never would. Staring out the window, the moon was low in the sky. It had been such a long, long night. The moonlight made patterns across the sky, filtering through the puffs of clouds. They looked solid enough to walk on. He thought he could use it as a ladder, step his way right back to GanEden someday. He looked at Jeff and said the thing that his heart kept telling him. "The 'Defectives' are about to change the whole world; you and I are gonna get to see it!"

Chapter Forty-Two

"DEFECTIVES"

"You're up, Jeremy. This is your moment!" Britton placed his hand on the young man's back. He kept shifting his weight back and forth. Jeremy had never spoken in front of an audience. Truly, Jeremy had only been able to speak for forty-eight hours. Britton nervously rubbed his hands together. "Jeremy, I really know how you feel. I stood in front of an audience, and I'd only been able to speak for a few days. It's not that different from when all your thoughts make circles in your head. It's a miracle that you get to share with them."

Britton squeezed Jeremy's arm; this young man...he was something special, all of them were. Since the night of the rescue, Jeremy was miraculously able to speak. At first it was short broken sentences. But even in tiny bursts, his brilliance was immediately apparent. He spoke with more and more ease as his confidence grew. "I can feel my story moving around in the back of my brain. Do I just tell my story?"

Britton spontaneously hugged the young man. "Yes, Jeremy. Just say what Adonai told you to say." He smiled so big his cheeks started hurting.

Jeremy nodded, turned to step out on the stage, but then turned back. "My, my dad is out there. He, he has never believed I was anything." Jeremy nervously clasped his hands and squeezed his fingers over and over.

Britton placed both his hands on Jeremy's shoulders. "Jeremy, Adonai has asked you to do this for Him. So that means He knows that you can do it. It is okay to say whatever is in your heart today. Your dad is about to receive a lot of truth all at once. Adonai will make good use of it; He always does."

Jeremy nodded. He still moved on stiff legs with his head down. Though autism had released its hold on his tongue, a lifetime of coping clung to him. He struggled with all the exposure of sharing his thoughts. It was something most people learned in tidbits over their lifetime. As far as Jeremy knew, Britton had been the only other person to experience what he was going through. It was like being thrown into a different culture, maybe onto a different planet, and trying to learn the customs. Life just wasn't an orderly thing. Rules of conduct weren't always clearly defined. What was acceptable between cultures, and certainly to a "Defective, " was difficult to explain. Jeremy felt like an alien from another world."

Britton paused, wondering if he should walk out with Jeremy, or just stand beside him.

From experience, Britton knew that it would be years before any of these "Defectives" understood how much of themselves to expose. He paused and under his breath he whispered the name "Defectives," then shook his head. He realized a new name needed to be found. It was such a derogatory name. The honest truth was that it applied to every single person in the world. But these young people were healed, and as whole as anyone else. He would ask them. Maybe they could have a real conversation about what they would like to be called. The thought caused him to tear up. A conversation...wow, who would've believed in such a miracle?

His clients would always be safe to share their hearts with him, with Asha, or anyone at the Center. He wished that he could have learned life's lessons easier. The knowledge burned a hole right in the middle of his heart. Maybe he could be a buffer between them and the world, at least in the beginning.

He reached out and tapped Jeremy on the shoulder. "Would you like me to go with you? I can be right beside you if you need any help." Jeremy's eyes were as large as an owl's. He leaned to look out at the audience. Those big eyes, so young and so old, held Britton's.

He nodded. "Please." Britton loved this young man; he loved all the "Defectives..." his clients, his friends. His heart was no longer his own. He took Jeremy by the arm and walked him out onto the stage. Familiar butterflies danced in Britton's gut. Jeremy's eyes were glassy, but he smiled at Britton. He gazed out at the large crowd, then turned his head. "Thank you for always believing in me, Britton. You gave me hope when I had none." Britton squeezed his shoulder, then nodded. "Let's do this, son. Just imagine Raphel out there listening...cause you know he is."

Jeremy stepped in front of nearly a thousand people, plus all those watching the live stream. Britton trembled when he looked out over the vast audience and wondered how they would be received. He reminded himself that how the people responded wasn't his job. The "Defectives" were to speak Adonai's message. The rest of it was up to the folks listening. The whole world was about to hear that message, and what a privilege it was to be here to watch it happen.

Britton stepped to the side and motioned for Jeremy to begin. Jeremy, still wide eyed, gripped the sides of the podium and swallowed three times before he could force any words out. "Your pastor asked me, well mostly it was Adonai that asked me." Jeremy looked down at his feet. Then he shifted back and forth in a sort of rhythm. It was something he'd done all this life to cope. When he realized what he was doing, he looked back at Britton in panic. He turned, his face flushed a bright pink. Britton saw the panic as he turned his back on the audience. "I'm acting autistic, aren't I? I can't do this or no one will listen to me."

Britton stepped forward, whispering in his ear. "They will listen. Adonai will soften their hearts and open their ears. You are Adonai's messenger. Just do your part; whether they listen or not, that's not in our hands."

Jeremy slowly turned back around and tried again. "I am here today to speak to you some good news." He looked down again, his feet shuffled, he shook his head and tried to stop them. "Adonai spoke to your pastor in a dream; he knew I needed to tell you this." The pastor waved to the congregation while nodding his head, then motioned for Jeremy to continue.

Britton patted his back, encouraging him. "Go ahead, Jeremy. Tell them what Adonai said."

Jeremy seemed to garner some courage and began to speak his heart. "Until only a few days ago, I was 'defective.' At least that's what the world says I was. A miracle happened, and there are now fifty "Defectives" that Adonai healed. He healed all of us, all at once." His feet shuffled and his face blazed red. "I am shuffling my feet because I am nervous. I hope you will still listen to me. Even people who shuffle their feet can be smart." A few people in the congregation chuckled. Jeremy dropped his head from side to side. He didn't understand much of what other people thought was funny. He felt Britton's hand on his shoulder, so he continued, "Adonai has given us a message of hope. This first message is about the virus that has come upon the world. Adonai has told us how to fight it, how to recover from it." Jeremy stopped speaking because so many in the congregation gasped.

He turned and looked at Britton for assurance. Britton said, "Keep going; you got this." He shuffled his feet for a solid minute, then looked up at the congregation; and to the church's credit, they were still listening. "The best news is that Adonai wants us to know how to destroy the virus. This virus is an attack. It was brought into the world by the dark spirits of the Netherworld."

The people in the congregation began speaking to each other and fidgeting around. The pastor stood and walked to the podium. Placing his arm around Jeremy, he assured him. "I am as sure of this message as anything I have ever heard in my life. This young man has been sent to share this message with the world. What a privilege that we...our church...we get to be the first to hear it." The murmuring died down, and the pastor motioned Jeremy on. "I think you can continue now."

Jeremy looked up; he still didn't understand a lot about how others received information. "Are the people angry? Why are they not happy at this good news?" The pastor patted his back and motioned for him to continue.

Britton stepped up closer behind Jeremy. "Remember, you are the messenger; deliver Adonai's message. Please don't worry about how the people feel about it. Adonai will take care of that part; I promise."

When he stepped back, Britton saw Asha in the front row, Maddie on her lap and Britton Jr. beside her. She beamed at Britton. Wow, he loved her. He felt a twinge of guilt over all she lived through just being his wife. She mouthed, "He's doing great!" She squeezed Britton Jr.'s hand, whispering, "Your daddy is so brave!" Memories surfaced, flooding her mind of all the interviews when Britton was first healed. Every time she pushed one memory away, a brand new group fell right into its place.

Britton cleared his throat. "My name is Britton Donovan. I'm here to support the former 'Defectives.'" He emphasized the word "former," and he loved doing it. "I want to encourage you to listen not only with your heart, but with your spirit. These young adults will speak only the truths that Adonai has given them. They were 'defective' only days ago. They know nothing of deception or lying. This is all Adonai's doing. He has healed them and brought them before you with clean hearts. You have no cause to doubt their motives. Please give them your attention, and maybe you could wait until they are finished before making a decision."

Britton Jr. stood up, clapping. "Yay, Daddy!"

Britton smiled and added, "That is quite obviously my son." Now his own face was pink. He decided to add, "I was also 'Defective.' though Adonai healed me a very long time ago.

I am...we all are living proof of His great love for us."

He stepped back, wanting to give Jeremy plenty of time to say all that needed saying. When he scanned the congregation, hoping for some kind of positive response, his eyes landed on Jeff; he blinked. Jeff, in church? It really was the time of miracles! Jazlyn was sitting up next to him. And when their eyes met, she lifted her left hand and wiggled her fingers. The diamond ring that sparkled on her finger was now accompanied by a wedding band. Smiles touched both ears across their faces. Britton gave Jeff the thumbs up. He was glad they decided not to wait. His heart was so full of joy, he couldn't imagine being happier.

Out of the corner of his eye, he saw red hair. His eyes stopped, and his mouth hung open. It was him. He was pretty sure he knew it was him. Light Warriors stood on the man's right and his left. Apparently, he was still a wanted man, but he was under the protection of The Great King. The man smiled slightly and then nodded. Britton's heart beat faster; everything was happening so fast. He struggled with happy tears. "Adonai, now You're just showing off." He couldn't imagine what this would mean for Asha. But he knew after all they'd been through, anything was possible.

Jeremy continued speaking, telling the congregation in the undiluted words of those with autism... "This is a spiritual darkness that has come on the world. It is like a predator, seeking who it can devour. The only way to be rid of it is the way we rid ourselves of all darkness; it is through repentance and Adonai's blood."

It was so quiet in the huge auditorium that Britton felt a type of vacuum. The atmosphere was electric with Light Warriors; it sparked and crackled with their power. Britton knew they were there because of the horde of dark ones hovering outside the church. They would be waiting to pounce, stealing the truth from any heart that held enough doubt. It felt like such a gamble, but truly it was war.

But Adonai was on their side. As difficult as the "Defectives'" story was to believe, the truth was in their recovery. His own miracle healing, and now this...fifty healed at once. It was Adonai's proof,

His stamp of approval on their message. "These signs follow those who believe."

He kept assuring each of them that no one could know who would choose to believe. But wasn't that the truth of all Adonai's messages? God's messengers put it out there; and each and every person had a decision to make. Britton felt his mind spinning. What a whirlwind these weeks had been. He realized he hadn't been listening. Jeremy finished and then turned to walk off the stage. Britton followed him, hoping. The people applauded. It was now in their hands.

The pastor stood at the pulpit and looked out over the congregation. He knew all of it was a lot to take in, but he refused to second guess what he knew in his spirit was true. He'd gone to bed early, only to find himself dreaming of the rescue of fifty "Defectives" from the Government Research Lab. He saw a fallen angel, of sorts, attacking them; a battle ensued that would make fighting with lightsabers seem like child's play.

That's when he heard Adonai speak and tell him to bring them all into his church for protection. His obedience would allow his flock to hear their message first. He even knew the man's name he was supposed to call. So he googled Jeff Cooper and found a Navy SEAL who was the first man in the United States to be diagnosed with this Claw virus. He had to be the one. So he called three Jeff Coopers in the wee hours of a Sunday morning. It took a few phone calls and two grumpy Jeff Coopers, but he got through to the right one.

He'd stumbled through the beginning of the conversation. "My name is Reverend Bruce Cameron. I am a pastor at Lake Pleasant Church in Houston, Texas." He knew that neither he nor Jeff Cooper would remember all he said. But this was an astounding miracle. He was more than grateful that Adonai trusted him to be part of it.

When the vans began pulling up to his church, he wasn't even sure what he was supposed to do or how to help. He remembered taking a deep breath and praying. "Adonai, I'm here; so please guide me. I promise to let You take the lead." But before panic started settling in, fifteen members of his congregation showed up. Each and everyone of them awakened and instructed to go to the church. The intricate pieces of this complicated puzzle were something only God could put together. Each member of his congregation showed up with the same urging that "some fugitives needed safe harbor." They just obeyed, even though they didn't know who or what. He sure was proud of them.

Pastor Cameron would someday tell the whole story, but for now, it would go down easier in small pieces. Today, this morning, he would let them hear from these miracles themselves. He refused to worry; Adonai had a plan. He always did.

****

The Beginning

Britton sat watching Adonai's plan unfold before his eyes. The rescue was only two weeks ago. The whirlwind of these past few days would be something he would remember all his life. When he got to the church the night of the rescue, there were fifty "Defectives" with the same story to tell. Each of them was baptized in the purple waters of GanEden. Adonai met them and healed them there. They all knew the source of the virus, and they all knew how to destroy it. Every single one of them, commissioned to tell the world.

Britton stood behind Jeremy. It was hard to keep his emotions in check. Over and over, the world chose to condemn those they deemed to be less than perfect. Even calling them "Defective" and forever lamenting the financial burden they created on society. Now it would be that same population that would bring healing, and most likely the message of salvation, to anyone willing to listen. These former "Defectives" would more than earn their place. They would be seen with new eyes. The "Defectives" would rise to serve those who despised them. Exactly as Adonai had done.

Can't wait to cross the veil again? Click here https://mybook.t o/cQDato experience the final adventure! THE LAST CHOICE, Book 3, is the LAST adventure in The Chronicles of the Shadowlands.

If you enjoyed reading No Choice, I would love it if you let your friends know. "Crossing the veil can be a life-changing experience." AND...I've made my books sharable on all platforms... share them with your friends! Books are driven by readers...by word of mouth, by REVIEWS! Click this link http://www.amazon.com/review/create-review?&asin=B0833JQ2PZand leave your review.

I'd enjoy reading your review, email me the link, at **teresaholm anwrites@gmail.com. I can't wait to read it!**

I love, love, love to connect. Through email, or social media. If you enjoy what I write and you could use an inbox with some encouragement...once a month, (sometimes less.) I share my journal entries. These are words I write to encourage myself. IF...you get worn out from all the political emails, and DYI's videos...Click this link, https://scavengers-of-hope.ck.page/0ba506d8e0and you'll be added to my email list. You can unsubscribe anytime. I don't sell my reader's emails; they are mine alone.

The Last Choice – Book Three https://mybook.to/ZEf mDzG

His bloodline is sworn to the service of The Great King. Can he stay true to his divine pledge when an impending war threatens all he holds dear.

A spine tingling screech shattered the cold night air. The crowd surged and ebbed like an ocean wave. The colors of humanity meshed into a purple and black bruise of motion in a type of agony. The hot sweaty bodies followed in blind allegiance...to what? Few of them seemed to think through who or what they followed. The crowd...they followed the crowd.

A mist of silvery grey feathered its way through the anxiety filled horde--the smoke in snaky tendrils inhaled in mass by those who lifted their heads in compliance. BenDavid blinked, squeezing his eyes hard...there had to be some explanation for all that was happening right in front of the whole world. But when his eyes fluttered open, there was no change.

The people pushed against each other in an attempt to move forward--or maybe just to move. BenDavid pushed his way through the crowd and stood with his back up against the glass window of a drugstore. "What in the world?" He combed his fingers through his sweaty curls and tried to come to some kind of understanding of all that was happening. But that wish felt futile; he didn't think he knew anyone in the crowd.

He squeezed his eyes again, straining to remember why he stood in this place with this mob. Outloud he voiced his confusion... "What am I doing here? What is happening? And who are we all following?" Of course he didn't expect an answer, but when the crowd surged in a sort of wave of humanity, his discomfort surged with it. He prayed...he always prayed when he was in trouble.

"Adonai, I don't know what's happening? I don't know what I'm doing here! Would You show me, guide me?" Before his prayer was finished, his eyes opened to a world that was hidden only moments before.

He turned his head toward the screeching sound--a groaning wail might've been a better description. The face of the spirit struck him first. The sharpness of the cheekbones, the large fanged teeth, covered any possibility of lips. The deep endless holes of nothing ness...and yet, they held death as clearly as if it were written there. The body was a ghostly apparition of smoky mist. He could make out arms, but no legs. It seemed to float forward, using the long sheer shape of fingers to beckon the throng. Cruelty misted the mass, soaking them with deception. The people didn't appear to truly see the spirit...at least not with their flesh eyes. They were pulled along in a type of Pied Piper sleep walk. Like the undertow of a large wave, the creature's mere presence was a powerful current, sucking the crowd to follow.

BenDavid pushed his back harder against the building's glass, wishing to disappear from what he begged Adonai to show him. The astronomical size of the spirit caused shivers to run up and down the back of his neck. His body vibrated with terror. The way the spirit drifted in front of the herd of bodies, each screech poured foul puffs of smoke from its slobbery maw. Its breath changed the air into wisps of grey with thorny threads of silver. It wove its way through the crowd--prowling, hunting, looking for victims.

BenDavid wanted to turn his face and look away when the young man standing nearest him inhaled a wisp of the animated vapor. The thread of smoke encircled the young man's neck and close around his throat. The startled man reached for his neck and gasped, but in only moments his bright green eyes dulled to a cement grey. His arms dropped to his sides, and he began to move in zombie rhythm with the rest of the crowd. BenDavid tried to discern if the man could still see, still breathe...but the answer wasn't easy; even from this short distance, it was impossible to discern.

"Adonai! Please help me!" He barely whispered the words, but he heard an instant reply with his spirit. Rushing to the highest place he could see, BenDavid shut the lid and crawled up onto a trash dumpster. He stood a good four feet above the restless crowd. He'd already made the "reckless" decision. "Guide me, Adonai. I don't understand so much of what is happening, but I do know it is Your voice I hear."

He placed his hands like a funnel in front of his mouth and yelled, "I set before you life and death! Choose Life!" He only yelled it once. His entire body shook with the intensity of power pouring from across the veil. The words hardly left him before he questioned himself. "What in the world do you think you are doing?" More doubt would've inevitably caused him to crawl off the dumpster and slink away into the shadows...except the reaction was so immediate.

Hundreds, who seemed so very lost in the throng, turned to stare at him. They rushed toward him and began lining up as if he had given instructions. Men, women, and children stared up at him as if he knew what to do. He'd swear he recognized some of their faces. These weren't just any souls lost in a crowd. These were friends, classmates, neighbors...family! He felt the pulse of fear and indecision throbbing in his throat. The only words he had time to mutter was... "Help me!" It was enough.

A blistering light of lustrous gold beamed in a blaze bright enough to force his eyes closed. The light carried warriors that rode the buttery beams--winged warriors that glided on fingers of lightning. They landed soundlessly beside the hundreds that heard his call ...none seemed to notice the appearance of the otherworldly. The warriors held spears that reached above the multi-storied buildings. These were not the angelic cherubs of children's books. These were seasoned warriors of countless battles--of timeless wars. Marbled faces that held serious expressions, rippled limbs of power and strength that sent a thrill through BenDavid.

He whispered... "Light Warriors." They bore very little resemblance to the pictures of angelic creatures he'd seen in Bibles. And they were nothing like the arrow shooting, roly poly cupids of Valentine's Day. He recited their name again... "Light Warriors." It was the first time he'd seen one of them. "Adonai, they are magnificent!" He didn't hear a reply, but he felt the warm smile of The One he knew was in charge. He was about to ask... "What's next?" when the warriors began a type of humming chant. The spears beat the ground in rhythm, creating a rumbling he could feel even on top of the dumpster. He knelt to climb down...but there was an urgency that he needed to be seen.

Everyone in both crowds felt the rumbling vibration caused by the pounding of the spears. With each drumbeat to the ground, light circled the tips of the spears. The light appeared as liquid swimming around each spearhead. Some of those who were lost in their grey-eyed trance were shaken awake, blinking in an attempt to remember which side was right and wrong. The possibility that BenDavid might sway them sent resolve through him. "Life! Choose Life!" He'd stood up and yelled the admonition without forethought. He'd yelled with all the volume his lungs would allow. He didn't truly know how he knew...but he was determined to prove *there was a choice*!

Some in the crowd that stood before him reached up toward the heavens, calling out... "Adonai!" For those who called out, a warrior would point his spear, and the spinning light would shoot into their hearts. The light filled their entire being, and their flesh began to glow. BenDavid wondered if the light was contagious. As one was filled, the beam of light moved to the one next to him, and the one next to that one...and so on, until most of those on "his side" were glowing.

Without warning, the grey-eyed souls were shaken "awake." and they shifted their gaze toward BenDavid. He motioned for them to move over--to join "his side." Some blinked away the darkness of the mist they'd inhaled and began coughing it back out. Moving as if afraid of falling back into their misty-eyed stupor, they quickly joined the others who had chosen life.

BenDavid held his arms up and continued shouting. He wasn't sure exactly what he was doing, but he felt like a cross between a marching band director and a minister of a large congregation. He directed the physical movements of the crowd, but the choice they were making was changing their souls...he relished the shift in the atmosphere from darkness to light.

Inside his spirit there was a tangle of emotions--something akin to exhilaration...and terror. The large silvery spirit spun in his direction, and they locked eyes. The deep gouges inside the face were like a vacuum...haunting, tugging at his soul; he struggled to pull his eyes away. Pressing his eyes closed, he yelled, "We Choose!" at the monstrous spirit..."Life! We Choose Life!"

The face grew in size and opened its large mouth as if it were yawning and then grew even larger in a silent scream. The body began to break into mist--long tendrils worming through the crowd. The mist, like smoke, ran up an invisible wall and when it reached the Light Warriors, repelled up and away.

BenDavid heard a sizzling sound as the mist retreated...the spirit regained form, releasing a darker smoke, exhaling out of its large open mouth. As the already subdued crowd breathed in the new smoke, their eyes turned to a flickering fire. They spun as one to face the group of defectors.

The Light Warriors slowly turned to face those who were still grey-eyed, raising their spears shoulder height...each spear making a metallic clanging as it made contact with the next. The spears and the sound created a wall of protection--a barrier around those who had chosen life...truth. Thick lines of gold light bronzed the sky against the western horizon. Light Warriors stood sentinel, not even mist passed the barrier their power created.

The air warmed around BenDavid; he felt heat through the soles of his feet. The warriors' bodies radiated not only power, but holy fire. It shot sparks into the darkened night, dressing the sky with hope. A thousand thoughts rushed through BenDavid's mind. He closed his eyes and let tears roll over his face, releasing both sorrow and unexplainable joy.

It was the sound of voices within the crowd that brought Ben-David back to himself. His heart swelled within--something he couldn't put a name to. The volume tore him from the overwhelming emotions. "BenDavid." His body trembled, gooseflesh ran up and down his arms. A hand on his shoulder...he turned to stare into the eyes of The One. It was a long, sober moment of love and acceptance. Their hearts were knit--there was no beginning and no ending--BenDavid's soul mingled there.

The sparkle in Adonai's eyes told him that this moment was not to be undertaken lightly. It felt like a pledge of honor, a commitment, a promise. "Life in this world is so different, Adonai. Sometimes I remember this other place--the place where love was born. I remember what it's like to walk from one moment to the next without fear."

Adonai reached for BenDavid's shoulders, still holding his gaze. His hands brought calm and peace to BenDavid's fallible flesh. "I Am The Way. I Am more than trustworthy, I Am The Truth. The Light of the World. Fear cannot dwell inside Love..." Adonai was always right; He always spoke the Truth...even when all those encased in flesh struggled for the power to reinvent it. He was and always would be—the Only Truth. ***If you gotta know what happens next, click here https://mybook.to/lPHN85gor use the QR CODE!

DEDICATION

To the unfathomable bravery of my son, Britton. This past year has brought endless seizures that no one has been able to control. You so rarely complain, you just get up and try again. Your bravery is so far out of my league; I am in awe of your strength. More than that, I am in awe of your perseverance. You are living proof that the human spirit cannot be destroyed. This story is in your honor. I tell the story of the life you dream about. The wife, the children, the seemingly unreachable things that the rest of us take for granted. Your bravery humbles me.

To my readers:

What is any book without you? It is for you that the story is trimmed and carved and sculpted. I see your faces in my mind, and I ask God what you need. I ask Him for ideas that will draw you nearer to Him. I ask Him to bless you. And...I admit, I ask Him for stories that soothe broken hearts and mend shattered dreams. I pray for Adonai to bless you daily. That the stories stay in your minds, and when you face impossible situations, you re- member to reach across the veil.

To my sister-in-love, Renee.

How will I ever pay you back for such diligence? For lost sleep, for determination...to be nothing but excellent? Thank you. You went far above the call of Sisterhood. You are a true blessing. I came to know your heart through our collaboration...it is a beautiful heart.

To my biggest fan....Randy Holman. How I love you. What did I ever do to be allowed to be your wife? You are my biggest cheerleader. My dearest friend, my number one supporter! Without your sacrifices, none of this would ever come to completion. You live sacrificial love every single day. Loving our son, and honoring me far more than I deserve. Thank you for always being willing to listen to "another chapter, yes AGAIN."

To Adonai...who chose me to write these stories, because I said, "Yes." You are the best friend and the most faithful companion any of us could ever hope for. I pray that I have done You justice in this story...no matter how much I wish to honor Your goodness, I know it will fall short. The English language is not vast enough to express Who You Are...

I humbly attempt to show others who You wish to be to them. How you are willing to reach past every barrier, every boundary, every prejudice. I have not always found you in the flamboyance of the lightning, nor the shaking of the thunder...but I have often found you in the gentle brush of the wind.

Chapter Forty-Four

DISCLAIMER

I t was the summer of 2019, long before the world was engulfed in the chaos of Covid 19.

This story came from a dream one humid June night when I struggled to sleep.

I was driving down I-45 almost to Galveston, Texas. I had just driven over the Causeway when the world

turned black...I was blind. My SUV barreled off the side of the bridge, plummeting 382 feet into dark waters.

In the dream, I contracted a deadly virus. The Virus took my sight, my hearing and I was paralyzed. I truly can't think of a more terrifying set of conditions. Alive, fully ALIVE inside yourself, but basically unable to prove it. The more I wrote the story, the more I realized that the virus in my story was of spiritual origin.

Reading my Bible one morning I came across this scripture.

Acts 28:27 "For this people's heart has grown dull, and with their ears they can barely hear, and their eyes they have closed; lest they should see with their eyes and hear with their ears and understand with their heart and turn, and I would heal them."

After writing **The Choosing**, I had no clue if I would ever write anything else.

I almost gave up the idea of this story...how would I explain that it was not based on the current events surrounding Covid?

Who would even believe me?

(Except for editor, author, writer extraordinaire...and friend, Deanne Welsh. She saw the outline and the first 17 Chapters before Covid19 was a word the whole world understood.)

I do however believe in prophetic dreams. Maybe some of the truths apply, maybe they don't...that decision belongs to you...the reader.

The characters from the first book moved easily into this story. Two new characters elbowed their way in, vivid and real. We became friends. They definitely make the story far more interesting. Much in our lives feels out of our control. We accept that we have NO CHOICE in much of what comes our way. It was important that I depicted that feeling...and then showed you that God is always, and forever with you. He is not always in the thunder and lightning...but you can often find him in the wind. It is my prayer that you hear him, and feel his breath as you read this story.

www.ingramcontent.com/pod-product-compliance
Lightning Source LLC
Chambersburg PA
CBHW051952240626
47153CB00005B/1722